Cygnus

Constellation Cygnus the Swan

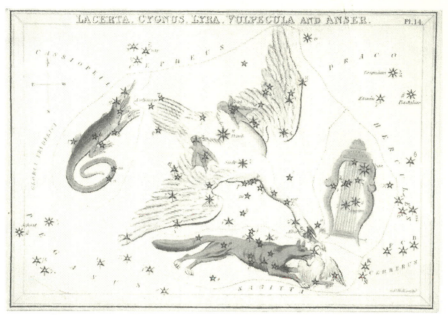

Cygnus as depicted in Urania's Mirror, a set of
constellation cards published in London, circa 1825.
Surrounding Cygnus and Lacerta, Vulpecula, and Lyra.

Cygnus

Linda Oxley Milligan

Library of Congress Control Number: 2019946133

Beak Star Books, Powell, OH

ISBN: 978-1-944724-02-3

Beak Star Books
Powell, Ohio 43065
www.beakstarbooks.com

Cover Design by Andy Bennett
www.B3NN3TT.com

Preface

Cygnus marks a shift in the Barry Short adventure novels. The series explores the past through archeological finds, but now the present comes crashing in through what most people call Science Fiction or what the initiated refer to as "legends of our time."

Keep in mind that legends as properly defined are narratives with core beliefs that at the time of their telling cannot be proved or disproved. While folklorists call these narratives legends, the people who tell them consider them "news" worth reporting. If a legend at some future date is "proven," it is no longer a legend but rather a statement of fact. Of course, this "statement of fact" comes much sooner to those who claim personal experiences that have proven to them, at least, that what was presumed to be a legend is in fact quite real.

Cygnus is the telling of such transformative experiences and what comes after. It begins when Barry Short reads a letter he has just received from his near nephew Paul who has had his own extraterrestrial encounter. The full telling of Paul's story is in a novelette titled *The Shadows that Haunt the Walls*. *Cygnus* picks up with Barry having received the letter describing Paul's extraordinary experience, which he is reading and discussing with friends at a Paris café.

Acknowledgements

My husband John's close reading of Dante revealed a passage with an uncanny similarity to the contemporary reporting of a UFO. It first describes and then reveals the nature of the phenomenon. It informs the reader of what it is not. Finally, it establishes the credibility of the observer. What is clear is that mysterious skyward observations have been made, imagined, and recorded for hundreds of years; and throughout these centuries, the structure of their telling has remained the same. What has changed is how the objects described are interpreted.

I began collecting UFO legends many years ago for a folklore course I took early in my career as a graduate student at The Ohio State University. Doctor Patrick Mullen was my professor who drove home the notion that oral traditions often conform to a pattern of telling that is both traditional and individual as the legend is passed from one teller to another and modified somewhat through the lights of each teller. Yet, in spite of individual modifications to the content, traditional structures tend to stay intact.

Don Jernigan, who would become my primary informant in what would become years of research into the legend that has dominated the 20th and now the 21st American centuries, was anything but what one would imagine to be a traditional man, unless one were thinking of a shaman perhaps. He opened the doors of my perception not only to the deeper meaning of the observations and reporting of observations that have become commonplace, but connected me to groups of what might otherwise be construed as ordinary people who explore the UFO phenomenon and create from it deeper meaning as to who we are, where we come from, and what lies in our future. To him most particularly I dedicate this novel.

Contents

For Stephanie who always sees nature anew

Cygnus

Chapter One

"She might as well have asked me to give her away. So I got the hell out of there, and here I am come to help you out," Stuart said, just having sat down at Barry Short's table at the Cafe Boulevard Saint-Germain in Paris.

"I'm sorry Stu," Barry commiserated, thinking it was Stuart who needed help. "I can only imagine Natalie doesn't understand how you feel. She's not a mean woman."

"Who the hell are Sartre and Beauvoir?" Stuart asked, his eyes fixed on a nearby street sign.

Barry sipped his wine. "Sartre was an existentialist. I read one of his books in college. Being and Nothingness, I believe it's called. Beauvoir was his paramour, I think. A feminist or something like that. They used to meet together around here someplace. Lived in the neighborhood."

Stuart signaled the waiter. "Do you have any Budweiser?" The waiter gave him a cold stare.

"Bring him a Kronenbourg," Barry said and pointed to his now empty wine glass.

"Being and nothingness," Stuart groaned. "I feel like being and nothingness." He brightened up. "So what's wrong with you Barry? I hear you've been drinkin' too much. The breakup with Madeleine?"

So they've been talking about me, Barry thought. "No, no, that was consensual. The best thing really. I'm just a little bored."

"With the museum and all that feminist crap?" Stuart said.

"I wouldn't call it that. No, the museum is grand. And they've given me a job, which is better than no job. But I'm a man to find things to put in a museum, not work in one."

The waiter set a glass of cold beer in front of Stuart and refilled

Barry's wine glass.

"Merci," Barry said. "The Institute in Chicago cut off my funds, you know. I've been put out to pasture."

"So they finally fired you."

"They didn't put it that way. Their funds dried up, and I was one of their cuts."

"It's tough all over. Natalie said even the Government Accounting Office has seen cuts. At least you weren't fired."

"I think they were being polite. They had every reason to fire me. I dropped the work they were paying me to do and took off for Egypt to see Hans Bueller. That was trouble right there. They don't like Bueller much. Of course, I thought at the time it would only be for a few days and of no consequence. But that trip had consequences all right."

"It sure did! She met this guy while I was over here rescuing you."

"What guy?"

"This guy she's gonna marry."

"I'm sorry Stu. I didn't mean to spoil your relationship. Then there was all that publicity."

"I thought you wanted it? When I left, you all were hustling to keep up with the press."

"Sure, it brought in a lot of private cash and support from the French government. But the news that I took an artifact out of Egypt without the consent of the Egyptian authorities did not endear me to the Institute. They don't want to be associated with a smuggler."

"You're no smuggler."

"Not in the ordinary sense. But I did take it, and I didn't have permission."

"I've been meaning to ask you why you didn't ask for it? You were a big wig in Egypt, right?"

"Once I was, before I got involved in Bueller's escapades. But that's not the reason. It would have taken years if they had given their permission at all. Hell, they didn't even know the statue exists. All I would have done is stirred things up. I wanted to find out who she is, that's all. And even in that I failed."

"I wouldn't say that," Stuart said after taking a long swig of beer. "You learned a lot about her and might have learned more if those bandits hadn't killed that old monk."

Sadness swept over Barry's face at the mention of Brother Thomas' demise. "That part I really regret. She's very important all right, but in the end we never learned her true name and had to guess her origin. And those bandits—murderers, I should say—well, one of their associates probably is responsible for me being stripped of my funding."

"That Felix creep?"

"He is an unsavory character all right. But he's got money, and he's well placed. That equals influence. I know it in my bones. The budget was tight and mine was the most convenient neck to string the noose around, but I'm convinced they wouldn't have hung me if it were not for him." He motioned the waiter to refill his glass. "I can't blame the Institute. Getting rid of me probably satisfied many of the demands being made on them. In fact, I wouldn't be surprised if by now they haven't gotten their funding back."

Stuart looked at Barry's reddened face as the waiter refilled his glass. "You'd better slow down."

"Who told you I was here?"

"Summer. I dropped by the museum looking for you."

Etienne sat waiting for Summer in the lounge at Le Musée de la Femme de la Mythologie when he heard the loud click of her boot heels in the hallway. He knew what that meant. He could hardly blame her for feeling perturbed. His sister Cinzia was so wrapped up in promoting her fiancé's musical career that she had left the running of the museum almost entirely to Summer and Barry. And Barry's depression had sent him to the cafe most days, leaving nearly all of the work to Summer. His grandmother Madame Conti had little time or talent for the day-to-day operations. She instead had become the public face of the museum, which had been very good for its image given her social position. And he? The European Central Bank had demanded most of his time as they and he attempted to keep Europe afloat following a banking crisis that threatened the fortunes of the entire Continent as well as his own. Etienne was about to deliver news to Summer that he thought would lift her spirits as well as his own and shore up their relationship, which had suffered under the strain of the situation.

3

"I thought we could go out to dinner tonight. I have a surprise for you."

"Fine, that would be nice," she said blandly. "But first I've got to take this letter to Barry."

"Can it not wait until tomorrow?"

"It could be important. It's hand addressed, and it's from Paul. Besides, it won't take me long."

"Where is he?"

"Guess!"

"Yes, of course. I will come with you."

"Sure, that would be fine. Stuart's with him."

"Stuart is back?"

"He just flew in today."

"Then we can have a party."

The walk over to the cafe was short and the weather was fine, but when Summer and Etienne glimpsed the two men huddled around a small table in a dark corner of the cafe it looked like winter, not August.

"Paris has not been good for Barry," Etienne sighed.

"No, he's happier in rougher quarters."

"He has been drinking too much. Maybe I should send him off on a project of some kind."

"I think he needs to dry out first."

"I know just the place, a resort near Switzerland: Spring water, fresh air, wholesome meals. Bonjour, mon ami!" Etienne said as he patted Stuart on the back in a warm embrace.

Stuart, not used to such outward affection, pulled back a little, but then let himself fall into the sentiment. He was in Paris after all.

"Well, well," Barry said, some of the old vibrancy coming back into his face. "What's the occasion?"

"You've got a letter from Paul," Summer said. "I thought you would want to read it right away."

"Sit down, sit down. Waiter, two more glasses and a bottle this time. Oh, and another beer." He studied the envelope for a few minutes. "It's thick. Maybe he's forwarding a sales contract from the realtor."

After the wine was served, the three of them chatted while Barry read. Summer and Etienne heard about Natalie's upcoming wedding, ill fated

4

from Stuart's point of view. They learned how he came to Paris to avoid being witness to her horrendous mistake and to meet up with his old friend.

"Has he been drinking like this a lot?" Stuart asked quietly but not beyond earshot had Barry been listening.

"All the time, I'm afraid," she said.

"It began in Bourges the night I had to carry him out of the dining room," Etienne added. "It has been going on ever since."

"Hmm, I don't remember that," Stuart said.

"You missed our fateful drive back to Paris. Remember, you had flown off to Egypt to retrieve Hans Bueller."

"Oh, yeah. It's funny how you forget these things," Stuart said and finished off his third beer.

Barry was oblivious to the conversation, so engaged he had become in the letter he was reading. He grunted and sighed several times, and then looked up at the table.

"What is it?" Summer asked.

"It's no sales contract, that's for sure." He paused briefly. "That boy has quite an imagination. He says here that extraterrestrial mice invaded my house. Not to worry, he says. They showed no signs of being hostile. He and a neighbor and a scientist from the Ohio State University were able to get them out. They were living in the walls, it says here."

"What?" she said. "He's got to be kidding!"

"That's what worries me. He's not. He calls them Bio-Nano Robots."

"He must have seen something like that in a movie," Etienne said. "Children confabulate."

"It's those Saturday morning cartoon shows," Stuart said. "They're full of crap like that. The kids love it."

"He writes here that Quentin—that's the scientist—says they came to the area because of Big Ear. Have any of you heard of Big Ear?"

"I have," Summer said. "SETI. It was a radio telescope array that used to exist in Central Ohio. It was pretty famous because it claimed to have picked up an extraterrestrial signal."

"That's what he says here. At least he's not making that up. He says the scientist believes that whoever signal it was came here to find out

5

who was trying to listen-in and whether the listeners are hostile. They sent these mice as probes."

"If it isn't a movie already, it should be," Stuart said.

"Why your house? Does he say?" Summer asked.

"I'm getting to that right now. He says here that my neighbor thinks they chose my house because I'm not there. Oh, and this neighbor has a UFO club."

"That explains it," Summer said.

"And they went to a meeting of said UFO club the evening of the night they saw the—what's he calling them now—BNR."

"Bio-Nano Robots," Etienne repeated. "That meeting must have been the catalyst for the confabulation."

"Yes, he says here that after the meeting he and his friend went into my backyard looking for UFOs, which he claims they saw. A storm blew up. They went inside and fell asleep. When he awoke he says he saw one of them, and then both he and his friend saw a whole—he uses the term 'peloton' of them."

"That is what we French call a pack of bicyclists who are racing the Tour," Etienne said. "He must have recently seen a bicycle race. He probably combined elements of the UFO meeting and the race into a strange nightmare."

"That doesn't explain the scientist," Barry said.

"You don't believe him, do you?" Stuart asked.

"Paul is pretty level headed."

"But he's a kid!" Summer said. "Kids imagine things. I remember when I thought I was an alien."

Etienne looked at her oddly.

"I was about twelve years old," she said defensively. "I felt so different from everyone, I thought I could be an alien."

"That's preteen alienation," Barry said. "Paul thinks he saw aliens. He says they appeared and disappeared into the walls."

"A dream," Etienne said.

"Well, I thought they existed too!" Summer asserted.

"Many people do, intelligent people," Etienne acknowledged. "But I do not think they would appear as mice hiding in the walls of a house."

"Yes, that's hard to believe," Barry said. "I hope the boy's all right. I need to get that house sold. I have to remember to call my realtor."

"Now," Etienne said, his tone marking a shift to a more important topic. "I have a surprise announcement that will impact both of you. I have hired a staff."

Barry's heart sank. Had he heard right? Had he just been fired?

"I know keeping up with the daily operations of the museum has been a tremendous strain on you both," Etienne continued.

Yes, it has, Summer thought. And I've done an excellent job. He could have consulted with me first.

"And your work has been superior," he said as if he suspected what her thoughts might be. "But I think it is high time Summer and I walk together in those lavender fields we were meant to walk in last year. And we should make it permanent."

"Did I just hear a proposal?" Barry said smiling broadly.

"Yes, you did," he said. "For all to hear. Will you?"

Summer turned red. "Yes," she answered meekly although she was not sure what she meant by yes.

"Do you desire that I accompany you in the lavender fields?" Barry said in jest.

For a minute or two Etienne did not get the joke or more importantly, the underlying question. When he did understand he had a ready reply.

"Oh, I see what you are getting at," he smiled. "No, that was not my plan. No, I think I have found something that will make you happier than that. I think I can help you find the funding for your continued pre-historical research, but first you need a rest, a vacation. My grandmother will welcome you to a wonderful health spa that she and Hans are enjoying near Lake Geneva. I am sure they would be pleased to welcome Stuart too. He could go with you."

An image popped into Stuart's head of Hans, Madame Conti, and other octogenarians enjoying the waters between luncheon and dinner, day after uneventful day.

"I've already planned a train tour of Europe," he said. He patted his backpack. "I've got my Eurail pass right here."

"You're going to vagabond around the place, are you?" Barry said. "I could go with you."

Stuart looked at Barry's now empty fifth glass of wine. "I think you could use the spa first. I'll come round and get you later after you've...."

"Dried out?" Barry said.

"I did not mean to imply...." Etienne said.

"I know you didn't. I have embarrassed myself," Barry said in the honest tone he is noted for. "You are just being a friend. Thank you. Let's quit talking about me and celebrate your engagement. Why, let's go out to dinner!"

"I've got to change my clothes first," Summer said.

"You look fine," Etienne said.

She looked down at her neatly pressed jeans. "If we just go to a bistro, these will be okay."

"I had something else in mind. I have made a reservation for the two of us at Le Club du Monde. I will add two to the reservation, and we will make a party of it."

"I should call my sister," she said.

"That can wait until tomorrow. Waiter, bring us a bottle of your best champagne. Such an occasion demands a toast."

I should feel relief, she thought in her current state of confusion, relief that I've been saved from a life of toil. Am I not Cinderella after all? She recalled all the people who in the past had made fun of her romantic imaginings and felt a morsel of revenge. In spite of their naysaying, the glass slipper had slid easily on to her foot. What she did not feel was joy: a modicum of relief, a morsel of revenge maybe, but no joy. Then another feeling welled up from the hidden springs of her childhood. She looked enviously at Stuart's backpack.

Le Club du Monde sat in a block in the Montmartre district that until recently had been graced with cafes and a row of shops selling this, that, or the other, whose value was inflated by the proximity of the shops to former artists ateliers, which were the real tourist draw. That was before the fire burned down the whole block. It was believed to have begun in a small candle making shop, although the damage was so extensive the cause could never be absolutely determined. Out of the ashes rose Le Club du Monde, a swank addition to Montmartre's nightclub district. Montmartre was also the home of one of the most beautiful basilicas in the world, Basilique du Sacré-Cœur. Etienne liked the combination of the sacred and the profane. For him this was the essence of life on Earth, and thus the club was aptly named.

Summer eyed the fashionably dressed dinner guests as the maître d' led them to their table. I should have changed my clothes, she thought. She looked up at her impeccable escort and believed that he would make up for the rest them in both appearance and reputation.

There was more champagne, more toasts, but Etienne had the distinct feeling something was wrong as he gazed apprehensively at his fiancée. This was not what he expected. She said little, which was precisely what disturbed him. Under ordinary circumstances she is quite talkative, he thought, and under happier circumstances even more so. These are the happiest of circumstances so what could be wrong?

Barry likewise took note of her odd behavior but thought it better not to say anything. He would talk to her later, tomorrow at the museum. His mind shifted to more important things. "I was just wondering, Etienne, if you don't mind my asking. How long before the new staff is in place?"

"Next Monday. Summer and you can spend tomorrow planning for their orientation, and by the end of next week, I am sure they will be competent to run the place without you."

She fumed. "It will take much longer than a week for these people to learn what took me months to learn."

"Oh, I am sorry, I didn't tell you. They have gallery background. I stole them from the Louvre."

She was even more furious. Barry could see it in her face, but Etienne failed to notice, he now being caught up in wedding planning.

"Nothing too elaborate," he said. "Grand-mère will help you plan. She will know who absolutely must be invited."

"I think I should go home now," Summer said before the dessert menu was brought to the table. "I do have to be at the museum tomorrow."

"Oh, yes, it is late. Tomorrow I will book our flight to Provence and make our hotel reservation."

"Can't we go by train?" she sighed. "We could escort Barry to Lake Geneva and see some of the country. Stuart, you could ride with us at least that far."

Stuart said nothing. Etienne appeared to be thinking over the request before he spoke.

"I suppose we could go to Évian and stay with Grand-mère for a few days. Yes, that is a very good idea. Good thinking. You and she can begin planning our wedding."

"Come on Stu," Barry said. "Just for a few days. It'll be fun."

By the end of the week the new staff hired away from the Louvre were barely capable of carrying out Summer's day to day operations. "No matter," she reported to Etienne. "They are quite able to open and close the museum and field general questions from curious visitors. That's about all. But we won't be gone long enough for them to do any real damage."

Training these new employees was empowering as it had highlighted her own competency. She realized Etienne had simply not understood that the help he lifted from the Louvre were used to a much larger staff and were not equipped to wear the multiple hats required to operate a small museum. That would take time, dedication, and a lot of energy on their part.

Barry behaved admirably all that last week, abandoning the cafe and working very hard to help train the new staff. He did not ask Summer too many personal questions because she had not created an opening for it. Her only complaint was Etienne's naive belief that she and he could be so easily replaced, but even that murmur lessened as the departure date grew near. Barry believed that complaint alone must have been the source of her moodiness at the ostensible celebration of her engagement at Le Club du Monde.

Etienne, on the other hand, felt perplexed that his plans had failed to alter Summer's mood. She puzzled him, perhaps as much as she puzzled herself.

The group arrived at the Geneva Cornavin Train Station, rented a van, and headed up the southern side of Lake Geneva towards Évian. Summer was bored with the prospect of the luxury that awaited her as they passed grand resorts with private golf courses, boating, and hillside views. They turned off the tourist thoroughfare and wound up an obscure country road, turned into a drive, and to her surprise stood a

10

much smaller hotel, but a lovely one, covered in flowers. She was delighted.

"I should have known your grandmother would choose gardens before golf estates," she said. "She has exquisite taste."

Etienne was pleased. He finally saw her smile.

Chapter Two

"Hold on for just a second," Barry said into his hotel phone. He raised his voice in answer to the insistent knocking at his door. "Come in, come in. Oh, Stuart, it's you. I'll be just a moment."

Stuart walked across the stuffy room, opened the balcony door, and took a seat.

"Yes, I know there's been a real estate slump," Barry said into the phone. "Has there been any interest at all? Okay, drop the price ten thousand dollars and get back to them. Yes, and thank you." He turned to Stuart. "I thought you were room service come to collect my tray."

"I noticed you weren't in the dining room for breakfast. Are you all right?"

"I'm fine," Barry said and sneezed. He walked over and shut the balcony door. "It's these damnable flowers." He sneezed again and not faintly. He grabbed a tissue from the bathroom and blew his nose. "I've got to get out of here. I can't breathe in this place."

"It sure is a ladies place," Stuart said sympathetically. "Summer likes it."

"I bet she does, but I'm allergic to something growing out there. Probably those flowery vines entwining the building. I feel like I'm suffocating."

"Maybe if we go outside," Stuart said.

"Outside! Have you looked out there? Just the sight of them!" He sneezed again.

"Pack up! You're getting out of here. I'll go downstairs and see if I can get a recommendation."

Fifteen minutes later Etienne and Stuart opened Barry's door and found him wheezing while lying prostrate on the bed.

"I will get a doctor!" Etienne said.

Barry opened one eye and then the other. He sat up. "I don't need a doctor. I need fresh air!"

"That's why I brought you here!" Etienne pleaded. "I did not know you are allergic to flowers."

"Neither did I," Barry said as he stood up. "Obviously not all flowers, but whatever is growing all over this place," he sneezed.

"I have found a hotel for you in town. It is flower free with a pharmacy nearby where you can get something for whatever troubles you, and I am letting Stuart have the van."

"How will you get around?"

"I can get something else. Here, let me carry your bag."

"I can do it! But thanks a lot for your help. I don't want to appear ungrateful. This is a very nice place. I just can't..." he sneezed again, "breathe."

He nearly lost his balance before catching himself on Etienne's arm. Stuart grabbed Barry's bag. Etienne helped him down the stairway to the outside, walked him to the van, and handed the keys over to Stuart.

"Give me a few minutes," Stuart said. "I've got to go back and get my backpack."

"I am so sorry I caused this," Etienne said as he helped Barry into the van.

"You didn't cause anything. Nature did."

"Summer and I will come visit you. We can have dinner together. I know she was looking forward to Stuart's and your company while here." He paused for a moment. "I do not know what has gotten into her. She seems unhappy about something."

"Sometimes good intentions aren't enough," Barry said gently. "Sometimes you think you are doing the right thing when you're not because you really didn't understand the problem."

"What did she tell you?"

"Not much really, but I don't think you entirely understand a woman like Summer. She's very independent, you know."

"Yes, I know."

"And you may be offering her more dependency than she ever wanted or could tolerate. I could be wrong, but that's my analysis. What she needs from you is a real appreciation for who she is and what she has accomplished at the museum."

"I do appreciate her. I love her!"

Barry glanced once more at the beautiful flowery vines that had entwined themselves around the hotel. "Then don't love her to death."

Etienne was stunned by the comment but before he could question him further Stuart returned with his backpack. The two men embraced and said goodbye. Barry watched as Etienne headed back across the parking lot towards the hotel and then turned his full attention to Stuart and the road in front of them, never noticing that Etienne veered away from the hotel onto a hillside path.

"What was that all about?" Stuart asked.

"Nothing much. Just gave him a little advice."

"Summer?"

"What else."

"I wish you'd give me some advice about Natalie."

"I remember I did once. Did you take it?"

"No," Stuart acknowledged. "Maybe I should have."

"That's what I thought. Natalie is not a mean person. She doesn't know what you feel."

"It's too late now. The wedding is only a few days off."

"Why don't you write to her, tell her how you feel"?

"Now?"

"Now. Tell her how you feel and let her decide."

Stuart went silent. But both he and Etienne would think long and hard that day about Barry Short's advice, advice, ironically, from a man who had never had a significant relationship with anything but his work. He was a wise man though, and they knew it.

Etienne left the path he had wandered up, cutting through wooded pines and across a grassy meadow that abutted an inviting lake. Birds danced upon the glistening water as they searched for a meal of insects. If he had had his rod and reel, he would have gone fishing, an occupation that in his youth had soothed his soul and settled his overactive mind. But neither rod and reel, playful birds, nor the peaceful chirps of insects and frogs could have induced his mind to quiet as he ruminated over Barry's accusation that he did not understand Summer.

Who did understand her, he mused. Certainly Barry had not understood how overworked she was when for the past several months he had left her alone to run the museum while he spent his afternoons at the

14

cafe. It was I, he thought, who had seen what Barry could not and determined to alleviate her problem without uttering even the slightest criticism of his behavior. She need not work. I even proposed marriage! Together we will walk in the lavender fields of love much as my grandparents did. And when my work keeps us apart, she can spend her days alongside Grand-mère doing charity work and dabbling in historical studies. And when I arrive home, she will be my devoted companion.

The picture popped: kerflooey! In spite of all his protestations, he knew Barry knew something about Summer he did not.

His reverie was short lived, his attention being drawn to a flash of light in the sky. He squinted and looked harder and recognized it was not a light exactly but more of a reflection like sunlight bouncing off a mirror. Initially he believed the flash was caused by a silvery bird about to dive down into the lake to attack its prey. But as the light descended he could see it was much larger than a bird and hovered more like a helicopter than a diver. It settled first upon the surface of the lake and then descended under the water. No helicopter he had ever heard of could do that. It was a large, silvery egg shaped thing that had submerged itself. He backed out of the meadow and hid himself in the pines, waiting a good thirty minutes to see what would happen. Nothing at first, and then he heard a loud rumble and splash. He came out of the woods to see the object raise itself out of the water creating whirlpools of waves, until it rose high into the sky and disappeared. He shivered as if he had been standing in ice and then sprinted towards the hotel.

A balding pharmacist eyed Barry with a look of concern, "Avez-vous une ordonnance?"

"Ne pouvez-vous recommander quelque chose? Allergies."

The pharmacist moved to the rear of his work area to retrieve an over-the-counter remedy.

"I could not help but overhear you," said a nice looking man with a mop of brown hair. "You are American?"

"My accent's that bad, aye?" Barry replied before he sneezed mightily.

"That is a very bad cold you have there."

"Allergies. I spent the night in a greenhouse."

15

The stranger stared into Barry's face for a few seconds. "I have something for that. It's natural and does not require a doctor's order. Are you staying near here?"

"I'm about to check into my hotel. I believe it's called Le Bain."

"Oh yes, I know it. One of the many curative spas here. Sorry, I should introduce myself, Luc Renard. I believe I do recognize you from the newspapers. Are you not the discoverer of the statue of the goddess of goddesses?"

"I didn't know I was famous," Barry said, his expression changing from distress to pride. "Yes, I'm Barry Short, and you are referring to Gitane Marie."

"Magnificent! I have been to Paris to see her, but I would be fascinated to know more. Would it be presumptuous of me to ask you to dinner? I do have a very good remedy for allergic rhinitis."

"That's very kind of you, but I'm not alone. You might like to meet Stuart. He's waiting outside. He was with me throughout the adventure."

"Of course!"

Barry quickly paid the pharmacist and grabbed a sack containing a bottle of pills. He led his new acquaintance over to Stuart who sat in the driver's seat of the van just outside the shop listening to Radio Nostalgie full blast.

"Will you turn that down?" Barry shouted. Stuart quickly complied. "I want to introduce you to Mr. Luc Renard. He has kindly invited us to dinner. He recognized me from the newspapers and is fascinated to learn more about our exploits in retrieving Gitane Marie."

Stuart looked at Luc suspiciously but remained silent.

Luc put out his hand. "If you would be so kind, I would be honored by your presence tonight for dinner. I have a remedy that might cure your friend more quickly and completely than aspirin."

"Is that all this stuff is?" Barry said looking at the sack. "And he charged me fifteen euros!"

Stuart reluctantly returned the handshake. "Sure."

"I don't live far from your hotel," Luc said. "Let me give you my card."

Barry looked at the card and then handed it to Stuart. "You are clergy," he said.

"In a way yes and no. The church does not take kindly to my explorations so I'm in retreat while I consider my options."

"I know the feeling," Barry said. "Yes, we would love to accept your invitation. It will be fun. What time should we arrive?"

"Eight o'clock would be very good."

"Well then, we'll see you at eight." He shook Luc's hand before climbing into the van.

Stuart quickly pulled away from the curb and headed for the hotel. "What did you do that for? He's a perfect stranger."

"Stu, you're too suspicious. My instincts tell me this is a man I want to know. My guess is that I will learn far more from him than he from me."

"Like what?" Stuart asked.

"I don't know. Whatever the fates have in store for me, I guess."

Etienne reached the hotel just before dinner. Summer approached him in the lobby. "Here you are! I thought you must have gone off with Stu and Barry."

"Of course I did not. I would have told you if I were going. I took a little walk, that is all."

"It must have been a long walk. Are you all right? You look pale. You look distraught."

"I am fine. I sprinted back here when I realized it was getting late, that is all. Did you and Grand-mère plan the entire wedding while I was gone?"

"We'll talk about that later. You probably ought to get ready for dinner now. Your grandmother tells me Hans must eat early. Dining late upsets his digestion."

"I will not be long," he said, relieved that the effort to make small talk had ended.

He had not wanted to tell Summer what he had seen, at least not now, not until he had sorted it out. He was too frightened to speak about it calmly, and at the moment he could not conceal that fact if he should speak of it at all. He began to question his own sanity as he considered how she would judge him. Had he confabulated the whole thing? Had

17

Paul's letter influenced his subconscious in ways he never would have imagined? And if it had, if his subconscious was able to produce such an experience with all the details he had observed, then surely he was going mad. No, he thought, I saw what I saw as sure as I see this sink I am washing my face in, as sure as I see myself in the mirror I am looking into. It was a UFO. There is some consolation in that terminology, he realized. He saw an unidentified flying object. He repeated the word "unidentified" over and over again as he stared into his reflection in the mirror as if he were forcing a correction of his thoughts.

"Are you ready?" came a voice at the door. It was Summer's voice summoning him back.

"Yes, I will be right there." He buttoned up a clean, white shirt and joined her in the hallway.

"I want to let you know before we see your grandmother that we had a slight disagreement while trying to make wedding plans."

He looked pained. "No matter, you will work it out."

"It's pretty fundamental," she said.

"What is it?"

"I want our wedding to be an adventure, outside, maybe on Mont Blanc. I want flowers in my hair. Maybe some children dressed as woodland nymphs. Some goats. Your grandmother can't think beyond a Parisian church."

"But we are Catholic!"

"Yes, but I'm not! And I am surprised that Madame Conti is so, well, stubborn about this."

Etienne looked at her for a moment and recognized that stubbornness was one of many traits these two women shared. It would take some finesse to work this out.

"Look at her interests, how she lives," Summer continued. "Her apartment in Rome looks like an ancient Roman water garden."

"My grandmother does have a very adventurous spirit, but in some things she is quite traditional. I am afraid marriage is one of those things."

"Her marriage, not mine!"

"Oh, Summer. Our family has a social standing that requires some sacrifice. She is thinking of the guests she must invite. They are not

18

mountain climbers. Many are very old."

She fell silent and was met with equal silence from Madame Conti who warmly greeted her grandson in the hotel restaurant.

"My dear, where have you been? We did not see you at lunch."

"I went for a walk, that is all. I should have told you and Summer I was leaving. Where is Hans?"

"He will be right down." She looked over at Summer. "I suppose she has already told you about our disagreement."

"Yes, Grand-mère. We will work something out."

"On a mountaintop, really!"

Hans Bueller looking jovial tottered into the dining room and over to their table like a man ten years younger than his age. "Etienne, so good you could come. I'm sorry I missed you z'is morning but I was sleeping in. I hear Barry is wi'z you. Where is he?"

"Good to see you too Hans. I'm afraid Barry had to leave. I spent the better part of the morning making arrangements for him in a hotel in Évian. He apparently is allergic to flowers."

"Z'at's too bad. I was so looking forward to seeing him."

"I will make arrangements for us to dine with him in town."

Etienne sat silent, eyes riveted on the menu. He felt increasingly uneasy. His head ached, his skin felt hot as if he had sat too long under a sunlamp. Who could he talk to about what had taken over his mind, he wondered as he looked up from the menu at the dinner guests. No use frightening Summer. And his grandmother? She had an open mind, perhaps too open. She could easily construct an ancient Greek odyssey out of the whole thirty-minute experience, he thought. It would have to be Barry.

"Dear, are you feeling unwell?" Madame Conti asked. "You look feverish."

"I am not feeling well. If you will excuse me, I should go to my room."

"Should I come with you?" Summer asked.

"No dear. He could be contagious," Madame Conti said. "I shall call in a doctor."

"I do not need a doctor," Etienne said. "Just some rest. I will see all of you in the morning."

He vomited up his morning breakfast and collapsed in the bed, feverish and out of sorts. Whatever it was that he saw at the lake must have made him sick, he thought. He rang the desk and asked to be connected to Barry at the hotel in Évian.

"I was checking to make sure the two of you found the hotel," he said weakly into the phone. "Do you find the accommodation pleasing? Good. No, I am all right, just a little under the weather. I have something I must talk to you about. Could we plan to have dinner tomorrow night?"

"Of course we can," Barry said. "All of you?"

"I expect so. Hans was lamenting your absence at dinner."

"Well, that's fine. I'll make a reservation for a party of six at the hotel. I'm glad you didn't ask about tonight though because Stu and I already have a dinner engagement."

"If the automobile rental office had been able to deliver a car today, I would have wanted to see you tonight. I had a very unusual experience after you left that I must talk to you about."

"You sound upset. Did Summer and you have a misunderstanding?"

"No, nothing like that. I do not want to mention it to her until I have sorted things out. It is too strange to even talk about on the phone."

"Well, you can tell me in person tomorrow," Barry said, unable to imagine how unusual Etienne's experience actually was. "Tonight we dine with a priest, one Luc Renard. He recognized me in the pharmacy from the newspapers. He's deeply interested in Gitane Marie."

"Luc Renard. The name sounds familiar," Etienne said. "If he is who I am thinking of, he is very famous in his own right, has quite a following."

"That wouldn't surprise me. There seemed something special about him. We will have a lot to talk about tomorrow. You can tell me about your experience, and I will tell you about mine. I've got to go now. We're due at his home in twenty minutes."

"À bientôt," Etienne said, no more relieved of his anxiety than before he had made the call. He went out on to the balcony of his room and looked out at the stars that were only now becoming visible. Mercury was swiftly setting just below the crescent moon, but on this night, Hermes had no message.

Luc Renard's town home was modest, but its decor was rich. The furniture, wall coverings, and carpets were not lavish. But the artwork, collection of books, maps and globes showed a man well traveled physically, historically, and philosophically. That perhaps was the crime that had put him on probation with his church. His mind was simply too broad to be easily squeezed into narrow theology. Barry felt instantly comfortable in his presence.

"So you are not absolutely sure Gitane Marie came from France," Luc said, following a lengthy discussion of their effort to identify her.

"No, not absolutely. Although the newspaper stories would have you believe otherwise. There is a good chance she was carved on what is now French soil though. Her markings, a language of sorts, are the very same found in the Paleolithic caves here, but less random, more organized. And the nanodiamonds found in the stone date back 12,000 years or more, following a massive comet strike that spread stardust across the globe. So, I postulate she was carved while the Magdalenian culture was still intact and somehow survived the devastation; or she was carved later, after the demise of the culture but before their language had been entirely lost. One of our party, Summer, calls the second hypothesis 'the time between.' I think that an apt phrase because it describes the time between the demise of Paleolithic cultures and the rise of pre-dynastic civilizations in the Nile Delta, a time we know little about."

"But you did find her in Egypt. Could she have been carved there?" Luc asked.

"I'm more inclined to believe she was taken from Europe and hidden there."

"The men who tried to chase us down and steal her were not Egyptian," Stuart pointed out.

"They were European," Barry said. "But to this day those culprits refuse to identify themselves or their leader."

"They are in prison, are they not?" Luc asked.

"Yes, except for the leader. He was killed in an unfortunate accident involving a chandelier."

"They clearly were on a mission," Luc said. "I suspect somewhere there is a group of men who know quite a bit about your goddess statue."

21

"Yes, that they don't want anyone else to know," Barry added. "Which is proof of her importance. But what about you? Pardon me if I'm being too inquisitive, but what brings you to the spas?"

"I guess you could say I'm in retreat until I gain some direction."

"A friend of mine, he will be dining with us tomorrow, said he's heard of you, that you have a following."

Luc took a few moments to formulate a response. "I did, and that may have proved to be my undoing, with the church at any rate, maybe beyond that. It never helps to be more popular than the local bishop, or more influential."

"Beyond what?" Stuart asked "Are you in trouble with the government?"

Luc laughed. "Governments do not dwell in my province."

Barry realized he and Stuart were intruding in an area far too personal for a first time meeting with someone he hoped to form a lasting friendship with so he quickly shifted the subject of the conversation.

"My friend that I mentioned to you, Etienne de Chevalier, will visit here tomorrow along with his grandmother and others of our investigative team. Summer and Hans Bueller will be along. Hans is the man who uncovered Gitane Marie in the basement of a monastery he resided in for a time in Egypt. I'm sure they would want to meet you. I was thinking you might join us tomorrow for dinner. I don't have the details yet, but I could phone you with them."

"Ah, I would be delighted to dine with a monk and members of the de Chevalier family."

"Hans Bueller is no monk, more like a thief!" Stuart said.

Barry gave him a look of indignation. "That's a bit of an overstatement." He turned to Luc, "Stuart is right that Hans is not a monk. He's an Egyptologist. Because of his age and an injury he sustained, he took up residence in a Christian monastery near the Red Sea. They made him their librarian, and that's how he made the find. He called me down there to help him, and that's when the whole thing began."

"Monk or not, it will be a privilege to meet him and members of such an esteemed family. Before you leave, I want to give you my allergy remedy. I have it all prepared for you. I'll be right back."

"Did you have to say that?" Barry said to Stuart once they were alone.

"The old coot is a thief," Stuart said.

"No more than I am. And you would not place that title on me."

"Your motives were different. You didn't profit from Gitane Marie."

"And neither did Hans," Barry reminded him.

"Maybe this time. But he sure has a record of profiting from his other finds."

"He has done what he has done in order to survive in his profession because he loves it. His supposed Austrian sponsors were a myth, and he had no university behind him."

"All you need to do is warm the carafe over a candle or something," Luc said when he reentered the room. "Not a stove or anything too hot or the glass will break. Then breathe in. Do it twice a day for a week and your head will be clear and the inflammation gone. Even tomorrow you will feel greatly improved."

"Just getting away from that vine covered hotel has helped considerably," Barry said.

"Well, then, it may not take a week."

"Thank you, thank you very much," Barry said when handed the carafe.

"No, thank you for an entirely enjoyable evening. It reminds me how important company is. Maybe I've been in retreat long enough."

Chapter Three

Etienne awoke from a dream, the memory of which slipped away as soon as he opened his eyes. Only the feeling remained, and it was not pleasant. Could yesterday's experience at the lake have been a dream too? He sat up and looked out of the window at the starry night. Dream? Maybe, he thought. He attempted to reconstruct the experience so he could search for clues.

"Not good enough," he said. He climbed out of bed, opened his balcony door, and stood outside looking up at the dark sky. The air had become sticky adding to the pungency of the flowering vines. Again he tried to visualize what he had seen. The slow descent of the object into the lake water. Its ascent and disappearance into the sky. Like a baptism, he thought, to be submerged and then pulled out of the water, holy and clean. But a man would have drowned in the thirty-minute interval between the descent and ascent. And the object was silver in color and brightly metallic. It was a machine and no dream!

That settled, he began to focus on a peculiarity of the experience, if anything could have been more peculiar than the entirety of the experience. He shut out the sticky air, returning to his room and bed. It was the object's disappearance that puzzled him. Not its rapid ascent into the sky, but the way it vanished once it got there. It seemed to disappear behind a door as he had just done had there been an onlooker below in the garden to observe his retreat from the balcony. But a door in the sky to where?

No answers came. Neither did sleep. He could not wait for the morning to come, the rental car to be delivered, and the chance to tell his story to Barry Short. He had to tell someone, someone who might help him sort through it, someone who could convince him he had imagined the whole thing. He had read about the power of confabulation on the mind. It gives an experience a heightened quality well beyond what the normal imagination can produce. Such a seeming memory has all the power of a real event. Some believe it can manifest physically like the

24

stigmata on the hands of those who believe they have made contact with angels. Were there angels inside that silvery craft, he wondered while under the influence of the slow moving night. He could not answer that question. All that he had seen was the craft, not who powered it; and he could not convince himself it was some sort of confabulation no matter how hard he tried.

Summer lay in bed listening to the rain. It started out hard but tapered off into a steady shower as a dreary dawn broke through the heavy clouds. She had not slept well.

Earlier that night before the rain came, her sleep had been disturbed by worry about her coming marriage and all of the unwelcome changes that it could bring. She had never imagined she would look on this day with dread, particularly with the prospect of marrying a man like Etienne. She had wrapped up in her cotton robe and gone out into the hotel garden to breath in the heavily scented night air and try to relax her mind. Minutes later, Etienne had come out onto his balcony and stared up at the few stars that poked through the clouds. She had thought to softly shout up to him, thinking what fun they might have together in the garden alone while everyone slept. But his appearance had silenced her. His face was obscured by distance and darkness, but his silhouette spoke volumes. Arms rigid, he clenched the balcony railing for support. His shoulders so bent, he struggled to raise his head.

Who is he really? she wondered. Had she allowed her youthful fantasies to shape an image that was not altogether accurate? Of him? Of herself? She watched until he retreated back into his room, and then returned to her own room and to sleep until the early morning rain awakened her.

Showers relentlessly fell as she lay in bed thinking. She wondered what had happened to him yesterday. He was distant and distraught and clearly withholding something. He had been missing for hours, and yet he claimed to have walked only a short distance to a nearby lake and stayed there briefly. There is something he is not telling me, she thought. She had known something was wrong as soon as he arrived back at the hotel but had not asked, so used she was to him keeping his private business affairs to himself. Could he be in trouble? And how could we be truly married if he keeps such secrets?

There was much she did not know about him, a man whose culture and breeding were foreign to her. Yet in spite of this, after a year in his company she knew quite a lot. She knew from his posture on the balcony last night that something was terribly wrong. Her phone rang. It was him.

"Are you awake?"

"Yes," she said. "The rain woke me."

"I need to speak with you alone, before the others get up. Can I come down?"

"Sure. Just give me a few minutes."

She washed and dressed, but before she could brush her golden hair Etienne knocked on her door.

"I think the best way to tell you this is to go out for a walk," he said as he stood in the doorway of her room.

"It's raining. Tell me what?"

"Come on. You will not get wet."

"I haven't brushed my hair yet."

"Hurry up."

He stepped out into the garden and opened a large black umbrella that he held over her head. "Remember how I was gone so long yesterday?"

"I've been wondering about that."

"I did not want to tell you what happened until I talked to Barry, but I cannot keep it back from you any longer."

"Barry!" she said. "What happened?"

"Let me explain." He guided her from the parking lot up the soggy path he had taken the day before. The rain let up. "Yesterday, after Barry and Stuart drove away, on an impulse I decided to take a walk up this way." He paused and closed the umbrella and thought about how frank he wanted to be. "I wanted to think through what Barry had said to me about you."

"Me?"

"He scolded me," he said as he smoothed her tousled hair. "He thinks I do not always understand you." She was silent. "You have not been as happy as I had expected you would be about our marriage, and I

26

asked him if he knew why."

"It could be a big change," she acknowledged.

"A happy change I had hoped."

"I am a little nervous, but I haven't talked to Barry about it."

"He too has seen your recent behavior. He claims to have more insight into its meaning than I. He says I do not understand a woman like you."

She was silent for a minute as they walked further into the fragrant pine forest.

"It could be a happy change," she said, "but it might not be if...."

"If what?"

"I'm not your grandmother! I love and admire her, but I'm not her!"

He wrapped his arm around her shoulders. "I don't expect you to be."

"But you do!" she said and pulled away. "You may not realize it, but you do. I'm not cut out to be a society wife. I want to work. I love my work!"

He was startled, not so much by her declaration as her moving away from him.

"Not only did you give my job away," she continued, "you've minimized my contribution as if anyone could fill my shoes!"

"I did not minimize your contribution. You have done excellent work, the work of three maybe four people almost entirely alone. Why do you think I hired a staff of experienced people from the Louvre to replace you?"

"And they still can't do my job," she said as she affectionately rubbed her head against his shoulder.

"No they cannot." He smiled and wrapped his arm around her shoulders. "But working as hard as you have has taken a toll on you. I only meant to free you from the burden."

"You could have asked me first."

"I'm sorry. I had thought of it as a gift."

"The gift was letting me run the museum in the first place. That was the gift!"

He went silent for a brief moment. "I promise I will ask the next time I make plans for the two of us."

27

Her voice softened. "I never knew your mother, but I must be more like her than your grandmother. She had a profession."

"She gave her life to it."

"I'm not that noble. But can you understand that well, I need an identity, a career, something more than just being a wife."

"Who will rear our children?" he asked, remembering how abandoned he had felt when his parents would go off to tend the suffering until finally they never returned.

She saw the pain in his eyes. Unable to find the words to alleviate it, she turned the conversation back to yesterday. "So what happened that kept you away for so long?"

He looked out at the lake that by comparison to what he had earlier witnessed now looked dull and lifeless. No birds danced across the water; no frogs chirped. All was quiet.

"Something very odd. Look up there," he pointed to the sky. Summer looked up but saw nothing. "Yesterday, a silvery ship sank from that sky into the water. I sat and watched until it rose up out of the lake and disappeared back into the sky."

"A UFO?"

"I don't know what else to call it. I would call it a product of my imagination if I could convince myself."

"Convince yourself of what, that you were dreaming?"

"Something like that."

"Why didn't you tell me about it last night?"

"I did not want to frighten you."

"Frighten me! This is too fascinating to frighten me. So, you stood here and waited all of that time for it to resurface and disappear."

"It was only thirty minutes or so."

"Thirty minutes! You left just after breakfast and didn't return until dinner."

He looked puzzled. "I had not considered all the time that had lapsed. Maybe I did fall asleep, and maybe I was dreaming."

"Or it went on longer than you thought," she said, excited by the revelation and relieved to know nothing seriously bad had happened. "I was worried that you were having business problems you weren't telling me about. That you were in trouble."

28

"If that is all that it had been!" he said, unable to understand how Summer could so easily brush off the revelation of his experience.

"It's really weird that Barry got that letter from Paul only a few days ago," she said.

"Yes, it is. I have wondered if hearing it could have influenced my imagination."

"That's possible I suppose; but then again, it may be only coincidence."

"It seemed so real," he protested. "Maybe Barry can offer some insight. I thought we would all go over to Évian once the rental car arrives."

"With your grandmother and Bueller?" she asked.

"I think they would enjoy it."

Summer sighed. "Maybe if they can tear themselves away from bridge. I guess you didn't know since you were gone most of the day. They're playing in some kind of tournament."

"What?"

"Some kind of bridge tournament. They've done very well. I think they're in the finals."

He broke out in laughter. "I didn't know. I knew my grandmother loves the cards, but somehow I never imagined Hans Bueller a bridge player."

"Apparently, a good one."

"Well, let them enjoy themselves. Maybe it is for the best that they do not learn about this event until I have had time to sort it out."

The smooth, flat surface of the lake grew pockmarked with raindrops, a herald to a rapidly approaching downpour. He opened his umbrella and held it over the two of them. "If we are going off on our own, we had better go back and greet them before we leave. Bridge!" he said, smiling.

Chapter Four

Etienne slowed to a stop when he saw two men standing under the awning outside the Hotel Le Bain. Summer lowered her window and shouted over the thunder at Barry and Stuart who climbed into the back seat.

"Sure is wet," Stuart said. He caressed the Mercedes' fine leather upholstery. "Nice car."

"Glad you like it," Etienne replied. "I was just about to park when I saw you outside."

"We've been waiting for you," Barry said. "Our plans have changed if you don't mind. Luc Renard has asked us to dine at his place tonight. "After having had breakfast at our hotel, I highly recommend that we do."

"Not good?" Summer asked.

"If low fat yogurt is all you want, it's fine," Barry said.

"It's a spa. They want you to get healthy," she said.

"Not that healthy."

"What prompted Mr. Renard to invite us?" Etienne asked. "Did you complain to him about your breakfast?"

"No, not at all. When I told him our party had dwindled to four, he made the suggestion unprompted."

"What do you think Stuart?" Etienne said.

"I think it's a nice switch. He's a good cook and an interesting guy."

"There, you heard it from an investigative expert," Barry said. "Luc has an interesting place. You will be impressed. Just turn right here, drive a few blocks, and we can park."

"Umm, it smells like chicken soup," Summer said when they entered Luc's townhouse.

Luc smiled, so unused he was to such informal introductions. "Yes, it's a chicken broth. I'm making a special recipe with plenty of eggs and spinach. Actually, it was my grandmother's recipe to cure my childhood colds. It will help Barry recover from his allergies."

Barry was momentarily speechless; a condition he rarely suffered from. He appreciated the concern but detested too healthy of a menu.

Etienne looked at the party of Americans he had arrived with, feeling a tad awkward that he had not been properly introduced. He extended his hand to Luc. "I am privileged to meet you. I have read about you and your philosophy, which has gotten you into so much trouble. I certainly support it. I celebrate it. The creation should be celebrated. I do not know why anyone would think otherwise."

"Thank you," Luc replied, shaking Etienne's hand. "I believe I've seen you in the news too."

"Yes, but unfortunately finding agreement on the means to secure the European economy is not nearly so life affirming."

"But it is necessary, and it is noble," Luc said.

Etienne blushed. He was not used to such praise, so dull were his endeavors in the minds of most people. But as Luc rightly pointed out, they were necessary.

"You already are acquainted with my friends here, but I do not believe you have been introduced to my fiancée."

"Ah, she who can appreciate the smell of a fine soup," Luc said.

"I'm Summer. Very glad to meet you"

"That wall map," Etienne said. "It looks very old."

"It's fifteenth century. I bought it because it recorded land travel routes. Very rare on a map so old. It amazes me how similar today's routes are, some exactly as they were."

"Only with a different pavement," Barry said, now that he had gotten his tongue back. "The Romans could find the shortest route between two points with very few instruments, and they never let a mountain get in their way."

"That's what I love about Europe," Summer said. "It's so old. In America, relative to Europe anyway, we've just paved over our cattle paths."

"Don't forget our Indian trails," Barry said. "Many of our first highways paved over very ancient Native American trails."

"You're right," Summer agreed. "But I wasn't speaking of the indigenous culture. A two hundred year old building is ancient in America but relatively new in Europe. And a two thousand year old roadway simply does not exist."

"Routes and trails—are we planning a trip?" Stuart said as a joke that would turn out to be decidedly prescient.

"Come with me into the kitchen," Luc said. "I want all of you to learn the secret of my soup. I've already strained the cooking vegetables and chicken from the broth. I used celery, carrots, onions, salt, and pepper."

He dropped the leaves of a bunch of freshly washed spinach into the bubbling broth and swished it around with a wooden spoon. "An extra egg for good measure," he said and broke three eggs into a small bowl, added a cup of freshly grated parmesan cheese, and beat the mixture. He stirred the golden cheesy mix into the broth, scrapping the sides of the bowl so as not to waste a drop. "Ready."

"Ready?" Summer said. "That's all it took?"

"The broth took all day. The rest a matter of minutes. Help me get it into this tureen."

Stuart grabbed the handle on the far side of the pan and together the two men poured the steaming soup into a brown glazed tureen.

"Smells good," Barry said in spite of his reservations.

"Food rich in health can likewise be rich in flavor."

"Can I help?" Summer asked.

"You'll find two loaves of bread and cheese on a tray in the pantry. And Barry, could you get the wine? It's in there too."

The meal was served, light but savory.

Each time Etienne attempted to bring up Luc's probationary state, Luc would deflect the conversation back to what they all shared an interest in, Gitane Marie, until they wore out the topic. It became clear that he did not want to discuss his personal religious crisis. After a fruit tart and several bottles of wine, Etienne had nerve enough to bring up what consumed him, his lakeside experience.

He turned to Barry. "I must tell you what happened to me after you left yesterday." He stopped for a moment and dropped his head. "I feel I will look foolish."

"No, tell him," Summer said. "There's nothing to feel foolish about."

"Go ahead," Barry said. "You're with friends."

"All right. After I left you and Stuart, I climbed up the hill from the parking lot into a meadow and made my way to a lake near a pinewood forest I had wandered into. I was thinking about what we had been discussing before you left when something miraculous happened. Out of the sky—well, by the time I saw it, it had begun to drop out of the sky." He paused.

"What had?" Barry asked.

"I'm not sure. It looked silver. At first it seemed to hover over the lake."

"A helicopter?" Stuart said.

"Well, that's what I would have thought, but it didn't look like one, and it descended down under the water."

"Could it have been a bird diving for fish whose appearance was altered by the sun?" Luc asked.

"No, it was too big for that. And it seemed mechanical, a machine."

"Are you saying you think you saw a UFO?" Barry asked.

"Yes, that's what I'm saying, but I'm not ready to identify exactly what this UFO was. Maybe it was some kind of submergible plane being tested. I don't know, but that would not explain its departure. After about thirty minutes or so…"

"Maybe several hours," Summer interrupted.

"That's another issue," Etienne said. "After what seemed like thirty minutes, the object rose up from the lake, high into the sky, and then seemed to just disappear. It did not fly away so to speak; it disappeared as if it had entered a doorway into the sky. Blip—it was there, and then it was gone."

An awkward silence followed.

Stuart grinned. "What did you say about Paul when Barry read his letter?"

"I know," Etienne said. "I suggested he confabulated the whole thing. And I have asked that very question of myself. It is possible, but I do not feel that I did."

"Who is Paul?" Luc asked.

"My near nephew," Barry said. "We've recently gotten a letter from him in which he describes having a UFO experience at my house in the States."

"And you knew about this?" Luc asked.

"Yes, yes, which is why I questioned my own experience. If I had not

33

had it myself, under these circumstances I would surely believe that Paul's letter had influenced the experiencer's imagination. But having witnessed the event myself, it is hard to dismiss it so easily. Although I would like to."

"He told me the event lasted about thirty minutes, but he was gone for hours," Summer said. "Something doesn't add up."

"You fell asleep," Stuart said. "It was a dream."

"That is possible," Etienne admitted. "I do not remember either falling asleep or waking up, but it is still possible. I have no other way to explain the missing time unless I simply lost track of it."

"That must be it," Barry said. "You fell asleep and had a very vivid dream. I have them all the time. Sometimes they're more like visions than dreams."

"But you know it when you do," Etienne said. "I have no awareness of either having a dream or a vision. It seems as if I saw what I saw, and I cannot explain it. Yet, maybe you are right."

"You know what they say about missing time experiences," Luc said. "I'm not suggesting this is what happened to you, only pointing to another explanation. This is the standard description of an abduction experience."

"UFO abduction?" Barry asked.

"That's what some claim," Luc said. "Hypnosis is sometimes used to help the experiencer remember, albeit a highly risky procedure."

"How so?" Barry asked.

"It can result in false memories, memories that seem as real as any other, but they have been planted or should I say constructed through subtle sometimes unconscious suggestions on the part of the hypnotist."

Straightening himself up in his chair, Etienne said, "I would never subject myself to such a thing. I only hope to find an explanation I can accept short of committing myself."

"I think Stuart is correct on this one. You fell asleep and had a very vivid dream. The fresh air up here could do that to someone," Barry said.

"There are other stories like yours, stories more miraculous in their interpretation," Luc said.

"What kinds of stories?" Summer asked.

Luc shut his eyes and looked deep into his memory, then began to recite:

Standing by the sea's new day
like travelers pondering the road
who send their souls on while their bones delay.

Low above the ocean's western rim,
through thick vapors
that form before the dawn burns red and slim.

A light appeared, moving above the sea faster than any flight.
A moment then I turned my eyes to question my sweet Guide,
and when I looked back to that unknown body
I found its mass and brightness magnified.

Then from each side of it came into view an unknown something-white;
and from beneath it, bit by bit, another whiteness grew.
We watched till the white objects at each side
took shape as wings, and Virgil spoke no word.

As that bird of heaven closed the distance
between us, he grew brighter and brighter and yet brighter
until I could not bear the radiance
and bowed my head...

He steered straight for the shore,
his ship so light and swift it drew no water;
it did not seem to sail so much as soar.[1]

"I've read descriptions like that before," Summer said. "A bright object, the mothership, and smaller craft that seem to come out of it."
"Dante?" Etienne said.
"What?" Summer said.

---

[1] Alighieri, Dante. The Purgatorio. Trans. John Ciardi. New York: New American Library. 1961

"It's from "The Purgatorio," Luc said. "Canto II, The Angel Boatman."

"Ancient astronauts!" Summer said.

"Something like that," Luc replied. "But something more. Angel boatmen, ancient astronauts, who knows? The point is humankind has been seeing things in the sky for centuries. All that changes is how those lights are interpreted. Just a minute, let me get the text."

He went to one of his many bookshelves and began a systematic search until he pulled out a volume.

"It's a very interesting passage when looked at in light of a typical UFO witness account. The first thing a witness attempts to do is establish his or her credibility. We are most impressed with reports made by airline pilots or astronauts because we trust their knowledge of the sky and therefore are more apt to pay attention to them. Of course, there were no airline pilots or astronauts in Dante's day, but look how he attempts to establish his own credibility at the beginning of the passage I recited."

The sun already burned at the horizon,
while the high point of its meridian circle
covered Jerusalem, and in opposition

equal Night revolved above the Ganges
bearing the Scales that fall out of her hand
as she grows longer with the season's changes:

thus, where I was Aurora in her passage
was losing the pale blushes from her cheeks
which turned to orange with increasing age.

"I see what you mean," Etienne said. "He establishes that he is learned, that he knows the sky."

"Yes," Luc said. "He is a man who knows the stars and understands the starry sphere and its rotations. And consider another important aspect of a UFO report. The reporting of what it is not."

"Like when we're told it wasn't a helicopter, a balloon, Venus, or some other natural thing?" Summer said.

"Exactly," Luc said. "Look how Dante does it, 'See how he scorns man's tools/ he needs no oars nor any other sail than his own wings/ to carry him between such distant shores.'"

"I see," Barry said. "Man's tools, in Dante's case oars and sails are the equivalent to planes and helicopters."

"Or our spacecraft," Summer said.

"Yes," Barry said. "But what about Venus, birds, or other misidentified natural objects?"

"He covers that too. 'See how his pinions tower upon the air/ pointing to Heaven: they are eternal plumes/and do not molt like feathers or human hair.'"

"When did Dante have this sighting?" Stuart asked.

"We don't know that he did," Luc said. "But he wrote this in the 14th century."

"Damn!" Stuart said.

"Yes, it reads like a template for nearly every UFO report I've ever heard," Luc said.

"Except Paul's. He actually saw the robotic mice," Barry said.

"There is a major difference, and this is very important, the interpretation of what was seen," Luc said before he began to read, "Virgil spoke, 'Down on your knees! It is God's angel comes!'"

"I know you are a man of the cloth," Stuart said. "But are you suggesting that Etienne here saw an angel?"

"I do not know what he saw. All that I'm suggesting is that it may not have been a dream, that people have been seeing these things for eons. What has changed is not the reported objects or how they are reported but our interpretations of what these objects are."

"There is another parallel between my experience and the passages you have read, the proximity to water. What does Dante say?"

"'He steered straight for the shore/ his ship so light and swift it drew not water/ it did not seem to sail so much as soar,'"[1] Luc repeated.

"That is not common in UFO reports, is it?" Etienne asked.

"I don't think so," Luc said, "Although I'm no expert in these matters."

"You seem pretty expert to me," Barry said.

"I know someone who has real expertise. A friend of mine who works at CERN. If anyone would know about UFOs, it would be him. He tells me they have many reported sightings over there."

"Near CERN?" Etienne asked.

"That's what he tells me. Maybe I can arrange a meeting with him."

"That would be wonderful if you could," Barry said. "It's a category of experts I'm not acquainted with."

"I do not think there are too many," Luc said. "He may know something. He doesn't live far, just across Lake Geneva. I'll phone him and get back with you. What's your schedule?"

"I am free," Etienne said. "And Summer too."

"We're all free," Barry said.

"It's too late to phone him tonight, but I will tomorrow and let you know what I can arrange."

"It's dark outside. What time is it?" Summer asked.

"Later than I thought," Barry said. "Time flies when you're engaged in interesting conversation. We had better get going."

Etienne stood up from his chair after looking at his watch, "It is eleven. I'm so sorry to have imposed on you this long. I had no idea."

"Don't apologize," Luc said as he and the others stood up. "It's been a long time since I've talked, truly talked with congenial friends." He walked them to the door. "Barry, I will phone you at your hotel tomorrow."

Summer and Etienne were quiet until they had driven out of Évian. Then the dam broke.

"Angel boatmen, what next?" he said.

"It's fascinating. I saw a special about ancient astronauts when I was a little girl. I've never forgotten it."

"What I saw did not look ancient, and it did not look heavenly either."

"It's an interesting perspective though."

"Yes, Luc Renard is a fascinating man. I wish I could have gotten him to talk more about himself."

"He seemed to dodge the subject whenever you tried. I wonder if he could be hiding something?"

"I believe he is. He had a lot of celebrity until the church disciplined him."

"What for?"

"I am not sure. That is what I had hoped to get him talking about. His celebrity may have been his real crime, but I believe he was accused of being a pantheist."

"I don't see why that would rile the church," she said. "What could be the problem with having a deep love of nature?"

"A deep love is one thing, but a pantheist could construe our lavender fields as being as sacred as Saint Peter's Basilica. But I doubt he ever claimed such a thing."

"Look at the different interpretations we heard tonight about what you saw. Claims and interpretations of claims can be all over the place," she said. "I wouldn't be surprised if his claims have been misinterpreted."

"I see what you mean. Maybe that is why he is reticent to speak about himself. I would be."

Etienne was likewise reticent to mention the throbbing in his head that had begun nearly as soon as they were alone in the car. It is nothing that a good night's rest will not take care of, he thought. Why worry Summer.

Chapter Five

"I wish you had told me sooner," Madame Conti said to her grandson at breakfast. "It saddens me that you did not."

He dropped his empty coffee cup on its saucer with a note of finality. "I was hoping to find an adequate explanation before I said anything. After yesterday, I am not sure I will."

"I could have helped you," she said, patting her mouth with her napkin and appearing to wipe her eye.

"I did not want to frighten you."

"Frighten me! Why would you seeing a UFO frighten me?"

"I felt exactly the same way," Summer said. "I told him, I'm too fascinated to be frightened."

Etienne was happy that Summer and his grandmother agreed on something even if their reaction negated his feelings.

"It may not frighten the two of you, but it frightened me."

"I'm sure at the time," Madame Conti said, "and with no one there with you."

"It still frightens me! I saw something extraordinary that I cannot explain."

"There are wondrous forces in the world," Madame Conti said, while straitening her posture and seeming to gaze off into space.

"What I saw looked powerful, advanced, and with purpose, not wondrous. You would have been frightened too if you had seen it. At least you should have been."

"Of course, you both may be right," Hans Bueller said. "Z'ere have always been wondrous, powerful forces in z'e world both friend and foe. I sometimes wonder if Imhotep was a visitor here. He was not of z'is world I don't z'ink. You say you told Barry?"

"He and Stuart thought I dreamed the whole thing. That is until Luc Renard offered his rather unorthodox explanation."

"Yes, Dante's *Purgatorio*," Madame Conti said and smiled. "Ah, Luc Renard. Interesting man. From what I have read of him he takes an original view of nearly everything. I would very much like to meet him."

"You may have your chance Grand-mère. He is to arrange a meeting with a friend of his from CERN. He thinks his friend may have some insight into what I saw."

"Marvelous! The bridge tournament final is this afternoon. Afterward, I believe we are free."

The morning passed with no phone call from Barry. Etienne was tempted to phone him himself. He did not however realizing that in all probability Barry had nothing yet to report. Lunch was served at one o'clock to be followed by the bridge tournament playoffs. He grew more impatient as he sat under the withering glance of his grandmother who thought it quite odd that Barry had not seen fit to call if only to lessen her grandson's anxiety. His head began to throb as it had the evening before as he and Summer were driving back to the hotel. It is only due to anxiety, he told himself.

"Are you all right?" his grandmother asked. "You look pale. I think it very rude of him," she went on. "He knows how upset you are, and I want you to be happy and relaxed at the bridge tournament this afternoon."

"I think you should phone him," Summer said. "It won't hurt anything."

"You are right." He raised himself from the table and went to his room. He first took an aspirin, reclined on the bed, and then punched in Barry's phone number.

Barry answered immediately as if he too had been waiting in earnest. "I thought you were Luc. We're about to leave for lunch, and I thought this might be his call."

"I'm very sorry for my impatience," Etienne said. "But my grandmother and Hans are in a bridge tournament final this afternoon. She wants me there for good luck so I will not be available until this evening. I wanted you to know in case you tried to phone me."

"Hans is playing bridge?"

"Yes, and very well." Barry laughed a good long minute. "We can talk later. Tell Hans—no give Hans a high five from me, and thanks for calling."

"Let's get out of here," Barry said to Stuart. "I need a steak."

41

"Did I hear you right, Old Bueller's playing cards?"

"Not just cards, bridge. I shouldn't laugh. If he's enjoying himself, good for him.'"

"It'll keep him out of trouble," Stuart said. "So Etienne's still wondering about what he saw the other day?"

"He didn't mention it, but he didn't have too. He phoned, and that's enough."

"Can't blame the guy. If I had seen what he saw, it would probably drive me nuts too."

The two men went down to the hotel lobby in search of two steaks when the concierge approached Barry. "Monsieur Short, I was asked to give this note to you when you came down."

Barry looked at the folded yellow paper he had been handed and then at the concierge. "Why didn't you bring it up to the room or at least phone me and tell me it was down here?"

"I was instructed not to by the gentleman who gave it to me. He said he did not want to disturb you until you were out and about."

"Strange," Barry said. "How long have you had it?"

"Roughly an hour I should say."

"Well, thank you very much," he said and read the note. "It's from Luc. He says to meet him at the pharmacy where we first met."

"What the hell is this about?" Stuart said.

"I don't know. I guess we'll find out."

The pharmacy was on the opposite side of the street, only a few blocks from the hotel. Luc stood in one of the aisles looking at a rack of newspapers. He looked up as if he sensed their entry and walked towards them. "I'm sorry to be so mysterious, but I have my reasons. Where are you off to?"

"We came out for some lunch," Barry said.

"A steak," Stuart added.

"You need something more substantial after a dinner of soup?" Luc said.

"It was very good soup," Barry said, "but to be honest, yes. I'm hungry."

"I know a good bistro nearby if you haven't already decided on a place. We can speak privately there."

"Fine, you lead the way."

"What's all this about?" Stuart asked.

"I'll explain inside," Luc said, as they entered an establishment just a half a block from the pharmacy.

The place was dark. Its few windows faced north, depriving the pub of natural light; and its faded army green walls soaked up most of the electrical light extending down from ceiling fan lamps.

"Well, at least it isn't a health spa," Barry said. "I trust the food is all right?"

"It's good. I believe the place opened during the occupation."

Stuart looked around. "The Roman one?" The men laughed.

The waiter put them in a corner booth across from a well-worn wooden bar lined with locals, not the spa set. He stood over them, waiting.

"Bring us a bottle of your house red," Luc said, "and a menu."

"Not for him," Stuart said pointing at Barry. "He's here for his health, remember?"

"I'll have a bottled water," Barry said. "Do you have steak and frites?"

The waiter nodded.

"Bring the two of us steak and frites. Luc?"

"Just a tomato salad."

The waiter sauntered off.

"Okay, so what's this all about?" Stuart asked again.

"I'm sorry. It does seem a bit ludicrous. The good news is that my friend, the one I told you about last night, is willing to meet with us. But he asked me to minimize any connection for the time being. So, that's why I've contacted you in such a roundabout way. I thought I would honor his request by limiting telephone contact, and I would ask you to do the same."

The waiter brought a bottle of wine along with a bottle of water straight from the springs of Évian to the table. He opened both bottles, poured out their contents, and strutted off. The conversation resumed.

"I can think of three reasons right off the top of my head why your friend doesn't want to be associated with us," Stuart said. "One, he thinks this UFO sighting is bats and doesn't want to be associated with it.

Two, he thinks there's something to it, and doesn't want to be known to be associated with it. Or three, it has nothing to do with UFOs and more to do with some kind of French politics or something. Which is it?"

Luc looked at Stuart with more admiration than he had heretofore shown him. "My friend was cryptic, but he usually is. All that I can tell you is that if he wasn't interested, he wouldn't bother, so he's interested."

"Good!" Stuart said. "That eliminates possibilities one and three. What's your friend's name?"

"He asked me not to tell you."

"I see," Stuart said. "Sounds like he may have good cause to be paranoid if he believes our discussion could broach on classified information."

"I would not know about that."

The waiter unloaded two plates of steak and frites and an exceptionally large tomato salad with the haughtiness often characteristic of French waiters but without the elegance. "Anything else?" he inquired in good English.

"That will be all," Luc said.

"At least he's willing to talk to us," Barry said. "So when do we go over to CERN?"

"We don't. He thought that would not be wise."

"So he's coming here?"

"No. He would like it to be a casual encounter among vacationers if by chance anyone should see us. He's taking a weekend trip to Lake Lucerne and suggests we do the same. He will contact us once we arrive, that is, if we choose to come."

"I hadn't planned a vacation from my vacation so soon," Barry said. "Do you think it's worth it?"

"That is not for me to say," Luc said.

"Stu?"

"Yeah, I do. There's gotta be something behind all this secrecy or it wouldn't be worth it to him."

"I will have to talk to Etienne, of course," Barry said. "But my guess is we are on."

"My suggestion is that we leave for Lucerne as soon as possible," Luc said.

The men were quiet throughout the rest of their meal, thinking or perhaps wondering what lay ahead.

Luc was the first to finish and get up from the booth. "You can phone me once you've confirmed Etienne's interest. Just pretend it is nothing more than a pleasure trip. Lake Lucerne is very beautiful."

"We won!" shouted Hans Bueller rather loudly for a man of ninety plus years. There was much applause as he and his partner stood up to take a bow.

The sponsor of the bridge tournament presented the beaming couple with a small silver trophy in the shape of an opened deck of cards. "We hope you will honor us by representing Évian next month in the International Championship Tournament," he said.

Etienne stood among a large group of onlookers and clapped for his grandmother and her dear friend. Until that moment he had no knowledge of the serious nature of the competition. He had thought it merely a small tournament among hotel guests, not the entire town. Neither had he realized that bridge was a serious sport in Évian, and thus the town had among its ranks many talented players. And most of all he never knew his own grand-mère was such gifted card player.

Madame Conti walked over to her grandson, hugged him, and whispered in his ear, "Life always offers something new. Never forget that." He kissed her cheek.

"International championship tournament!" Summer exclaimed, "Wow!"

"Yes, it's exciting!" Hans said. "Just last year I was exiled from Egypt believing my best days were done. And here I am with a whole new life." Madame Conti kissed his cheek.

A photographer approached the foursome for permission to begin his shoot. He took pictures of the championship couple, one of which would appear in the next day's newspaper along with photos of the group of four as a memento of this grand evening.

"We should have a fine dinner with lots of champagne," Etienne said.

"There is no disagreement here," Madame Conti said. "But I should go to my room and rest for a few minutes and change. I am all in a sweat."

"You do that Grand-mère and Hans too. I will see to the reservation. Hans, is eight too late for you?"

"No, no, I'm all a flutter, not tired a bit."

"Good, then we will meet in the dining room at eight."

Etienne made the reservation quickly giving him the necessary time to phone Barry and ready himself for dinner.

"He won't tell us his name," Barry said. "I'm not even supposed to be talking to you about this over the telephone, but I can see no way around it."

"And we are supposed to follow this man, whoever he is, to Lucerne?" Etienne said.

"The way I look at it is this. If he's a friend of Luc Renard's, he must be all right. I suppose he is anyway," Barry said under his breath. "He works at CERN; it's highly secretive. Stuart thinks that explains it."

"I cannot help it. I have a bad feeling about this."

"I wouldn't take it personally," Barry said, mistakenly thinking Etienne interpreted the man's unwillingness to be publicly associated with him as a social slight. "I think it has more to do with what you saw than who you are."

Etienne grew quiet as he contemplated the import of what Barry had just said. If this scientist from CERN believes a secret meeting is necessary, if a meeting is to happen at all, with all the travel time and convoluted instructions Barry had just laid out, what does it mean about what he saw?

"Are you there?" Barry said into the phone after a long period of silence.

"Yes, yes, I was just thinking. Of course I am available to go. There is Summer, and my grandmother will want to go if I tell her Luc Renard will be there. Then of course Hans will come with her."

"Under these circumstances I wouldn't bring them all," Barry said. "Just a minute. I've been overridden. I'll hand you over to Stuart."

"It might be a good idea to bring them all," Stuart said. "If the point is to look like tourists on a holiday, they would add to that impression. Just don't tell them anything."

Framed this way, Etienne's mind was made up. "I cannot endanger them," he said. "I will tell them something to keep them here."

Stuart paused briefly as he took in Etienne's resolute tone. "I see where you're coming from, but it would look more natural if your family was with you."

"I cannot turn them into props in what could become a misadventure."

"All right. We'll pick you up in the morning before everyone is up, let's say eight."

"Good, I will think of something to tell them. I've got to go now. Summer is at the door."

"Etienne, are you there?" she said from the hallway.

"Come in," he said and let her into his room.

"I was wondering if you were here," she said.

"I'm sorry. I was on the phone."

"Barry?"

"Yes, it was." He headed towards the bathroom. "I will be just a few minutes."

"What did he say?"

"Not too much. I will tell you after I have washed."

Etienne looked at himself in the mirror as he washed his face. He would have to think of something fast. He dried, combed his hair, put on a clean shirt, and reappeared. "Come on. Let us go to dinner and celebrate. I am wildly hungry!"

"What do you mean Barry didn't say much. Didn't he talk to Luc?"

"Yes, he did, but the fellow Luc hopes to introduce me to is currently unavailable, a vacation or something like that. It will have to wait."

"Oh." After a few silent moments she added, "Maybe tomorrow we can do our own investigation, get Barry and Stuart over here and go back to the scene of the crime." She smiled amused at her own overstatement.

"I will not be here tomorrow or for several more days. I've been summoned to Brussels to help arrange very important debt financing."

"You never mentioned this before."

"I only just found out. Barry is not the only person I talked to. The French minister of finance phoned."

"Oh," she said. "I'd like to do some shopping in Brussels."

"No, no, you must stay here and have your vacation."

47

"With your grandmother and Hans?"

"I will leave the car with you. The three of you can go on an outing or two while I am gone. I will take the train to Geneva and fly from there."

"I'll drive you to the train station," she said.

Summer did not feel much like celebrating at the celebratory dinner that evening. Neither did Etienne for that matter, so uncomfortable he was with having told such a whopping lie to his fiancée. He knew his intentions were pure; nonetheless, he could not kick the feeling he was betraying her trust. And there was something else. He could not kick the feeling that this trip was ill fated. He was not sure why. It was all the secrecy, he supposed. That did not dampen Madame Conti and Hans Bueller's celebration, however; toasts went round until midnight. And it did not dampen Etienne's appetite. He ate enough lamb for two men.

Later in his room Etienne once again phoned Barry. "I'm sorry to phone you so late, but I just got back to my room."

"What's up?" Barry already asleep mumbled.

"There must be a change in our plan. Summer is dropping me off at the train station in Évian tomorrow. She thinks I am going to Brussels on business. So you must pick me up there and not here."

"At eight?"

"No, make it later, around nine, after the train has departed."

"Will do. Bonne nuit."

Chapter Six

"**I**'m surprised the French finance minister would call you at the last minute like this," Summer said while she drove Etienne to the train station. "He's never done such a thing before. And while you're on vacation! "

"It is an emergency."

"I would have liked to come along. I enjoy visiting Brussels."

"Another time."

She was surprised he had so little to say and few apologies. It was not like him to hold back, except... She recalled only a few days earlier he had held off telling her about his UFO sighting. Could that have something to do with his sudden departure? She became suspicious, so suspicious that after she dropped him off she parked the car a block away and returned to the train station on foot. She concealed herself in the doorway of a shop across the street to watch, not really expecting to see anything but to reassure herself. She was confident he would board the train to Geneva as he had said he would. Yet a part of her overruled those expectations, so she set out to spy if nothing more than to relieve her doubts. Twenty minutes later she recognized the van that had carried them all from Paris pull up to the entrance of the train station. Stuart was in the driver's seat. Etienne emerged from the doorway of the station carrying his suitcase. She darted out from the shop doorway to confront him.

"Where are you going?" she shouted as she crossed the street.

He stopped in his tracks and turned around to confront her. "You found me out," he said, too embarrassed by his own behavior to question hers.

Barry got out of the passenger side of the van and went over to the couple. "He's only trying to protect you Summer."

"From what? Where are you going?"

"I am going to Lake Lucerne to see the man Luc Renard contacted," Etienne replied ashamedly.

"You told me that man was on vacation, that a meeting would have to wait," she sobbed.

"I thought it best," he said.

"The circumstances are a little strange," Barry explained. "This man is secretive. He won't tell us his name and doesn't want anyone to know about the meeting. That set off a few alarm bells and Etienne..."

"I didn't want you or my grandmother to get in the middle of trouble if there is any," he interrupted. "I thought it best to...."

"To lie to me? We have a problem," she said, her tone having changed to anger. She turned to walk away before she turned back to him. "You keep making decisions about me without consulting me. Don't you think I can handle making them for myself?"

"What do you want to do?" he said.

"I'm going! You will very likely need my insight."

"You have no clothes with you."

"I'll buy some!"

"You had better sit in the rear with me," Barry said to Etienne. "Summer, you get in the front with Stu."

"Fine!"

"You're going to have to be my navigator," Stuart said, handing her the road map.

"Fine!" she repeated. She studied the map for a few minutes. "It looks like we should drive around the eastern tip of Lake Geneva to Montreux, then head northeast up to Bern, drop south toward Interlaken and northeast into Lucerne."

"Why drive north then south then north again?" Stuart said. "Can't we cut across?"

"Sure, you can do that," Summer said. "But it will take longer. The roads will be narrower, and I get carsick circling through tight mountain curves."

"Summer is right," Etienne said from the rear seat. "You forget we are going to Switzerland. We should stick to the main highways as much as we can. We can stop in Montreux, get a snack, and do a little shopping."

The drive to Lucerne was short, taking only four hours even with a stop in Montreux where Summer picked up a few items of clothing and toiletries. Her mood had softened; the views of the gentle, lush

50

countryside contributed to an improvement in everyone's spirits. Once the van turned south at Bern and drove into Interlaken, the sight of the mighty Alps became spectacular. Yet it was the lakes not the mountains that had been the theme of their holiday thus far. It was into a lake, after all, that Etienne had seen a UFO submerge and then raise itself out of the water and disappear into the sky. Évian itself was lakeside. And they traversed the entire southern shore of Lake Geneva from its eastern edge to Montreux on its far western side. They skirted the lakes of Thun and Brientz before turning north again to Lucerne, which is situated on a lake by the same name. Their hotel in Lucerne was likewise lakeside, with watery views from the expensive rooms that Etienne's travel agent had been able to book them even at this busy time of year.

This fact had not escaped Etienne who had begun to fantasize about unknown presences lurking below as they sat out on the hotel terrace overlooking the water. Luc had become nearly as mysterious to him as the unnamed man they would soon meet. He asked their waiter for a phone and dialed up Luc's number, but there was no answer. He left a message to assure him they would wait dinner until he arrived and to let him know about the hotel's unusual entrance, a glass funicular housed behind glass doors that carries its guests from the street below to the lofty hotel lobby. He secretly wondered if Luc might not return the call. Had his course been altered, he wondered as he recollected the intensity with which he had recited those lines from Dante two nights before. In hindsight he realized that Dante was a part of Luc's meditation, a private meditation that was perhaps his reason for retreating to Évian. Could he have fallen into Dante's pit, he thought, while to the others he voiced only a concern that he might have walked past the entrance and become lost. Etienne knew firsthand of clergy who had fallen into the pit's core. His speculation ended when Luc phoned back to say he had in fact walked past the entrance but had found it now thanks to his message and would be right up.

When Luc arrived the foursome was enjoying wine and hors d'oeuvre at the terrace restaurant. He seemed friendly and relaxed, not at all the troubled penitent Etienne had imagined. Etienne chalked the contradiction up to his own state of mind, which he acknowledged had been unsteady since the sighting. He continued to feel headachy, hot, and always hungry in spite of the fact that just that very morning he had had to loosen his belt a notch. His judgment had been askew. He had been wrong to lie to Summer. He had been wrong to even imagine Luc, who had after all arranged this trip to Lucerne, would not show up. And he probably was wrong in his suspicions about the nameless man from CERN. As Luc and the others exchanged greetings and small talk about the beautiful views afforded by the terrace, Etienne turned inward and pledged that he would temper both his imagination and his appetite.

"I'm sorry this has turned into such a roundabout way of meeting Roland," Luc said. "But his job is sensitive, and he wants to keep it."

"Roland," Barry said. "So it's all right now if we know his name."

"Only his first name," Luc said. "He abhors scandal, and does not want to risk drawing any such thing to himself. I cannot blame him. Any scandal and poof, he's out of a job. That is just how things work at CERN."

"I see," Etienne said. "UFOs sightings are scandalous."

"They can be for a scientist," Barry said. "They're so often associated with hoaxes that it could put anyone's career at risk, even my own."

"You misunderstand me," Luc said. "It's not your UFO sighting he's worried about. It's the claims you've made publicly about Gitane Marie."

"What! I never imagined unearthing Gitane Marie to be scandalous," a disbelieving Etienne said.

"Don't get me wrong," Luc said. "I don't feel that way, but I am a theologian, not a scientist. I can accept it. In fact, I welcome the view that Gitane Marie embodies the divine creative force. But the scientific community does not view reality through the same lens as I."

"They would have been happier if we had posited something more along the lines of further evidence for Australopithecus Afarensis?" Barry said.

"Something like that, I'm afraid."

"That seems rather narrow," Summer said. "There's plenty of evidence for a mythic reality unless you choose to entirely discount cross cultural, cross historical belief from our lexicon of knowledge."

"So true," Barry said.

"That's what we show in our museum," she said. "The thread that runs through time and place that links us all, a kind of spiritual, psychological umbilical cord."

"Good image Summer," Barry said.

"I won't argue with you," Luc said. "I have visited your museum and found it, well, inspiring. But I am speaking of hard scientists here."

Etienne was stunned by the eloquence of Summer's defense. He began to doubt that a scientist such as Luc described could offer him help. "Do you think a hard scientist, as you call him, could possibly understand what I saw?"

"Roland is not so hard as many," Luc said. "If he were, he and I probably would not be such good friends. Although he well knows the terrain he must live in. He also knows a bit of the terrain around sightings such as yours."

"Well, that's good," Barry said. "A fair hearing is all we want. When will we speak with him?"

"He has asked that tomorrow we take the train up to the top of Mount Pilatus and meet him at their outdoor cafe. No one will be up there but other tourists, climbers, paragliders, and the like. We will be quite inconspicuous."

"That's agreeable," Etienne said looking up at the distant mountain peaks.

"Yeah, that's way up there," Summer said.

"Nearly 7000 feet," Luc said. "Just the breeze and the cow bells."

"Cow bells?" Summer said.

"You hear them in the distance, sometimes even see a cow or two on the way up."

"Sounds like you go up there a lot," Stuart said.

"I like to when I'm here," Luc said. "I like high places."

"Let us have some dinner," Etienne said.

The following morning they ferried across a foggy Lake Lucerne to the village of Alpnachstad where they boarded one of the red cars of a cogwheel train that began its steep climb up the mountain, passing a lonely farmhouse and barn perched sideways on the slope. The loud clang of cowbells broke through the silence as they inched along. The deciduous forest intermingled with fog until they were so high there was only pine. After the mist dissolved, there were no trees at all.

"Look over there!" Summer shouted pointing to a woman dangling in the air from a hot pink canopy.

"She jumped from up there," Luc said pointing up to the mountain summit.

Stuart, never comfortable with heights, cringed while Summer looked on in delight.

"I'd like to try that," she said. "I've always wanted to fly."

"Paragliding is not like bungee jumping. It requires training," Luc said.

Etienne instinctively wrapped his arm around Summer's shoulder as if he were poised to protect her should she leap from the train.

"Summer, when's your birthday?" Luc asked.

"Why do you ask?"

"I'm just curious. You don't have to tell me your birth year, just the month."

"I was born late November."

"Ha! I knew it."

"Knew what?"

"You are a Sagittarius."

"I know I am. So what?"

"Those ancient stargazers had more wisdom than we give them credit for."

"So what?" she asked again.

"Sagittarians are tightrope walkers, adventurers, dare devils if you will. Now, I've known Sagittarians who are none of these things, but you fit the bill. I love to meet pure signs."

"Sagittarius is an archer too," Barry said and began to laugh. "Better not give her a bow and arrow. We might all be in trouble."

The wind picked up. They had arrived at the craggy top.

Chapter Seven

Clouds moved in driven by brisk westerly winds. Until only a few moments earlier, the sky had been quite blue and the sun brilliant. A black bird dove low over the outdoor table where the group sat and deposited a rather large dropping that read like an invitation to leave.

"Let's go inside," Roland said having just dodged the disgusting splatter. "I can hardly hear you over the wind."

"But it's beautiful up here!" Summer said. She rose from her chair and wandered to the edge of the great concrete deck; stretched out over the thin screen railing and admired the peaks, cliffs, and trails above and below. "That lake down there looks white."

"Those are clouds," Roland said.

"We're above the clouds?"

"You can see it all from inside" he said, guiding her away from the edge and towards the door. His actions did not go unnoticed. Etienne stepped between them, putting his arm around Summer.

Roland had the meticulous good looks of a concert pianist, she thought as they followed him inside. Brown hair neatly combed, a starched white shirt under the jacket of a freshly pressed black suit. He looked ready to go on stage or to a funeral and not how she had imagined a scientist to look. Which was it? she wondered. He turned around and looked at her after leading them into the restaurant. A hint of a curl dislodged by the wind softened his melancholic brow. Yet there was no grief in his expression; instead, she saw a soulfulness that all of his formality was meant to conceal, a mask to hide the heightened sensitivity of an artist. But he isn't an artist, she thought, he's a scientist.

Barry eyed him more critically than did Summer. If he wanted to blend in, he thought about the stranger he had just been introduced to, he could hardly have done a worse job. So out of character was his dark suit with the casual sport dress and athletic gear worn by the rest of the tourists who had ventured to the top of Mt. Pilatus.

Formality was the norm for Roland, one that he could not break with even when inappropriate. The reverse was true of Barry, which would explain why this usually genial man felt a tinge of contempt.

The building they entered looked a little like a cylindrical can composed of alternating bands of aluminum and large panoramic windows. Their table in the restaurant pressed against one of the windows, and indeed their view of the mountains was glorious.

"You are looking at Jungfraujoch," Roland said to Summer. "You should go there before you leave the region."

"Ah, yes, the Sphinx Observatory," Luc said. "They call it the top of Europe."

"Nearly twice as high as we are now," Roland said.

"Can we go?" Summer said to Etienne.

"I will order us a large cheese fondue," he graciously offered, and without answering her question left the table to place the order.

"I like that name," Barry said. "I did a good deal of work near the Sphinx not too many years ago. The terrain and temperature couldn't have been more different. Dirty work digging in all of that sand," he added looking pointedly at Roland's pressed suit.

"Barry is an archeologist," Luc said to Roland. "He and his friend Stuart are the men who brought the statue of the goddess back to France."

"I read about it in the paper. A most remarkable exploit, smuggling it out of Egypt."

"It was mostly hot," Stuart said, not picking up on the innuendo.

"We were stowed away in the belly of several ships without sunlight or fresh air," Barry explained. "The funny thing is that at the time I didn't think of it as smuggling, although your assertion is arguably correct. No, it felt more like a liberation, and in fact that's what it proved to be. Gitane Marie had been held captive in the basement of a very old monastery for a very long time. My friend who called me down there hadn't realized this. He had only wanted me to take her back to Europe to identify her. He was sure that's where she came from. We do that sort of thing all the time in my line of work, attempt to learn the background of our finds, put them in an historical context if you will. What he didn't know, and neither did I, nor did the abbot, is she had been intentionally buried away there probably for hundreds of years."

"I read that in the papers too," Roland said. "You were pursued by men who wished to steal her back, were you not?"

Summer held up her arm as if it were wounded. "One of them ripped off the sleeve of my nightgown. He would have...." She paused, unable to finish her sentence.

Barry patted her arm as if to console her. "We tried keeping all that nasty business quiet. But reporters will be reporters. There's no stopping them."

Etienne returned to the table with several bottles of white wine and some glasses in time to hear the latter part of the conversation. He added, "They invaded my sister's home. There were only women there at the time. They were very brave and fought them off. I believe they would have murdered them if their leader had not died first."

"I read impaled by a chandelier," Roland said.

"Yes, a replica of the Cross of Camargue," Summer said. "It was pretty horrible." She turned away as if the gruesome scene had just flashed before her.

"I saw the corpse myself," Barry said. "The cross at the bottom is formed in the shape of an anchor. The fluke caught him in the heart as he and the others were shoving a heavy dining table at the women in an attempt to pin them against the wall."

"Grisly! You were lucky to have escaped," Roland said looking tenderly at the girl. "The paper was not clear about who these men are."

"Neither are we," she said. "They never gave their names, not even the name of the deceased. They went to jail without doing so."

"The surviving men were finally arrested in Paris," Barry said. "They tried to steal the statue from one of the girls at Saint Sulpice during a concert we were attending. That one there," he pointed to Summer, "kept one of them pinned down on a park bench until the police came."

Roland tried unsuccessfully to hold back a smile as he imagined the pretty girl before him piled atop her assailant on a Paris park bench. Such beautiful eyes, he thought. "So you think what?" he said to Barry his voice tinged with skepticism. "You think they are a cult of some sort who meant to steal her back and return her to oblivion?"

"Yes, exactly," Barry said, sure now it was not just Roland's immaculate grooming that bothered him.

"Could they not have been ordinary thieves whose goal it was to steal her and sell her to the highest bidder?"

"There are a number of other details that make us think otherwise," Etienne said. "Let me assure you. These were no ordinary thieves, and Gitane Marie is no ordinary artifact."

"How do you know that?" Roland persisted.

"Have you gone to Paris to see her?" Luc asked.

"No, I have not."

"Then you should. Look into her eyes, and then tell me she is ordinary."

Roland grew silent on the topic. At that moment it was Summer's eyes that had caught his attention. "But we are not here to discuss the statue," he said turning to Etienne. "Luc tells me you have had a sighting."

He says that too casually, Etienne thought before he responded. "Yes, I saw something I cannot explain. We came here because Luc thought you might offer some insight."

One of the restaurant staff placed a spirit burner on the table and the kitchen cook followed behind with a large pot of cheese fondue that he proudly placed over the flame. The staffer returned with two baskets of large chunks of crusty bread, plates, fondue forks, and napkins. Etienne ordered another bottle of wine and a large plate of fruit, and they all ate.

"So, tell me more about what you saw," Roland said.

"I had taken a walk into the pinewoods near our hotel outside Évian and came upon a small lake. I stopped there and rested when out of the sky came a silver object. At first I thought it might have been a helicopter, but I saw no blade. And then it began to descend. It continued to do so until it was entirely submerged. I waited a good thirty minutes."

"It was longer than that," Summer interrupted.

"There is a time discrepancy we can talk about later," Etienne said. "It seemed like thirty minutes or so. And then the thing rose up out of the water way up into the sky, and in a blink of the eye, it disappeared."

"Were you alone? What was the time of day?"

"It happened in the late morning. I remember it was very sunny, and I was by myself. I had just gone to take a walk."

"Let's go back to the time discrepancy," Roland said. He turned to Summer. "What do you mean?"

"He told me he came right back to the hotel afterwards, but he had been gone for hours."

Roland looked over at Etienne.

"Well, yes, I cannot explain that. The whole event took about forty-five minutes, an hour at most, and I did return to the hotel immediately. In fact, I ran back."

"Could you have been abducted?"

"Impossible!"

"Abductees rarely know it unless they undergo treatment for a trauma of an unknown origin."

"Hypnosis, you mean. Never!"

"Hmm," Roland sighed. "What do you think happened?"

"I don't know. I thought I might have confabulated the whole thing after hearing the letter from Barry's nephew, but it seems so real that I cannot quite believe I did."

"Little more than a week before the event I had a letter from my nephew," Barry explained. "He isn't my nephew really, he's Summer's sister's nephew, but he's like a nephew to me. He's taking care of my house back in the States while I try to sell it. He wrote me a detailed letter, which I read to these folks that describes his own UFO experience. Well, actually, it was more than that. He reports that he and others saw what he called Bio-Nano Robots, robotic mice inhabiting the inside of the walls of my house. That is until the mice were chased out by high frequency sound and taken aboard a flying saucer in my backyard. I read parts of it out loud while we were still in Paris, and we speculated about what could have caused Paul to report such a thing."

"Your nephew is attracted to the fantastic, reads science fiction?" Roland asked.

"He's quite imaginative in the positive sense of the word," Barry said. "But up until now I never would have described him as fantasy prone."

"Could you make me a copy of his letter for my files?"

"Sure. I have it with me back at the hotel. I'll mail you a copy."

Looking at Etienne, Roland asked, "So you think this letter may have influenced your imagination, and you unwittingly concocted the whole episode?"

Etienne paused for a moment before answering. "No, I do not. I think I wish that were the case."

"I don't think you confabulated the experience either," Roland said. "I don't know you well enough to speculate about your personality type, but I do know the episode you describe. I have read it reported several times in this region. I will look in my files for the details."

"I thought you would know if that were the case," Luc said. "That's why I brought these folks to you."

"Why do you suppose in this region?" Stuart asked.

"The proximity to CERN. The research projects at the Sphinx Observatory. More science goes on here than in many parts of Europe."

"So, what are you saying?" Stuart said. "Do you think these things might be some kind of secret research project?"

"They could be. The questions are who does this invention, this flying saucer you saw, belong to? And what could be its purpose? I've been keeping an eye on these stories for years with these questions in mind."

"What can we do to assist you?" Etienne asked.

"I would like you to write down everything you have said to me, including the discrepancy in the time line of events. Include all the details you can remember: weather conditions, color of the object, sounds it may have produced, and other natural conditions at the time. It would be useful if you can make a map illustrating the exact location of the lake. And I would like a copy of the letter from Barry's nephew. I will be able to compare your account with like accounts in my files and see what conclusions, if any, I can draw. That's the best I can do for now. Following this, I may make other investigative suggestions."

"You should see his files," Luc said. "The organization, the attention to detail. I've never seen anything like it."

Roland did not respond to Luc's compliment. What was a matter of amazement to Luc was a matter of course to him. Instead, he unexpectedly rose from his chair. "I think that is all we can do here for now. I will keep in contact with Luc. I should ask you to act quickly. These cases can grow cold very fast." He looked over at Summer. "You are a brave and passionate girl, wonderful attributes in a woman; but do

60

not let them overwhelm your judgment. You could be hurt." With that, Roland left the restaurant and made his way back down the mountain alone.

Etienne felt a rush of possessive jealousy. Summer, never one to resort to the kinds of flirtations and psychological games that arouse such feelings, had never given him cause to feel jealousy in the past. And she had not now, but Roland had.

"This was a brief meeting, particularly when you take into account how far we had to travel for it," Barry said.

"Roland's a bit of a philosopher," Luc said. "A philosopher of the human soul. I think that's why he keeps so much to himself."

"Why so?" Barry asked.

"When you look too deeply into the soul of men it can be troubling," Luc said. And then realizing his point could be misinterpreted he turned to Summer. "That's not what he saw in you, the troubling part, I mean. To the contrary, he paid you quite a compliment, particularly coming from him. I think what he sees in you is the exception, something quite extraordinary."

She stayed silent, not knowing how to respond to the compliment.

"Summer is very special to me," Etienne said.

The words "to me," repeated themselves again and again in her head where they were soon divorced from the intended compliment. They bothered her, but she did not know why.

"We might as well go back to Évian tomorrow," Luc said, pointing to the fog that had begun to envelop the mountain. "I wonder if I might hitch a ride?"

"I had hoped we could go to Jungfraujoch," Summer said.

"On another trip," Etienne replied. He had grown tired of mountains.

The area around Interlaken was shrouded in fog the next day eliminating any chance to see Jungfraujoch and removing any temptation Summer might have had to press her case to ascend the mountain to the Sphinx Observatory. They reached Montreux around noon, just as the sun broke through and roused the sleepy passengers who began to discuss what had been on their dreamy minds while Stuart chauffeured them through the Alps.

"We never gave Roland an opportunity to talk about his work," Barry said.

"Yeah, what does that guy do besides chasing down UFO stories?" Stuart asked.

"He does research related to neutrinos," Luc said. "He doesn't talk about it much; I suppose it must be proprietary."

"You mean secret," Stuart said.

"What are neutrinos?" Summer asked.

"A kind of subatomic particle. They've been in the news lately. I haven't asked Roland if he's involved in the controversy because we have this sort of unspoken agreement that I won't ask too many questions."

"So ours isn't the only controversy to have made the news," Barry said. "What's his?"

"I'm not sure of his level of involvement or if he is involved at all, but it has been reported that some scientists at CERN are asserting that neutrinos can travel faster than the speed of light."

"I thought that's impossible," Summer said. "I thought the speed of light is as fast as anything can go."

"That's the controversy," Luc said. "Einstein's theories rest on that belief. But they shot neutrinos from their lab here in Switzerland to a sister lab in Italy some 500 miles away that they claim went faster than the speed of light. It's been in all the papers."

"I thought our discovery was controversial," Barry said. "At least ours didn't threaten to overturn everything science thinks it knows about physics."

Luc shot him a glance that turned into a wide smile. "Just religion," he said sarcastically.

"Ours is a corrective, to be sure," Barry replied.

"I don't see why you can't ask him about it," Summer said. "If it's been in the newspaper, it's not a secret."

"You can," Luc said. "If you're interested, you should. It's just not how he and I relate."

"How did you meet him?" Barry asked.

"He was a speaker at a conference I attended. He was very good. 'The Meaning of the God Particle,' I believe was the title of his lecture."

"God particle?" Etienne said.

"Odd terminology for scientific inquiry, isn't it? But aptly named, " Luc said.

"What is it?" Summer asked.

"According to this theory of the universe, the God particle is what gave mass to matter after the big bang."

"A little out of your territory, isn't it?" Barry said. "You being a theologian."

"A little, but less than what I would have thought before I met Roland. You've heard of the big Hadron Collider they've got over at CERN. They're shooting proton beams through this thing creating huge collisions they hope will replicate the big bang and unmask the elusive God particle."

"Oh, I see. 'Let there be light,'" Barry said.

"Let there be matter. Slightly different perspective, but otherwise the same thing."

"So, the God particle is what turns light energy into matter?" Summer said. "That sounds a lot like the Sophia."

Luc looked at her inquisitively.

"The Sophia. The final emanation, that which is closest to us," she said. "You know, she is supposed to have created the physical world from God's light."

"Whatever was, whatever will be is in her care/ For she is the maker of the world," Barry recited from Gitane Marie's poem.

"Very interesting," Luc said. "The Higgs boson, the God particle, the Sophia."

"Gitane Marie," Summer added. "How does this collider machine work?"

"It's very large, about 17 miles round," Luc said. "The proton beams travel at incredibly high speeds clockwise and counterclockwise ramming into each other to produce explosions that leave a debris. The debris is where they hope to find the Higgs boson."

"It sounds dangerous."

"It hasn't caused the end of the world yet!" Luc said in jest. "They've taken precautions. It's 500 feet underground. It hasn't produced the Higgs boson yet either, but Roland believes they are hot on its trail."

"The Higgs boson may be as elusive as the Sophia," Etienne said.

"I don't know about that," Barry countered. "We unearthed her in Gitane Marie. It seems fitting somehow that her scientific counterpart should be revealed now, just after she was brought into the light. All secrets out in the open. It seems fitting to me somehow."

Stuart pulled up in front of Luc's townhouse shortly after they had arrived in Évian.

"Thanks for the lift," Luc said, as he was about to exit the van.

"Wait a minute," Stuart said. "What's our plan?"

"Roland wants a map of the area around the lake," Etienne said.

"We can do better than that," Stuart said. "Let's map your entire walk, from the parking lot to the lake and back to the hotel."

"Good idea," Barry said. "Do it while the event is still fresh in your memory. A running account of what you saw would be helpful too. I have a lot of experience with that sort of thing."

"So do I," Stuart said. "Roland also wants a copy of Paul's letter."

"I've got a multipurpose printer that makes photocopies," Luc said. "You can bring it over tomorrow, and I'll make copies. Why not come over for lunch."

"But the mapping?" Barry said.

"Etienne and I can handle that," Stuart said. "Besides, you're too allergic."

"To those god forsaken flowers, not to pine trees!"

"Barry, you go to Luc's," Summer said. "Stuart, you come have lunch with us at the hotel. Afterwards, we can follow Etienne's path. You two can do the mapping, and I'll write down the running commentary."

It was settled.

Chapter Eight

"I left the path here," Etienne said. "I walked up there into the pinewood."

"Okay, so the parking lot's here," Stuart said while looking at the map he was in the process of drawing. "I'd say we've come about a mile on the path."

"About one and a half kilometers," Etienne agreed.

"How are you feeling?" Summer asked him.

"I am fine."

"That's good," she said, relieved that what he had feared most had not happened, the rekindling of what for him had been a nightmarish experience.

"I am past it now. I am sure of it," he said.

"It's the talking," Stuart said. "Talking about it diminishes the shock. Holding it in has the opposite effect."

"I think you must be right. Now, it is as if you all had been there with me."

Stuart looked into his face. "That's what it's like when you share. You don't feel so isolated."

"You sound like you know from experience," Summer said.

"I do, sort of. Nothing like this. I've never seen a UFO, but I was in combat. Saw a lot of horror there. It was tough when I got home. I felt isolated. At times I thought I was crazy or would go crazy, so I know of what I speak."

"I didn't know you were in the military," Summer said.

"I don't know much about what you were doing twenty years ago either."

"She was just out of nappies," Etienne said and smiled.

"I was not. I was older than that."

The threesome walked out of the sunlight into the cool shade of the pine forest.

"I love the smell of pine needles," Summer said after taking in a deep breath.

"I walked along until I came out into a grassy field near the lake," Etienne recounted. "It should not take long to get there."

"What were you doing twenty years ago?" Stuart asked Etienne.

"Funny you should ask. I was just thinking about it. I was a very pious teenager, still at the lycée. I was inducted into what I believed to be a very special organization for pious young men. I thought it was an honor at the time. So did everyone else."

"It wasn't?" Stuart asked.

"Not for me."

"What happened?"

"I knelt and kissed the ring of power thinking it was the ring of God."

"Sounds pretty esoteric."

"That was the problem; it was not. As I said, I was a very pious young man and very naive."

"You're still a little stiff," Stuart said.

"If you think I am stiff now, you should have seen me then. I have since learned to accept the world but on my own terms. I was born into privilege, which is why I was initiated into the group at all, but I did not know that back then. I could laugh at myself now."

"You've never told me about this," Summer said.

"You have never asked about my youth."

"I just supposed—I knew what happened to your parents, and I haven't wanted to bring it up."

The mere mention of his parents was like a knife blow to his heart. For a moment he relived the bitter pain that had overwhelmed him after his mother and father had abandoned him for their mission, leaving him to the mercies of a clandestine group of men to whom he had unwisely transferred his parental affection. Tears came to his eyes.

"Thank God for my grandmother. She helped me get past the disillusionment, and she was there for my sister and me after my parents were killed."

"Didn't you say they died in one of those wars down in Africa?" Stuart asked.

"Yes, murdered while they were treating the wounded."

"We all have had our disillusionments," Stuart said, "except Summer here."

"Life hasn't always been a bed of roses for me either," she said. "But nothing that bad has happened. Not like you two. I suppose I've been lucky."

The sun came coursing through the trees as they neared the edge of the pinewood. The trio cut through the tall grasses to the lakeside.

"This lake's bigger than what I had expected," Stuart said. "Does it have a name?"

"Nothing is posted," Etienne said. "I should look on a map."

Summer opened her notebook. "So, what did you do when you got here?"

"I sat down and took it all in. Over there, on that log."

The three of them took a seat on the log and stared out into the still lake.

"Do I hear frogs?" she asked.

"Over there." Etienne pointed to a shallow spot with an abundance of reeds. "It is just like it was on that day."

"So what happened?"

"I sat here meditating. And then I noticed something in the sky. I did not know what it was, which is why it intrigued me. It was far too big to be a bird, but it did not have the blades of a helicopter. I did not know what I was looking at. It was silver. It quit hovering and began to descend. After it submerged itself into the water, I knew it was not like anything I had ever seen."

The three of them looked out at the lake as if to create a mental picture of his description when suddenly the still water grew unsettled, as if a heavy boulder had been dropped into its center sending out rippling waves.

"Did any of you see anything fall into the lake?" Etienne asked.

"No!" Summer said.

"A bird must have dived in going after a fish or an insect," Stuart said. He paused for a moment. "How could I have missed that?"

"Or a frog," Summer said. "They quit croaking. Did you notice?"

"Yeah," Stuart said and became very quiet.

The silence was broken by loud hissing sounds coming from the center of the lake.

"What's going on?" Summer shouted.

"What the hell! That's no bird," Stuart said.

Ripples of water became great swirls pushing out from the center of the lake towards the shoreline, and up it came. A great silver object rose into the sky, sheets of water sliding off of its rounded sides splashing into the deep empty well from which it had ascended. Whitecaps splashed violently over the lake edge soaking the threesome who sat on the log.

"Get back!" Stuart shouted, as he back flipped over the log. They fled into the tall grasses and hunkered down. Not wanting to miss the show, Summer stood up to take in the whole spectacle.

"Get down!" Stuart shouted.

"This is fantastic!" Summer exclaimed still standing.

He pulled her down. "You don't want to be taken do you?"

She stared at him first in disbelief and then in recognition. Etienne had gathered himself into a ball, head buried in the grass, and she knew.

"No, I don't want to be taken."

The object flew up but not away. Up and then poof it was gone; the invisible door had silently closed in front of it. A few minutes later the water had receded from the shoreline, and the frogs resumed their chorus.

"Etienne," Stuart said rubbing his back. "It's okay. It's gone." He did not move, but lay still, curled up in the grass.

Summer grabbed his arm and raised him up. "Come on. Let's get out of here."

The threesome retreated into the pine forest exhausted and confused. They wandered back towards the hotel in silent meditation as if individually they were trying to shape the foreign image into an utterance.

"You should both go to your rooms and shower then rest," Stuart said. "I'm going back to my hotel room in Évian. After I've rested I will write down every detail of what I saw. I suggest you do the same."

"I'm the secretary," Summer said. "I record the commentary."

"Good," Stuart said his voice steady. "The commentary, the images, the timing, everything you can think of. We will talk about it later, share our notes after we've rested."

Etienne wrapped his arms around Stuart and Summer and the threesome hugged. Stuart, always uncomfortable with outward shows of affection, was the first to pull away. He stood back and looked at Etienne reassuringly. "You will be all right. You just need rest. You too Summer."

He knew Summer would be all right. She was the stronger of the two. He was not so sure about Etienne. At least he has Summer, he thought.

Stuart climbed into the van and from out of its window stared blankly at the entrance to the path they had just taken. Seeing a UFO is very different than hearing about them, he thought. Not that he had doubted Etienne's words exactly, but he had doubted his perceptions until the events of this day confirmed them.

It's like war, he thought. No one really gets it unless they've been there. They can listen, they can sympathize, but they never really get it. His psychiatrist hadn't gotten it. Returning to civilian life was like being hurled out of one sort of chaos into another that only communion with his peers could pull him through. Together they made some sense of what they had witnessed, as much sense as it is possible to make from experiences that had obliterated everything he thought he knew about himself and the world. He had to find a new kind of order, one that took into account the extreme conditions of war. Here was the healing, the recognition that in spite of what he and his men had done and seen, they were not monsters. They were victims too. He had never told Natalie any of this. He refused to speak to her about the war when she asked, so sure he was that she would not understand. Maybe he should have tried.

Were there monsters inside the craft he had just seen? How many? What had they done to Etienne and why? This thing, this UFO, requires another kind of understanding, an explanation for what it is, whose it is, and what it's doing here. That could be a shocker too, he realized. But the damage had already been done. The planet he had thought he inhabited, spinning around the giant lighted orb it shared with other planets, yet singular among them with its abundance of life, like a lone ship sailing in a universal night filled with distant, empty stars—that world was gone now. The surety of it at least. He would have to reconstruct his place in the world. But first he would have to learn the world's place in this new inhabited universe.

He drove the now familiar road back to the hotel in Évian in perceptual automatic as his mind was engaged elsewhere. He darted to the room he shared with Barry fully expecting to find him returned from Luc's and waiting expectantly to hear the bizarre tale of what had happened that afternoon. But the room was empty. He could hardly bear the silence, the aloneness. He picked up the phone and direct dialed Natalie's number. Her recorded voice answered. He paused for a moment thinking whether to leave a message. What could it be? he thought. Come for me Natalie, come and comfort me. I will tell you all. He did not speak. He stripped down, showered, dressed in clean clothes, and shot out of the hotel, rapidly walking the seven blocks to Luc's townhouse. But before he arrived he met up with Barry who was walking back to the hotel. Seeing him, he felt relief.

"Is everything all right?" Barry said. "You look flushed."

"If you mean am I safe, if all of us are safe, yes," Stuart said.

"I didn't mean quite that. Safe from what?"

"I will tell you when we get to the hotel; I will tell you everything."

When they arrived Barry said he would pick up a bottle of wine and some glasses from the bar to bring up to the room.

"Get two. One white and one red," Stuart said.

"Or maybe you'd rather have a beer," Barry said, remembering beer was Stuart's preferred drink.

"Wine is fine. That way we can enjoy it together."

Barry ordered a bottle of Pinot Grigio, nicely chilled, and a robust red wine from the South, and the two men disappeared into their room.

"Natalie always ordered this," Stuart said, sipping his first glass of Pinot Grigio.

"You miss her, don't you?"

Stuart did not speak, but his face said everything.

"Have you written her since you got over here?"

"I tried phoning earlier today. She didn't answer."

"Too bad. So, what's all the excitement?"

"I saw it."

"It?" Barry paused for a moment. "Oh, lord!"

"We were retracing Etienne's steps. Got to the lake, and he started describing what he saw last week. And then up it popped right out of the middle of the lake. Huge! Silver! Alien! We were covered with water.

Ducked into some tall grasses to conceal ourselves. The thing shot up into the sky and disappeared. It didn't fly off. It just disappeared."

"Having you there to see it must have reassured him. At least it confirmed he wasn't dreaming."

"I wouldn't say so. I mean he didn't react positively if that's what you think. He curled up into a ball, what do they call it, into a fetal position. We pulled him up off the ground and he couldn't even speak. Didn't talk all the way back to the hotel."

"Huh, I wouldn't have expected it," Barry said, and then refilled their glasses. "Do you think he will be all right?"

"Summer's taking care of him."

"How did she handle it?"

"She was fine, fearless and fine. He's rolled up in a ball in the grass, and she's standing up staring at the thing practically announcing herself. I had to yank her down before she was taken too."

"So that's what you think happened to him. You think he was taken the other time."

"I don't have any other way to explain his breakdown. That, and the missing time. It adds up. That's all that I'm sayin'."

Barry shook his head. "Summer won't be able to help him by herself."

"He's going to need more help than I can give him or you either."

"You seem fine, at any rate."

"I wouldn't say fine exactly. It was a real shocker. I've heard about them, but seeing one is a whole new experience."

"You seem to be handling it."

"Yeah, but I wasn't taken."

The room phone rang. Stuart picked it up. "Yeah, yeah," he said after several minutes of conversation at the other end. "Let me talk to Barry, and we'll get back with you."

"Who is it?" Barry whispered.

Stuart covered the phone. "It's Summer. She says Etienne needs help pretty bad. He's starting to remember what happened."

"Hmm. Tell her—tell her I will call Luc Renard right away and see if he knows what to do." He got up off of the bed he had been reclining on. "I'll just open this second bottle," he muttered under his breath.

71

Barry handed Stuart a glass of the red. Stuart took a long, slow sip. "She sounded panicked. Are you going to call Luc?"

Luc was stunned when Barry brought him up to date about what had gone on earlier that day while the two of them were having lunch, chatting, and making a copy of Paul's letter. He was at a loss when he learned about Etienne's breakdown. "I could minister to him," he said, "but I'm not sure what I could say under the circumstances. I think Roland would prove a far better counselor than I." He promised to contact Roland promptly and counseled Barry and Stuart not to worry too much. "Many times things seem far worse, more frightening in the middle of the night than they are. In the light of morning, Etienne will likely be much improved."

The phone conversation was brief but consoling. Barry and Stuart finished off the red wine and retired. Two hours later they were awakened when Luc called back with a new message and a changed tone.

"Roland is coming," he said in earnest. "I would have waited until the morning to phone, but he was adamant that I should warn all of you, particularly Etienne, to keep what you know to yourselves. He said he's learned some things. He said it could be dangerous."

"Who would believe us," Barry said with a nervous chuckle.

"Apparently someone," Luc scolded.

"Well, it's too late to call Summer now. I'll warn her in the morning."

Chapter Nine

Bang! Bang! Bang! Bang! Stuart thought the racket must have been coming from outdoors, repairmen ripping up asphalt on the street or something like that until he opened his eyes. Night still reigned outside his window. Silence. He closed his eyes again until the next round of hammering. Thoroughly roused, he recognized the noise was coming from the door, which he opened slightly to Roland who stood in the dark hall dressed in a neatly pressed black suit.

He looks like an undertaker, Stuart thought. Unable to restrain himself after having stayed up half the night, after having seen a UFO, after having consumed a bottle of wine, and after having been rudely awakened, he greeted Roland with, "Who died?"

Roland, taken aback, at first did not recognize Stuart's brand of humor; but he caught on fast, smiled and answered, "No one yet."

Stuart pointed to a long pile of blankets on the twin bed near the window. "Barry's not up."

"Could you wake him? Luc and I will be down in the lobby waiting. If you don't mind, we would like you to drive us to Etienne's hotel."

"Drive? Sure," Stuart said.

"You look like you could use some coffee."

"What time is it?"

"Nearly five-thirty."

"We didn't turn in until after midnight. Luc woke us up sometime after that," Stuart said pointing to the log on the twin bed that had not moved in spite of the conversation. "Couldn't you give him another hour or two?"

"I didn't sleep all night after Luc delivered the account of yesterday. I took the late night train so that I might arrive before further damage is done."

"Okay. I'll get him up, and we'll meet you downstairs. You'd better have a big pot of black coffee waiting for him."

He shook the man under the pile of blankets. "Barry, get up!" The pile didn't move. Stuart pulled the blankets down from over his head and repeated the order much louder. Barry emitted sounds this time. "Roland's here," Stuart said very loudly. "Luc is here too. We're heading out to see Etienne. You'd better get up!"

"What?" Barry said, eyes still closed.

"You heard me. I'm getting in the shower first. You're next. So get up!"

Roland and Luc were seated in the dining room when Barry and Stuart plopped themselves at the table barely able to support their own weight after a night with little sleep and a lot of wine.

"We have time for you to get some breakfast before we leave," Luc said, looking pityingly at the two. He pointed to the buffet table.

Without prompting, the waiter crossed the floor, turned over their cups, and filled them with black coffee as if the two men's appearance was signal enough.

"Thanks," Barry said.

"What do you want?" Stuart asked.

"Eggs if they've got any. None of that granola. And no yogurt! Some toast if they've got some."

"I'll be right back."

"So what's this about danger?" Barry said. "Stuart told me you were worried enough to take the night train over here."

"Yes, I did. I've been making some comparisons with what I knew of Etienne's account. By the way, I'd like to read the letter from your nephew."

Barry patted his breast pocket. "I've got it right here. I was going to mail you a copy today."

"Can I see it?"

"It's rather long," Barry said and handed him an envelope.

"I'll read it later. While searching through my files I noted several accounts that included reports of temporary abduction. The outcome was never good for the victims."

"They didn't return them or what?" Barry said.

"No, the victims were returned, and first reports were they suffered only from mental disorientation, which one would expect under such circumstances."

"So, what happened to them?" Barry asked again.

"Once I pulled all of my files and started comparing notes, I noticed a pattern I had not seen before. You see I try to follow these things and the people involved over time as best I can. I keep my files updated."

"You should see his files," Luc said. "They take up an entire room, and they're extraordinarily well organized."

"Well organized yes, but I failed to see this obvious pattern until I pulled all of the files with reports from this area."

Stuart returned to the table and placed a plate of scrambled eggs and toast in front of Barry. "I hope you appreciate this. They made them just for you."

"Thank you Stuart. I really do appreciate it. I see you've got some too."

"I asked if they had any bacon, but no such luck."

"This is a health hotel," Luc reminded him.

"Sadly," Barry said. "At least they acknowledge the wholesomeness of a good bottle of wine. So, you were saying you saw a pattern."

"I have reports of about a dozen cases from this area involving UFO sightings. I suspect there are more that went unreported. Three of these cases describe abduction. In all three the abductee was reported dead within six months of the original news account."

"Dead! What killed them?" Stuart asked.

"A drowning in one case, a car accident in another, and a fall from a very high place in the most recent. None of the cases was investigated."

"Maybe there wasn't anything to investigate. The cause of death was obvious," Stuart said.

"Yes, precisely, but I fear that may be a testament to the skill of the murderer."

"Why are you so sure they were murdered?" Barry asked. "Maybe these really were accidental deaths."

"I can assure you, the mathematical probabilities of that are infinitesimally small."

"So, who did it then?" Barry asked.

"I don't know. What I do know is whoever or whatever is responsible is operating in this area. That for reasons yet unknown, they do not want any of these contactees to survive. Oh, I should tell you. All three abduction victims reported further contact with their abductors after the original event. That's why I refer to them as contactees. They seem to have been abducted for some purpose, and future contact was part of it."

"Oh, lord!" Barry said. "How does this future contact take place?"

"All three victims reported telepathic messages. One claimed he was receiving plans for a design of something he was to build. The other two talked about warnings, changes that were about to take place, that sort of thing, as if there was some kind of preparation going on."

"For what?" Stuart asked.

"It's not clear from their stories, and I should point out that these later stories, those describing contactee experiences, were not from reliable press sources. I cannot be sure of their veracity."

"Grocery store tabloids? Give me a break!" Stuart said.

"The truth is always in question in regard to stories of the fantastic," Roland admitted. "But the original accounts of the abductions were in the local newspapers."

"That doesn't make them true either," Barry said.

"No. But soon we will have Etienne's account to add to the list. Do you trust him?"

Stuart reflected on his recent encounter and Etienne's reaction to it. "Yes," he said.

"We had better get out there and warn him," Barry said.

"You haven't yet? I explicitly told Luc to warn you right away before anyone else learns about this."

"I phoned Barry and Stuart straight away," Luc said.

"It was too late by then to call Summer," Barry said. "We had better get out there."

"My dear boy," Madame Conti said to her grandson. "You are not the first to be summoned by the gods. There is a long, long history of such events. The only difference I can discern is the vehicle you describe. Not a winged messenger but a silver craft."

"No winged angel either," Etienne said. "The only features I remember were their eyes. Large blue, watery eyes staring at me, looking at me as if they were looking into my soul."

"Z'e Eye of Horus, of course!" Hans Bueller said. "Some call it z'e Eye of Ra."

"In an Egyptian tomb, yes," Summer said. "But in a UFO?"

The breakfast table went silent. Madame Conti, not to be deflected from her main point, spoke up, "What is the difference, after all? All visitors come by one means or another. Do they not?" She directed her question to four of her bridge friends who sat at the table next to them who were obviously listening in on the conversation.

A man at the table asked, "Did I hear your grandson say he was taken aboard a UFO?"

"Yes, you did. Just up the path from the hotel."

"I've heard reports like that for years, but you are the first person I have ever met to have had the experience. Happy to have met you," the man said to Etienne as he and his three smiling friends got up to leave the dining room.

Etienne nodded politely to the stranger then whispered to his grandmother as they were walking away, "You should not discuss my private affairs this publicly!"

Madame Conti's eyes brightened. She waved across the dining room. "We have more company. I'm not sure I have been introduced."

Summer turned around and saw Barry and Stuart followed by Roland and Luc Renard. "Oh, that's Luc," she said. "And his friend, the scientist from CERN."

Etienne stood up and greeted the foursome. "We were just finishing breakfast, but if you like, you could pull up some chairs and join us."

"We've already had breakfast," Barry said, "but I could use some more coffee."

"My, you are up early!" Summer said.

"You're right about that," Barry said. "Where's that coffee?"

Etienne motioned the waiter who brought cups and saucers and a fresh pot to the table.

"We have just been discussing Etienne's encounter," Hans Bueller said.

"I don't believe we have been introduced," Madame Conti said, directing herself to Luc and Roland.

"Grand-mère, this is Luc Renard."

She smiled approvingly. "I have wanted to meet you ever since my grandson told me he had made your acquaintance. I have read your book and was quite impressed. Ah, I agree with you, life is not to be denied but celebrated."

"That's reassuring," he said. "Unfortunately, not everyone was as impressed as you."

She smiled weakly, not sure which detractors he was referring to.

"And Grand-mère, this is Roland the scientist from CERN I told you about who offered to help me."

Roland bowed slightly and kissed Madame Conti's hand. "It is a pleasure," he said.

"We were just trying to cast some light on my grandson's experience with the help of my dear friend and eminent Egyptologist, Dr. Hans Bueller."

Roland bowed slightly then glanced at Summer who sat next to him.

"Of course, you have already been introduced to Summer," Madame Conti said.

"Yes, we met on Mount Pilatus. Tell me, did you go to Jungfraujoch as you desired?"

"No, not yet. But I did see the UFO!"

"Yes, I've heard." He smiled. "You don't look the worse for it."

"Hans has suggested that Etienne has witnessed the Eye of Horus," Madame Conti said.

"It is not as odd a surmise as it sounds," Etienne said. "I remember now I saw eyes, very intense eyes looking at me."

"Or through you, " Madame Conti said.

"Yes, like they could see into my soul."

Roland who was seated across from Etienne looked at him earnestly. "I would like you to recount all of the details you can remember."

Etienne closed his eyes. "It was as if I were inside a fish bowl." He opened them again. "I've often wondered what captured fish think as they look at us looking at them. Now I know."

"Why do you say a fish bowl?" Roland asked.

Etienne's eyelids softly closed. "I was behind clear glass, enclosed. It was shaped more like a tube than a bowl. I could not touch those eyes that peered at me nor did they touch me."

"You say eyes. Can you describe the rest of their features?"

"There were none," Etienne said now quite wide-eyed himself.

"How tall were they?"

"They were—the eyes were in rows. I'm not making myself clear. What appeared were disembodied eyes. I would say about a dozen or more. They were grouped...."

"Here," Roland said handing Etienne a fresh paper placemat and his pen. "Draw what you saw."

Etienne began to carefully sketch while Hans continued the conversation. "Z'at is just as I suggested z'e Eye of Horus. It appears disembodied, and has much cultural import."

"For another culture perhaps," Roland said.

"I beg to differ," Barry said. "These very ancient symbols generally cross cultures, transcend time. I think Hans has made a very interesting observation."

Stuart pulled an American dollar bill out of his billfold and placed it on the table, the eye in the pyramid side up. "There," he said.

"I get your point," Roland said.

Etienne's sketch showed the figure of a man inside a glass tube not much wider than his own girth. Outside the tube was a grouping of about a dozen large eyes looking in.

"How do you explain it?" Etienne asked.

"I cannot," Roland said. "I can say a few things though. I would guess that like a fish in a fishbowl, the glass tube might have provided you the necessary environment to breathe, which suggests that would not have been possible in their environment. Or these entities may have wanted to protect themselves from infection, from any bacteria you may be carrying, which would suggest they are biological in nature and unused to Earth's microbes. And too, they may have been protecting you from themselves for the very same reason. The tube provided you very little space for movement or sitting, which suggests they had no intention of keeping you for long. But what they are and what their motives for taking you were, I do not know."

"Roland has uncovered some very interesting details in his files that might tell you something more," Barry said.

"I found twelve newspaper accounts of sightings such as yours in this area of France and Switzerland," Roland said. "All twelve describe ships having submerged themselves into bodies of water. Three accounts describe abduction."

"Who made those reports?" Summer asked. "Maybe we should talk to them."

"I'm afraid all three abductees are dead."

"How?" Madame Conti asked.

"Officially, as a result of accidents."

"And you do not believe it," she said.

"I do not."

Stuart turned away in frustration. Summer was right. Etienne should talk to someone who has shared his experience for reasons beyond what she could have imagined.

"What do we do?" Summer cried.

"We must keep this out of the newspapers at all costs," Roland said. "All of the deceased names appeared in newspapers and follow-up accounts in other publications devoted to such things."

"Which means there could be others!" Stuart said. "Others who are still alive whose accounts were never published."

"Precisely," Roland said. "Still alive because their accounts were never made public."

"But the eyes, whoever they are, the alien eyes know!" Summer said.

"I'm not sure the abductors are responsible for these deaths," Roland said. "None of the reports indicate the abductees were in real danger when they were taken, and whoever or whatever took them was apparently interested in some kind of ongoing communication."

"Are you suggesting they might try to take Etienne again?" Stuart asked.

"I cannot tell you any more than what I've read. And I should warn you that these publications are not always reliable. But they do report that all three victims described some kind of continuing communication until their demise. Telepathic, they said. Tell me, do you have any unusual marks on you, small wounds that have appeared since your abduction?"

"No, nothing. Why?"

"If there were an implant of some sort, that could explain how ongoing communication takes place. But without such a device, I have no idea how they would communicate."

"Telepathy my dear man," Madame Conti said. "You don't need a device; you only need a mind."

"We need to find some of these suckers who are still around, talk to them, compare notes. Find out what they think is going on," Stuart said.

"If any exist, it's apparently because they didn't go public. Unless you think all those accidents were really accidents," Barry said. "So, how do we find them or even know for sure there's anyone to find?"

"I'll think about that for awhile," Stuart said.

Etienne looked down at his plate. "This is not what I would have wanted."

"You've been chosen," Madame Conti said. "That's not always easy, but it is an honor of sorts."

Her comment fell on deaf ears. Etienne was not only terribly uncomfortable with his current situation, his mind cast back to his youth when he was also chosen as an initiate to a clandestine group. That did not turn out well. Now he was threatened with death. He grunted something nearly inaudible and drank some more coffee.

As if she could read his thoughts, his grandmother said, "Maybe this time they will be worthy of you."

"I want you to keep a log of any unusual thoughts you may have," Roland said, "visions or anything like that. I will visit the lake and do my best to work out the physical nature of the event, but you must keep me apprised of the psychological."

"The psychological!" Etienne said upon hearing this request. His countenance changed from distraught to sick and his head again began to throb. "I should go lie down."

Luc's mind drifted to childhood stories of saints and innocents who had witnessed miracles and visions as he followed Stuart and Roland to the lake. The magic of such possibilities had drawn him into the priesthood. Since the publication of his book and the rebuke from the Church, he had begun to question his vocation. In his solitude he had pored over Tillich, Rahner, Kiekegaard, Meister Eckhart. He studied the landscape poetry of Shelley and Wordsworth. But it was Dante's treatise on heaven and hell that had inflamed his imagination and inspired him to write his own poetry. If I could only see like Dante, he thought. I need a Beatrice of my own.

They left the path and walked through the pinewood where the crunch of pine needles underfoot were the only sounds to disturb its quietude. Natural pictures such as this had infused his verse since he withdrew from the worldliness of his vocation to the forests and lakes surrounding Évian. He had imagined himself a young Francis who would seek and find a greater truth, a purity in nature. But no visions had come in this year of his retreat, no epiphany, no miracle to renew his faith. He studied the still pool once they arrived at the lake. He would write about it, he thought. He would use his words to paint a picture of its silent beauty. But that is all the further his words had taken him. Visions come not to those who seek them. They come upon those who least expect it. He envied Etienne.

Stuart showed Roland and Luc the log Etienne, Summer, and he had sat upon; pointed to reeds where the frogs still croaked; described how the frogs went silent when the center of the lake splashed open sending out waves of displaced water as if a great boulder had been hurled up from it. The waves grew larger and more violent, he said, drenching them in water. When out of the center of the whirlpool popped this great silvery thing, rounded, almost egg shaped. It rose into the sky and disappeared in the blink of an eye. He described how he had ordered Summer and Etienne into the long grasses to hunker down and wait, how Summer stood up until he forced her back down, how Etienne rolled up into a ball. He said that's when he knew what had happened to him. His extreme reaction, the missing time, it was the only thing that could explain it.

Roland took off his shoes and socks, rolled up his pant legs, and waded into the water to try to ascertain the depth and makeup of the lake. He returned when his foot felt the drop-off.

"I couldn't go any farther," he said. "It must be very deep."

"It must be," Stuart agreed. "The UFO had to be a good five stories high, elongated, longer than it was wide, silver. It shimmered in the daylight as folds of water washed down its rounded sides."

Roland and Luc stared out into the lake's center working up an image from the details Stuart offered.

"I will look into the geology of the area," Roland said. "That might tell me something about the lake's depth, its source, whether it was formed from a natural spring."

"If we had diving gear," Stuart said, "we could go down there and see for ourselves."

"I think you could not go deep enough," Luc said, imagining a well whose depths reached to the other side.

"That's all we can do here for now," Roland said, looking up wistfully. "It's not coming today. We had better go back."

The three men returned to the hotel and found Barry and Hans Bueller engaged in conversation in the lounge.

"Where are the others?" Stuart asked.

"Etienne went to his room," Barry said. "He's not feeling well. Madame Conti said she wanted to read. Summer went out into the garden."

"This is where you had trouble with your breathing, isn't it?" Luc asked. "I only ask because you seem in fine shape now."

"It's that brew you gave me. I took it this morning before we came out here to protect me from these noxious flowery fumes."

"They're very beautiful," Luc said looking out into the garden at the rich, red blooms, and the lovely girl who sat among them. Loud laughter from the dining room broke into their conversation.

"What's going on in there?" Luc asked.

"I don't know. Let's see," Barry said as he walked inside and spotted Madame Conti among the other revelers gathered round a table playing cards.

"Oh, you have returned," she said. "I was just telling my friends how you went off to the lake in search of the UFO my grandson saw. Let me introduce all of you." She turned back to her friends. "This is the scientist I told you about from CERN. And some of you may have heard of the famous theologian, Luc Renard. Dr. Barry Short and Stuart brought back the Gitane Marie from the monastery in Egypt. My, my! We are in such good company!"

Roland blanched. He thought he had made it clear that silence was necessary to protect Etienne's life. He looked at the four strangers gathered around the table with Madame Conti and said, "You will be very quiet about this. Madame's grandson's life could depend upon it."

"Oh, sure, sure," one of them uttered contemptuously. The others laughed.

Madame Conti looked confused. "I thought it was only the newspapers we were concerned with."

"Yes, the newspapers," Roland said, not wishing to cause her further embarrassment, "but we don't want his identity spread in other ways. We do not know who or what we are dealing with." He looked back at the others. "You will be silent on this?"

"Sure, sure. We won't tell anyone about that UFO or her crazy grandson."

Madame Conti, mortified, shot a withering glance at her friends as they got up and departed the room. "I shall henceforth remain silent," she promised.

Chapter Ten

Stuart surmised that his agency must have kept tabs on UFOs since they keep tabs on everything deemed important. Sure enough, files popped up on his computer screen containing the whole history of UFOs including summaries of the most notable books on the topic. But what he wanted were reports far more recent and specific than files laden with innumerable accounts of the 1947 UFO crash near Roswell, New Mexico along with Air Force disclaimers of the incident. He wanted names and locations of recent witness accounts. When he could find none, he made a call to a friend back in DC.

"No, I have not lost all my marbles," he said, repeating the mocking phrase that had just been hurled at him. "I saw it myself! The guy who was abducted saw it real close. No, we weren't smokin' anything. Ha, ha yourself. So stop the foolin' around. I want access to the recent stuff. Okay, call me back, and make it pronto." He slammed the phone down. "Jerk!"

"Not going well?" Barry said, his voice hoarse from the day's encounter with the flowering vines.

"They won't let me in."

The phone rang and he grabbed it. "I don't have the proper security clearance! What the hell? Look, could you do me a favor? What I need is someplace to take my friend where he can talk to other people who've been taken up into these things. If you could put me into contact with some of those folks, tell me who they are, that may help. Yeah, I'm over here in France. Okay."

"Blocked?" Barry said. He sneezed mightily and blew his nose. A foghorn could not have been louder.

"You should do something about that. I lack proper credentials," he said in a voice mimicking the man he had just spoken to. "Oh, hell, the guy's all right, really. He can't change the rules."

"Do you think he's gonna give you the names if you aren't a good security risk?"

"He didn't say I was a bad security risk, and yeah, I think he'll give me somethin'."

"All of this security," Barry said as he put the carafe of brew for his allergic rhinitis over a candle to warm it up.

"Yeah, they take this stuff more seriously than they let on."

The phone rang again. Stuart grabbed it. He wrote down a name, "Swiss Associates. Got a phone number? Okay, I'll Google them. Thanks."

"Swiss Associates doesn't sound like a UFO group," Barry said. He took a deep breath and let the fumes from the carafe rise up into his nostrils.

"That stuff smells bad," Stuart said and got up from the computer to open a window before sitting back down and entering the name into his search engine.

"It works; that's what counts. Don't you think you should run it past Roland before you go any further?"

"There's nothing wrong with parallel investigations. He can do his thing, and I can do mine. We have different motives anyway."

"What do you mean?"

"My motive here is to put Etienne in touch with people he can talk to before he flips."

"He seems okay to me."

"It'll only get worse."

"Fine," Barry said. "I hadn't noticed, but if that's what you think go ahead and look them up. I'm going down to the bar for a bottle of wine before dinner."

Stuart continued his search. "Jackpot!" he shouted when Barry returned with the wine.

"What is it?"

"I hope you brought champagne. There's a conference going on right now, in Geneva no less, sponsored by the World UFO Collaborative. You'll never guess what the conference topic is?"

"UFO abduction."

"How'd you know?"

"What else could it be when you put it like that. 'You'll never guess,' " Barry scoffed. "So the plan is to go. Do we take Etienne?"

"Hell yes! This is the best opportunity to connect he's likely to have."

"And Summer?"

"She'd only distract him. He needs time for himself."

"You tell her that, not me."

The phone rang. The timing could not have been better. It was Summer.

Barry handed the phone over to Stuart. "She wants to talk to you."

"Was she reading my mind?" Stuart said before he took the phone.

"I wondered if you had heard the news?" Summer asked.

For a moment he thought she too had found out about the conference, but then thought better of it. "What news?"

"I just spoke to my sister. Natalie cancelled the wedding. I thought she might have emailed you or phoned or something."

"No, I haven't talked to her since I flew over here. What happened?"

"I hoped you would know because Rosalind doesn't. She said she didn't learn about it until she and John got to the church so it must have been a last minute decision because the church was already decorated with flowers. The groom's family made the announcement. They apologized if the cancellation had caused anyone any inconvenience. Rosalind said she was about to say it cost them over a thousand dollars in airfare and hotel, but she didn't."

"I'm sorry for their inconvenience," Stuart said while mentally adding up how much it had cost him to flee the ordeal by coming to France. "Natalie hasn't written me anything about it. She hasn't written me at all since I've been over here."

"I'm sure she will now. Please tell me all about it when she does. My sister said she wasn't anywhere to be found, neither was her mother. Oh, well, I suppose we'll see you tomorrow."

"Wait a minute," Stuart said before she hung up. "Now that I've got you on the phone I should tell you what Barry and I have planned for Etienne if he wants to do it."

"He's right here. I'll put him on."

"No, let me tell you first. I just learned there's a UFO conference going on right now in Geneva addressing the abduction issue."

"Wow! We should go. Definitely."

"Yes, he should, but maybe not with you this time."

Summer thought Stuart was playing the boys club routine again as he seemed apt to do. "I don't see why not. I'm interested in this too."

"I know you are, but hear me out before you get mad. Etienne needs to talk to some people who have gone through experiences similar to his."

"He's been talking to me about it."

"It's not the same as talking to others who've been taken up."

"Oh, like group therapy."

"Exactly. I've been tryin' to figure out how to find a group for him when I learned about this conference. It could present a good opportunity."

"I still don't understand why you've disinvited me."

"It's simple. You'd distract him. He needs to focus on himself."

Summer rather reluctantly saw the sense of what he was saying. "So, what will I do while you are gone off to this fantastic event?"

"You can think of something."

"Sure," she said reluctantly. "Here, I'll put him on the phone."

"Hello," Etienne said. "What do you think of the news?"

"I'm not sure what I think," Stuart said coolly. "She never suggested she was having second thoughts. Right up to the last time I talked to her she insisted she was doing the right thing."

"Insistence sometimes masks doubt."

"Kind of like trying to talk yourself into somethin'. Right?"

"Quite right."

"I don't mean to change the subject, but I was about to call you. There's a UFO conference that's just about to start in Geneva that Barry and I want to take you to. We thought there may be someone there who knows a thing or two, and it's right up your alley."

"I've been thinking," Etienne said with some hesitancy. "I would rather put it behind me if I can."

"I know how you feel, but let me tell you something, you can't. At least not until you've resolved it internally. This might help."

"What do you think?" Etienne asked Summer. She shook her head. "She thinks it's okay," he told Stuart.

"Good. We'll pick you up in the morning."

"Whoopee!" Stuart shouted when he hung up the phone. "Did you hear that?"

"Etienne's going with us?" Barry said stone-faced. Stuart looked blank. Barry broke out in a broad grin. "If I understood correctly, Natalie didn't follow through with the wedding."

"John and Rosalind were witness to it."

"What are you going to do about it?"

"I don't know. Congratulating her probably isn't the right thing to do, although that's what I feel like doing. That guy's a jerk."

"You're probably right not to, not now at least, not until you learn what happened."

"Can you call her mother?" Stuart asked.

"Madeleine. It's been a long time since I've talked to her."

"You're still friends aren't you?"

Barry sighed. "We were the last time I talked to her, but it's been months. Oh, well. What time is it over there?"

"It's about one in the afternoon," Stuart said and shoved the phone over to Barry.

"Madeleine," Barry said. "Yes, it's been quite a awhile. No, nothing bad has happened over here. I was wondering about you and your daughter. Yes, I just heard what happened and wanted to offer my condolences. Natalie must be very upset. Oh, she's there with you now. She's okay, good," he said, looking directly at Stuart. "You're right, it would be a tough decision. Oh, well then it was for the best. When did she find out about him?" He was silent while he listened for a good ten minutes. "I agree, it was a lot of trouble to put you through, but it can't be helped now. Yes, I'm fine. I'm over in Évian vacationing with Summer and Etienne. Yes, Summer just called me. Okay, I'd like to talk to her too. Hello Natalie. I was sorry to hear what happened, but after talking to your mother I see it was for the best. Stuart, yes, he's here. He's vacationing with me now. Don't you worry, I will tell him."

Stuart, mouth agape, finally spoke. "She asked about me?"

"Yes, she did. I think she feels abandoned."

"Well, what happened?"

"Apparently, it happened some time ago, but news of it got to Natalie right before the wedding and she opted out."

"News of what?"

"Her fiancé was indicted by the government in some kind of billing

89

fraud. She had known there was an investigation, and she had hoped he'd be exonerated. In fact, she stuck her neck out for him. Well, he wasn't exonerated, and she's now convinced he did whatever he's being charged with. The worst of it is that her agency is one of the agencies he's charged with bilking." Barry shook his head. "This must be very embarrassing for her."

"Now I know where the guy got enough money to tool around in a BMW Z4 while he pays alimony and child support to his ex-wife."

"I hope Natalie's still has a job when she gets back."

Stuart shook his head in agreement. He was happy she didn't marry the guy, but unhappy she found herself in such a situation.

"Madeleine said Natalie's boss kind of forced the truth on her. The day before the wedding he took her into his office and presented her with all the evidence gathered against this guy just from his agency alone. She and her mom drove back to Ohio that very night."

"I suppose she's got time off," Stuart said. "She must have put in for time off for her honeymoon."

"Well, you had better write her," Barry said.

Stuart opened his laptop. *Dear Natalie*, he wrote. He paused as he thought about what he would say. He wrote quite a long letter for Stuart. And then he sent it without a word to Barry about what he had written.

After he witnessed Stuart press the send button, Barry looked at his watch. "It's time to meet Roland and Luc over at the bistro. In fact, we're a little late. Are we going to tell them what we're up to?"

There really was not anything to conceal. UFO conferences were no secret to either Luc or Roland who had attended several in the past and had very little interest in attending anymore.

"I think I'll have to turn you down on this one," Luc said. "Those kinds of events are always a disappointment."

"How so?" a deflated Stuart asked.

"More faith than fact. True believers."

Stuart could not help but laugh.

"I know," Luc said. "Who am I to talk? But my faith comes out of a centuries old tradition. Their faith goes back to 1947."

"Roswell," Stuart said. "The agency files are full of it."

"It's the holy grail of Ufology," Luc said. "When it comes to matters of science, I'm more interested in what scientists have to say." He looked over at Roland.

"Most scientists have very little to say about UFOs," Roland said.

"They're skeptical, you're saying?" Barry said.

"True skepticism is a good thing, but the basis of true skepticism is study. They will not even submit UFOs to study."

"Well, I'm not going there to solve any debate," Stuart said. "I saw the thing myself. My goal is to find people Etienne can talk to, people who've been through it themselves."

"Maybe you will, and maybe you won't," Roland said.

"Good luck!" Luc added.

"So I take it neither of you are interested in going," Barry said.

"Not really," Roland said. "I think the four of you can cover it."

"Summer's not going so there will only be the three of us," Barry said.

Roland looked up from his steak. "I'm surprised. I would have thought she would want to go. She is so adventurous in her outlook."

"That she is," Barry said. "Stuart convinced her it wouldn't be in Etienne's best interest."

"She'd take up all of his attention," Stuart said. "No, this time it's got to be all about him."

"I see," Roland said. "I should caution all of you to be careful not to speak with a reporter looking for a good story."

"Thanks for the warning," Stuart said.

Roland sighed. "Do you mind if I hitch a ride with you in the morning? I thought I might come out to take some more measurements of the lake. And since Etienne's going to this thing, it might be wise if I prep him before he leaves."

"You're always welcome."

"Fine. I'll come round your hotel at eight."

Luc looked surprised. "I thought you were going back to CERN?"

"That can wait."

Chapter Eleven

Etienne was less than enthusiastic about attending the conference when Stuart, Roland, and Barry saw him the next morning. In fact, he seemed uncomfortable about attending, so uncomfortable that Barry began to question Stuart's wisdom in insisting that he go.

"Roland's not too interested in the conference either," Barry said. "He's going to stay here and take more measurements out at the lake."

"You might find it more interesting than I would," Roland said. "I've been to a number of them already."

"Dull?" Etienne asked.

"Not dull. Perhaps a little too imaginative. I think my time will be better spent if I take further measurements before I return to CERN."

"Dull, imaginative, who cares!" Stuart argued. "The goal here is to find people you can talk to who will understand in a way none of us can."

Stuart's comment only increased Etienne's discomfort. He was not sure he wanted to share his experience with those who he imagined would attend: geeky boys who spend their days and nights on their devices playing star wars games. He knew Summer was of a different opinion. She found the idea of the conference exciting and thought it would be attended by intriguing scientists like Roland.

What will she think of me if I decline to go? Etienne wondered. Will she think me dull?

"There will be plenty of people interested in your story if you choose to tell them," Roland said. "Every new incident adds to the evidence, but be careful with whom you speak or you could find yourself in the newspaper."

"If we go, we should use false names," Etienne said.

"That would be wise," Roland agreed.

Summer wandered into the hotel garden where the men were gathered in time to catch the drift of the conversation. "So you're going incognito," she said wistfully. "It sounds like an exciting adventure."

"Roland does not think so. He is not coming," Etienne said, hoping he might persuade her into believing it was Roland who was dull.

"Why not?" she said. "I thought you would be the first to want to attend."

"Not this time. I've heard most of these speakers at one time or another, but it may prove useful for Etienne. I thought instead I would go out to the lake to take a few more measurements if you would like to come along."

"Yes, Summer, go with Roland," Barry said, thinking he would feel much better if she had something planned to do.

"Sure, maybe the UFO will come back," she said.

"You are not frightened?" Roland said and smiled as Etienne's expression darkened.

"I think she had better stay here in the hotel where she will be safe."

"Certainly, if that's how you feel, but she would be safe enough with me."

"I will decide what I'm doing for myself," Summer insisted. "If you're going off on an exciting adventure for the entire weekend, I should find my own entertainment. That's what you said this morning."

"Yes, you should take Grand-mère and Hans for a drive. I suggest Montreux for lunch."

Summer turned sullen. "Maybe I should like to go to Jungfraujoch instead."

"Grand-mère would never agree to that," Etienne said dismissively.

Roland thought that if he deferred to Etienne, Summer would be furious, and Etienne would be furious if he did not. So he remained silent.

"I think Summer will be fine," Barry said. "Roland's expert in these matters. He won't let anything happen to her."

It had been a wet summer. Late season wildflowers still bloomed in green fields. Roland followed Summer down the path leading to the pine forest. He watched as she stopped to gaze at flowers or pirouetted to catch a glimpse of a nearby bird. The light caught loose strands of her long, golden hair turning them into a mesh of radiance. Nothing could be more perfect, he thought, than this girl walking through the meadow. If he had had a butterfly net, he would have been tempted to capture her and keep her forever.

Her mood changed slightly when they entered the pinewood. He saw her take on all the mystery that lurked in the shadows of the deep wood as if her psyche was a harp upon which nature played. He wondered what animated her, what made her different from other women he had known. As they came to the edge of the wood that would soon open up into the lake, he smelled mint in her hair. He wanted to pull her near to him, hold her close, but dared not.

She sat down on the lakeside log and looked up into the clear sky. He sat next to her. "Do you think it will come back?" she asked.

"I would guess it will sometime since we know it has been here at least twice, but I doubt that it will come while we are here."

"That would seem too coincidental," she said. "But what do they say about the third time?"

"I'm not sure I know what you mean."

"It's just a saying we have in America. The third time is the charm."

"And what would that charm be Summer?"

"Oh, I don't know. They would get out of their spaceship and talk to us maybe. Tell us who they are and why they're here."

"Would you like that?"

"Oh yes, I think, unless they aren't friendly."

"Do you think they're friendly?"

"You would know better than I." He looked puzzled. "I mean you've been studying this stuff after all."

"Right," he said. "It could be both."

"What do you mean?"

"Who is to say how many of them there are. If extraterrestrials are visiting here, who's to say they don't come from many worlds."

"And they could have different motives," she said.

"Yes, and they might not even like each other."

"Enemies," she said. She stood up and looked out onto the lake as if she were readying herself to leave. "So, what measurements are you going to take?"

He pulled a laser tape out of his pocket and pointed it at different angles across the lake. "It won't take me long. I need a better read on its size," he said as he wrote some figures down in a pocket notebook. "I'll be just another minute." He took off his shoes and socks and rolled his pant legs up to his knees. "I'm just going to wade out a bit."

Summer watched as he waded out and carefully searched for the drop off he had earlier noted. She saw him stop and point the laser down into the lake approximately five feet from where he stood, then ten feet, then fifteen feet. He noted the figures, and then he waded back.

"You could measure the depth of this lake with that?"

"Yes, it's a laser tape," he said holding it up. "The lake drops off quite rapidly. I could measure that. But the last measurement I attempted failed. All that I can say is it goes very, very deep, deeper than my instrument could detect at that angle."

"I've used laser measuring tapes before, but I didn't know they could do that."

"This one is probably far superior to anything you've used. What would you like to do now?" he asked.

"If I could do anything, I'd like to go to that conference. Next to that, I'd like to go back to the mountains."

"Jungfraujoch?"

"Oh yes! If it wasn't so far away."

"If we go now, we could be back Sunday evening when the others return. I could probably get special permission to take you inside the observatory."

"You could?"

"I have my contacts."

"Etienne left me his car."

"Let's go back to the hotel, and I'll make a few calls."

"You don't have a cell phone?"

"I never carry one."

She thought that fact curious but said nothing since she too had left her cell phone in Paris. But she was on a holiday and did not want to be bothered by the newly trained staff at the museum. Roland, on the other hand, was here for an entirely different purpose.

The conference was easy enough to find. It filled the entire lobby of a Lake Geneva business hotel with people, merchandise, registration tables, and all manner of signs and flashy posters directing attendees to various events. Getting in was another matter. They had to register, which meant they had to provide names.

"We're going to need aliases," Stuart said, "at least until we know who we're dealing with."

The men exited the lobby door they had just entered to powwow in front of the hotel. Their movements did not go unnoticed.

"I'll go as Walter," Stuart said.

"That's the phony name you used in Egypt," Barry said.

"Yep, the same. Less confusing that way."

"Well, I'm going to have to think about it a minute," Barry said. "How about Bob, Bob from Chicago. Hard to track me down with that kind of moniker."

"What about you Etienne?" Stuart said.

"René. That was my grandfather's name. That way I will not forget."

"Fine, okay, let's go," Stuart said, turning to lead the men back into the lobby. Their reentry was momentarily blocked by a large man who pushed through the door while taking a pack of cigarettes out of his pocket. When he saw Barry he let them fall back into his suit coat.

"Hello Brad!" the man said, swinging his long arm around Barry's shoulders. "How did that session in Marin County go last month? I haven't seen a thing in the news over here, but you know how it is. Did you bring anything down?"

"I don't believe we've met," Barry said, pulling away from the arm that wrapped around him.

The man looked puzzled. "Brad?"

"No, I'm Bob."

"From Chicago?"

"Yes, Chicago, but I have no recollection...."

"Maybe I got the name mixed up. Bob, Brad, close enough. But I could swear it was Brad from Chicago."

"You've mistaken me for someone else. I'm Bob, Bob Connor from Chicago."

"Well, maybe you know him? You could be his twin."

"Hmm," Barry said, curious to know more about his look alike. "What does he do?"

96

"He calls them down."

"Calls them down?" Barry repeated.

"UFOs," the man said. "He's quite adept at it."

"Oh, yes, UFOs. No, I'm afraid I've never met Brad."

The man studied Barry's face closely. "You look just like him. He was here last year. Gave a presentation. I thought maybe you had come back."

"No, I'm not him. I've never met him," Barry said.

"Oh, well, coincidences do happen. Pardon me for not introducing myself. I'm Raymond Lepont, chairman of this year's conference. I'd like to welcome you."

"Thank you very much," Barry said. "I'm Bob Connor from Chicago and this is my friend Walter, a business associate also from Chicago, and René here from Paris."

"Paris is a beautiful place," the man said.

"Yes it is," Etienne replied.

"What business may I ask?"

Barry paused but only for a moment. "We buy and sell old things, very old things. We are, I guess you would call us an import/export business of well, treasures."

"Antiques," Etienne said, lest their business sound illegal.

"So, you came all the way from Chicago to be here?"

"No, we were in the area, in Paris," Barry said.

"I saw the conference advertised on the internet," Stuart explained. "We decided to drive over."

"Hmm," the man said. "So you have an interest in UFOs?"

"In abduction," Stuart said. "We hope to meet some abductees."

The man led them back inside toward the registration table. He looked at the crowd milling about the lobby. "The morning session must have let out. Lunch will be served. You should register now. I'm sure you'll meet some people who know a thing or two about abduction. I'm sorry you missed the morning session. Excellent speaker on the Rendlesham Forest episode. Right up your alley."

"Rendlesham Forest, is that around here?" Stuart asked.

The man looked slightly perplexed. "No, it's in England, near what used to be an American Air Force base. I'm surprised you haven't heard of it. Most people interested in abduction have."

"I'm pretty new to this," Stuart said.

"You must be."

"So, how recent a case is it?"

"It's recent all right. I believe it happened in 1980."

Stuart's hopes began to falter. The case was so old it was probably in his agency's unclassified files. "Is anything more current coming up?" he asked.

The man paused to think. "We've got an expert here on crop circles. I believe he will bring us up to date on the latest evidence from England."

"Crop circles!" Barry said. "Are you referring to those lovely designs found in farmers' fields?"

"Yes, and elsewhere."

"Tell me, what do they have to do with abduction?"

"Well, everything is connected in some way or another," the man said. "You just have to find the link."

"Or invent it," Barry said, forgetting where he was and who he was speaking to.

"You're not reporters are you? Not that we mind them being here, but we would prefer you identify yourselves."

"I am not a reporter," Barry said. "No, I'm here to learn."

Etienne, who had grown quite impatient with the conversation, cut to the chase. "Are you aware of any UFO activity in the area?"

"I'm glad you asked. Collecting UFO reports is our primary function René. Our organization operates as the European central clearing house for all known activity."

"I thought you were an American," Etienne said. "You sound American to me."

Raymond gave him an icy stare. "Our organization is international in its reach."

"What do you do with the reports?" Stuart asked.

"We file, we investigate, and we keep our findings confidential until after we've had time to thoroughly study the event in question." He turned away from Stuart and Etienne effectively ending the conversation. "Brad, lunch is about to be served. You and your friends should find a table. The dining area is to your right. Your identification badges will get you in."

"Whew, that was awkward," Stuart said after Lepont had marched off.

"You asked the wrong question," Barry said as the three men headed into the dining room. "He thinks you're too nosey. He thinks we're undercover reporters."

"Yeah, for the 'World Inquisitor,'" Stuart laughed.

"I do not think he liked any of us," Etienne said.

"I got that impression. After he found out I wasn't Brad."

"Your saving grace is that you look like him," Stuart said. "Summoned any UFOs lately Barry, Brad whatever your name is? Maybe you caused that thing to appear at the lake."

"Very funny."

They seated themselves at a table in the rear of the banquet room. A bespectacled woman sitting across the large, round table fixed her attention and her horned rimmed glasses on Etienne. She said not a word but smiled and nodded at him as if she were engaged in cross table conversation. He felt awkward, believing it would be impolite to turn away yet unable to decipher any of her meaning, although he was sure by her countenance she meant something. He wondered if she were deaf and had learned some new form of communication that he was unacquainted with until she finally spoke.

"What's your name?" she asked over the din of other conversations and waiters serving boxed lunches.

"René," he answered but said nothing more.

She nodded and smiled again, and then raced around the table and whispered in his ear. "You're psychic, aren't you?"

Etienne felt both puzzled and uncomfortable. Had all that nodding and smiling been a test?

"I could sense it from across the table," she said.

"If you mean by psychic that I can read other people's thoughts, you are quite mistaken."

"It's more subtle than that," she insisted.

"I am perceptive if that is what you mean. I sometimes know what someone is thinking, but it is from reading the context, not mind reading."

"I knew it!" she said. She smiled knowingly as she backed away to her side of the table. To his great relief she began conversing with a woman sitting next to her, a conversation he could neither hear nor mind read.

"What brings you here?" a white suited man seated next to Stuart asked. Stuart noted his coiffured blonde hair. He could be a daytime TV personality, he thought.

Getting right to the point, he answered, "I'm here to meet abductees. I'd like to interview a few."

"That's my interest too," the man said. "I didn't see you in the workshop this morning."

"We just got here."

"It's too bad you missed it. It was very good training."

Stuart grew interested. "For what?"

"To take their reports. I want to help them, but feel woefully unprepared to provide what they need."

"I know what you mean," Stuart said. "It's hard to know what to say to someone who has had a traumatic experience that you yourself haven't had. Their best medicine is to talk to people like themselves."

"If they can find any. So few of them survive; or if they do, they don't remember a thing."

Stuart thought he might have found a good lead. "I've heard they often die by accident, something that looks like an accident that is."

"Most of them disappear never to be seen or heard from again," the man said. "The few survivors, if they remember anything at all, are so traumatized they need extensive counseling. That's what I hope to provide, help and protection."

"If they disappear, never to be seen or heard of again," Stuart said, repeating the man's words, "how do you know they were abducted by extraterrestrials?"

"The statistics! Do you know how many people go missing every year and are never heard from again?"

"I'm aware there are quite a few. But why do you think they are victims of UFO abduction?"

"That many people didn't just disappear off of the face of the earth, unless...."

"Oh, so you think they were taken off the planet by some kind of extraterrestrials and never returned?"

"What else could have happened to them? If they were here, they would have shown up somewhere."

"For what purpose would they be taken?"

"Medical, research, food, whatever. Like the mutilated cattle."

"What are you talking about?" Stuart asked, having grown impatient with a line of reasoning he was having difficulty following.

"Surely you're aware of the mutilated carcasses of cattle found all over the American West."

"I can't say that I am. So, did the wolves get them? I don't see the connection."

"No, the wolves didn't get them, unless wolves have developed advance surgical skills," the white suited man said sarcastically. "These carcasses are found with their organs surgically removed, the blood drained from their bodies."

"Ugh! Are you suggesting that is the fate of missing persons?" Stuart choked out.

"The population needs to be warned! And the survivors need to be protected lest they be taken again!"

Stuart got up from the table and excused himself leaving his boxed lunch half eaten. Barry and Etienne followed. The man eyed them suspiciously as they were the first to leave the dining room.

"Roland was right. There isn't anything here for us," Stuart said.

"Not for me," Etienne said. "The eyes that held me seemed nothing like vampires drinking blood."

"Don't be impatient," Barry said. "The organizers can't control who comes to these things. Let's at least go to one of the afternoon sessions."

They stood together in the lobby studying the program.

"They've got a session on crop circles," Barry said. "That'll have the new stuff according to Raymond Lepont."

"Not relevant," Stuart said. "For a conference on abduction there is very little of it here. Hmm, some former Air Force major is going to offer an historical survey of secret military investigations up to 1962. Probably more about Roswell. I'm looking for something current."

"The session in the Oak Room looks the best," Etienne said. "Disclosure," he read, "If the truth becomes known," he continued.

"Sounds interesting," Stuart agreed. "Not right on target, but at least it's dealing with the here and now."

"We've got a good twenty minutes before it starts," Barry said. "Let's look around. Maybe we can find what we're looking for over at one of those booths."

Many of the books for sale had been listed on Stuart's agency's website. He thumbed through several and noted the cases described were old, dating back to the last century or before. If it had not been for Etienne's mishap and his own sighting, he would have thought UFOs had ceased to exist in the twenty-first century. He spotted Barry across the aisle holding up a rather large crystal while talking to an attractive blond. He joined them.

"So you say by holding this crystal, I can see back in time?" Barry said to an ethereal woman wearing a long, glittering dress.

"Yes, if you hold it long enough and concentrate hard."

"Like a crystal ball?" Barry asked.

"Not exactly. It can only tell you of the past it has experienced."

"Oh, I see. So if I wanted to know what had happened in let's say— on the Giza Plateau during the reign of Tutankhamun, I would have to find a stone from there like this one to tell me?"

"If it's the right stone, and if you meditate on it."

"Thank you," Barry said and laid the crystal down on the table. "If you're right, crystals could make my work a lot easier."

"Try one," she said, but the two men walked away with no crystal in tow.

"Hey, did she say what those crystals have to do with UFOs?" Stuart asked.

"No, she didn't, and I didn't ask. I think they have more to do with some of the people who come to these events than UFOs."

They approached Etienne over in the next aisle who was engaged in conversation with a very earnest young man.

"So what's up?" Stuart asked, insensitive to the fact that he was breaking in on an unusually intense discussion.

"I know this must sound crazy to you," the young man said to Etienne while stealing a furtive glance at the two strangers who had just arrived at his booth. "But it's all true; I can assure you."

102

"What sounds crazy?" Barry asked.

"This young man was just telling me about a great war going on, a great war we have not yet seen that we could become the victims of," Etienne said.

"It's true! It's true!" the boy said, looking beaten down, which served as evidence that he had spent the day arguing with a conference full of skeptics. "If you go to our website, you can learn more than I can explain." He looked over at another young man, slightly older than himself, who appeared to be prompting him.

"You are new to this, aren't you?" Etienne said to the boy, while recognizing himself as a youth in the earnestness of the young man's face.

The boy flushed, feeling caught. "Yes," he replied.

Etienne felt great pity for the boy. He wanted to tell him to get away from these people who would control him, who would use him for their own ends, but he knew that would only cause the lad greater pain. The boy would have to find out for himself. Instead, he took the flyer the young man handed him and assured him he would look at the website. He meant it, and the boy knew it.

"What was that all about?" Barry asked Etienne as the three men walked to the session.

"He's in some kind of cult. Led by a man who claims that he and only he can save us from the demonic shenanigans of some evil race of extraterrestrials. He has that boy terrified. His fear is nearly contagious."

"Are you sure you want to go to this thing?" Stuart said. "We could leave now."

"No, we are here."

"I'm sure glad we didn't book a room for the night," Barry said.

"Yes, I look forward to returning to Summer this evening," Etienne agreed.

"Won't she be surprised when we're back so soon," Barry said.

"When she finds out what a bust this thing is she won't be so mad at me," Stuart said.

"She is not angry with you," Etienne said.

"Yes she is."

They stood at the entrance to the lecture room looking for somewhere to sit when Barry was accosted once again by Raymond Lepont.

"Hello Brad. Are you having a good time?"

"Very informative," Barry said.

"I'm sorry. I don't believe I got your name right," Raymond said.

Without a pause Barry answered, "Bob Connors from Chicago."

"Yes, I keep mistaking you for Brad. You look remarkably like him. I see three chairs over there," he pointed to the back of the room near a rear exit. "I'm glad you decided to attend this session. It should prove most interesting."

"It looks like everyone else thinks so too," Stuart said.

"I'm afraid attendance will be quite small at the other sessions," Lepont said. "I should have made this the keynote. I will speak with you later." He walked up to the front of the room where he took the microphone to loud applause. The room grew silent.

"I'm very happy to introduce our next guest, Claudio Postremo. Many of you know his work already, but today he will discuss his latest and most intriguing book." He paused for a second and looked at a distinguished gray haired man seated behind the podium. "Did you say it will be released in four months?" The man shook his head. Raymond turned back to the audience. "Today you will become privy to his latest, not yet released work, *Blindfolds Lifted*."

There was wild applause as Dr. Postremo rose out of his chair, shook the hand of the man who had introduced him, and took the microphone.

"Thank you," he said to the applause. "My English is not so good. But I will speak it today because you come from many places, and sad to say, English has become the common tongue."

"Postremo," that is Latin," Etienne said.

"Latin's no longer anyone's tongue," Barry said.

"After having spent the better part of my life researching the cultural history of UFOs," the speaker said, "I thought it time to look into the future, our future, at this critical time when many believe full disclosure is about to take place. The past saw waves of UFOs, but they were always understood within the cultural boundaries and, I should say, the limitations of the people who observed them. Thus, the biblical description of Ezekiel's Wheel associated what was clearly a UFO with the manifestation of the Lord. And this is only one instance of mistaken identity."

Etienne thought of the lines from Dante that Luc had recited on their first meeting after he recounted his own experience at the lake. He was impressed. He wished Luc were here with them now.

"Cultures from all over the world have seen these objects," the speaker continued, "and have interpreted them through their own cultural lights. Lights, that's the common denominator, isn't it? I think of the ancient British legends that identify lights in the forests as fairies gathered around a fire. Wheels within wheels. Angel, god, or fairy. These interpretations coexist with a phenomenon that has been observed since before recorded time. But today I'm here to talk to you not about the past but about the future, a future with full disclosure. How will it change us? How might they, the visitors be changed by us?"

As intriguing as the thesis was, the follow through raised more questions than answers in the three novice UFO investigators. The most fundamental was how could we assume that our own interpretations of the phenomena would be any more accurate than our predecessors? Are we not as subject to cultural interpretation as they? And how do we know that past interpretations were not accurate, at least up to a point?

"Maybe the fairy folk and the Angel Boatman were just as real as what I saw," Etienne whispered to Barry.

"True, that is possible. They just gave a name to it, which you have not yet done," Barry said.

"What the hell are you saying?" Stuart said. "Tinker Bell flew down in that silver egg I saw lifting up out of the lake?"

"No, that's not what I'm saying," Barry whispered and then grew silent as he continued to listen to the impressive Dr. Postremo.

"The most obvious question that arose as I thought about what full disclosure would mean," Postremo went on, "is what would it do to our sense of our place in the universe. That we have always understood in terms of either science or religion. What would become of those great fonts of wisdom? Would God as we have understood Him still exist? This is a more profound question than you may have realized. Religion poses a hierarchy of being, with God ascendant and supernatural beings, his servants, between God and us, his children so to speak. But if other intelligent life forms far more intelligent than we exist, and if believers

105

come to know this absolutely and undeniably, that ancient order evaporates. What will arise in its place? And where would be humankind's place in this new order? For those of us more attuned to science than religion, we must contend with the very same problem. For within the family of man we also have an ascribed order with scientists ranking in or near the top of the intelligence ladder, depending on one's point of view, that is."

The audience laughed, a long knowing laugh as if they were all privy to an inside joke.

"Where will our scientists rank if humanity comes face to face with beings far more advanced than ourselves? And although some of you may think they will reap their just desserts, you must ask yourselves this. If scientists, those who are esteemed to be the most intelligent of our species, are dropped down a notch or two or three or four or five, where does that leave the rest of us?" He paused for a moment. "In Pandemonium, I tell you! We will have lost all sense of self, fallen so far in rank that we may go mad or at best retreat into permanent childhood."

Boos were heard where there had been applause. Someone shouted from the audience, "They will teach us what they know!"

"What makes you think so?" Dr. Postremo shouted back. "Why, after observing humankind for millennia would they want to empower us to travel across the universe? They may look at what we can already do with apprehension."

The room grew silent, and the speaker continued. "I thought like you at the beginning of my work. I thought what wonderful things we could learn and know after disclosure takes place. Yes, cures for cancer, traveling beyond the speed of light, or through wormholes that would make such speeds unnecessary. Or perhaps we would learn how to travel back into the past or into the future. I thought of all of those things just like you until I considered that if they had wished to bestow those wonders upon us, they would have already done so."

"We weren't ready yet!" someone shouted from the audience.

"Why would you or they think we are ready now?" he replied.

Silence fell across the room.

"We are not ready," he continued. "I do not know that we ever will

106

be. We seem not to be evolving as we had once thought we were, at least not socially."

"They can teach us!" someone insisted.

"Perhaps they have already tried," he answered. "Perhaps those references from the distant past that we interpret as misidentified UFOs were meant to be misidentified. Perhaps those ships carried teachers to ancient men who called them gods or God or angels or fairies. Perhaps through those misidentified teachers they have tried."

"But what would happen if we knew them as men?" another member of the audience asked in desperation. "We might learn through logic instead of superstition as a pupil from its teacher."

"We might," Dr. Postremo conceded. "We might if we were humble as a child is to her reading instructor. And they might try if they thought it possible we would open up to instruction and not rebel. But without that combination of attributes, teaching mankind the secrets of the universe could bring about, well, disaster."

Barry spoke up. "Yes! Yes! I know what you mean. The ancients understood the problem. Imhotep, the great teacher of Egypt, he knew the danger."

The two men stared at each other in profound understanding, Barry Short and Dr. Claudio Postremo.

"Look what we did with Einstein's discoveries," Postremo said. "We should not wish for disclosure," he continued. "I did for many years but no longer. Not after thoroughly considering what it could mean. It was a false hope. If we are to evolve, if that is possible, we will have to do it in our own time. We are in deep need of ethical guidance, but for guidance to be accepted I'm afraid the source must remain concealed. Historically we have rebelled from sources outside ourselves, whether they be laws or gods. It must come from within, or at least it must seem to. What did Shakespeare write? 'What a piece of work is man, how noble in reason, how infinite in faculties in form and moving how express and admirable, in action how like an angel, in apprehension how like a god.' Such words seem false flattery, but they are necessary. If we are to evolve it will be because we believe we can, we believe in ourselves, we believe we have a destiny. We must believe even if we elevate ourselves on a false platform, a manmade hierarchy if you will. No, we can never become the suppliant child at the knee of a great teacher. Our spirit is too rebellious. Our sense of worth, wisely understood, is the pathway to genuine elevation if we are to attain it. So we must be guided carefully, discretely. That is all I have to say."

Dr. Postremo dismounted the small stage, walked towards the main entrance door and out he went. Barry rose from his seat in the back row and darted through the rear exit door after him. The audience was silent, and then, slowly, gradually there was mild applause mixed in with grumbling.

Chapter Twelve

Summer and Roland drove into the Bernese Oberland on their way to Grindelwald, the town where Roland had booked their rooms. They drove at a leisurely pace, stopping in Bern for lunch and a visit to the city's mascots, the Bern bears, before heading south to the quaint town of Thun. From Thun they skirted the lake by the same name and followed the River Aare into the Interlaken region. The fast moving currents of the Aare churned past green rocky foothills; the flinty grayness of its water contrasting sharply with delicately colored wildflowers and sturdy evergreens that rose up on either side. Tidy chalets arranged in picture perfect order added domesticity to the scene. Above them stood the towering and inhospitable mountain peaks of the Jungfrau, quite visible on this sunny day.

"This reminds me of somewhere I've read about but have never been," Summer said.

"It is its own kind of place," Roland said. "I love it here."

"It reminds me of where Tolkien's hobbits and elves live and the Misty Mountains," she said as she looked out toward the peaks.

"I've never read Tolkien."

"You should. You would love him if you love this place. When I was young the settings in his books seemed nearly real to me, and here I am now."

"You are young Summer. You see the wonder in things."

She didn't know how to accept the compliment, although she liked it very much.

"We turn in just a few more kilometers," Roland said as he studied the map. "You will love Grindelwald. I think it will be very much like those villages you've imagined but have never seen."

The hotel he had found them was lovely, and her room had a wonderful, clear view of the mountain they would ascend the following day. They were to have dinner at the hotel, Roland having arranged for them to share a cheese fondue. Nothing could have been more perfect if she were not distracted and hurt by what she had left behind, the conference and Etienne. She felt wounded but found some solace in the fact that he had not tried to deceive her this time. Though she wondered why he would have chosen to cut her out of an experience they truly could have shared. After all, she had seen a ship too. She felt isolated from him, kept at a distance, but mixed in with these feelings was her curiosity to know what might be happening at the conference she had been disinvited to. In fact, her curiosity had so trumped those negative emotions that she was able to enjoy this evening in the mountains.

Barry came crashing through the hotel lobby door catching Dr. Postremo's notice just as he was about to step into a cab. He recognized Barry immediately, the only man he had connected with after having endured shouts and hostile questions from a defensive audience.

"Do you have a few minutes?" Barry said. "I've got a man with me I hope you will hear out. You're the only person I've met here I can trust."

Postremo stepped out of the cab just as Stuart and Etienne came stumbling through the front door to catch up with their friend. He looked over their shoulders into the lobby as if he feared the entire lecture room audience would come shouting and hissing behind them.

"It is only us," Etienne said, reassuringly. "The rest of them were too stunned by your sudden departure to act quickly."

"They're still trying to figure out whether to applaud or boo," Stuart said.

"These are my friends," Barry assured Dr. Postremo. "Etienne is the one I was telling you about. I would love it if you would hear him out."

"Get into the cab," Dr. Postremo said. "I know a cafe. Have you had dinner?"

Etienne climbed into the front seat with the cab driver as the others squeezed into the back. He was thinking of Summer. This was the kind of adventure she would have loved, pursuing a brilliant lecturer who had just walked out on a dazed audience. So mysterious, she would have thought. All the reasons for not bringing her vanished. He was sorry he had listened to Stuart. More painful was the thought of her having to entertain his grandmother who, for the time being, could think of nothing but bridge.

"I used to come here when I was a student," Postremo said as he dined on ouefs et mayonnaise. The others ate the daily special, grilled salmon. By the look of the place it had not changed much; it was quiet, dark, and nearly empty.

"So you didn't immediately recall that you had been abducted?" Dr. Postremo said.

"No, not at all. It was only after I realized I had been gone from the hotel much longer than I could explain that I started putting the pieces together."

"Could you have merely fallen asleep, lost time in that way?"

"I wondered if that could be the case until we went back."

"You went back?"

"Yes, a few days later with Stuart here and my fiancée Summer, and we all saw it."

The doctor looked over at Stuart.

"I'm afraid he's right," Stuart said. "I saw it too."

"Can you describe it?" Postremo said.

"It was just like Etienne said, round, kind of egg shaped, big, silver. I didn't see it land. It must have gone down before we got there. I saw it rise up out of the lake and disappear."

"You both said it disappeared. What do you mean by that?"

"It was as if it went through a door and the door shut behind it," Etienne said.

"Yeah," Stuart agreed.

"What did you do?"

"I told everyone to get back and duck out of the way. I pulled Summer down because she insisted on standing up, and I didn't want them to take her."

"And how was your friend here, Etienne through it all?"

"Bad," Stuart said. "That's why I brought him here. He collapsed on the ground, folded up into ball."

"He looked traumatized?" Postremo said.

"Yes, traumatized."

"You don't seem traumatized now," Postremo said to Etienne.

"No, I feel much better. It was after that second encounter that I remembered what had happened. Them taking me; the eyes staring at

111

me."

"What do you think they wanted?"

"I do not know. Maybe nothing. It felt like I was being assessed though, but I do not remember being asked any questions."

"Hmm," the doctor said. "Maybe that is what they wanted. You happened to be there, and they took the opportunity."

"Yes, it seemed something like that. It was nothing like what you read about. No probes, no forced sexual encounter, that sort of thing."

"So, you are aware of the abduction literature?" Postremo said.

"I am now. Before I was not, but since then, since I remembered, I began to research the topic on the internet. What happened to me was nothing like what I read, at least not what I remember."

"Have you considered hypnotic regression?"

"Never!"

"Wise," the doctor said. "So what kind of assessment do you think they were doing if they asked no questions and did not probe your body?"

He sighed. "It felt like they were looking deep into my mind."

"Maybe that was the case."

"But what about what Roland found," Barry said. "The abductees who were written about in the newspapers who were later reported dead, having all suffered some kind of accident."

"Well, if that is true, it tells you not to be too public," Postremo chuckled.

"We know that," Barry said, "which is why we didn't tell anyone at the conference. Not that any of them would have been much help. But we don't really know what the danger is or who poses it."

"Neither do I," Postremo admitted and turned to Etienne. "I'm not sure what the danger is. But of this I am sure. If those who took you desired to kill you, you would not be here now."

"It was also reported that people who had been taken received some kind of telepathic communication from their abductors after they were returned," Etienne said.

"Have you received such communication?"

"No."

"Well then, you may not. Such stories as these are often

112

embellishments that have no basis in fact."

"Do you know who they are?" Etienne finally asked.

Compassion spread across Postremo's face as he saw the anguish in Etienne's. "I do not know. What I can tell you, what my research has led me to conclude, is whoever or whatever they are, they have visited Earth for a very long time. No harm seems to have come from it up to now. I take comfort in that. They do not seem to want us to know too much about them. Very few people are privy to their existence at all so you might consider yourself one of the lucky few and take some solace in that. As to their purpose, I have many theories, none of which I can prove. You having had the experience are the best judge."

"You believe me then."

"Yes I do, but you must know that most people will not."

"I do not intend to tell most people."

"A wise choice."

The meeting ended with cordial handshakes as Etienne was anxious to return to Summer that evening and it was already dark. Barry and Postremo promised to keep in touch after Barry congratulated the doctor for having the courage to take an unpopular position.

"Maybe I will find new admirers," Postremo said. "New ones to replace the old ones."

"Like me," Barry said.

Darkness had settled in on Grindelwald by the time Summer met Roland for dinner. Otherwise, the hotel restaurant dining room would have offered a magnificent view of the mountains.

"I'm sorry you cannot see them," he said.

"That's all right. I saw them earlier from my room. Thank you for making reservations at such a beautiful place."

He said nothing. The server who brought out their fondue and placed it on a warming dish interrupted that moment of awkward silence. The server then lighted the candle warmer, along with the yet unlit candle on the table.

It was as romantic as it was meant to be. Summer looked about the dining room and saw by its patrons that this was not a family hotel. She felt embarrassed.

Sensing her discomfort Roland said, "We will have to get up early in the morning. I want to get to the top before the crowds arrive."

"It gets crowded up there?"

"Yes, very."

"But it looks so..."

"Inhospitable," he said.

"Yes."

"That's why it's so popular. It's a chance for people to go to the moon."

"Oh," she said, "that desolate."

"It would be if it were not for the crowds. That's why we should go early, and why I have arranged to take you inside the observatory."

Clouds had moved in blocking any light the moon might have offered. The dining room lights had been turned low, leaving only their single candle and the light below the warming dish blushing amber. With no other distractions to draw her attention, Summer focused on Roland in a way she had not before as the two of them dipped their crusty bread chunks into the swirling fondue.

His eyes are blue like mine, she thought, but not quite like mine. His are deeper, much deeper, the color of dark seawater or the night sky before the sun has fully set. She pulled herself back in her chair lest she fall into them. Now at a safe distance, she raised her eyes to his again. They are beautiful, she thought. Out of sync with the stiff and formal Roland she had thought she knew. Not his eyes, she thought, they are anything but stiff.

He could feel her looking at him and knew it was for the very first time. "I brought you here," he ventured hesitantly. "I brought you here so that we might get to know each other a little better."

"There's not much to know about me," she said. "I manage the museum in Paris. But what about you? I know about your scientific interests, but what about the rest? Have you ever married?"

"No," he said, looking down at his hands that rested on the table. "I've been too busy with other things."

"You can never be too busy with other things not to think about it," she said. "It's humanly impossible."

He looked at her squarely. "Look at your friends," he said. "Has

114

Barry ever married or Stuart?"

"You're right about that," she acknowledged. "Barry has never met the right woman. If you ask me, he has spent too much time studying the caves and suffers for it. Stuart is another story. He has met and loves the right woman. He's just afraid to tell her."

"He's afraid she will reject him?"

"That's what he acts like. But I think the truth is that he is afraid of that kind of commitment."

"I can understand that," he said. "And you?"

"I am engaged," she said.

"I know, but you do not seem in any hurry to marry."

"There are some problems."

"Commitment?"

"That's not exactly it. I've been trying to sort it out."

He looked at her in expectation and she complied.

"I've always been an independent person. A self-starter. Life wasn't handed to me on a silver plate so I had to work very hard for what I've wanted. I won a scholarship to a very fine college. I worked my college radio station experience into a job in New York City after I graduated. And I worked that job into managing the European office of a very interesting record label. Last January I began the task of putting together Le Musée de la Femme de la Mythologie and have been almost single-handedly managing it since it opened in June, and very successfully I will add. I always thought I wanted great wealth, but now I'm not so sure."

"You're afraid it could rob you of your ambition?"

She shook her head yes. "And more, my independence. I've come to realize something about myself I hadn't known. All that time I spent working so hard I had wished I were rich so I wouldn't have had to work so hard. I realize now that I loved the work. I loved the challenge. I love the adventure of it."

"You love adventure. I could see that about you from the first."

"Yes, I do. And the prerequisite for adventure is risk. If things are too easy...."

"I understand. I love it too. The challenge, the exotic nature of new things."

Summer had never imagined Roland an adventurous type. His stiff

115

formality had seemed quite the opposite. In the latter regard, he seemed a little like Etienne. "I guess there can be adventure in science," she said. "And other things."

She thought it too intrusive to ask what those other things might be so she did not, and he did not offer to explain. But that evening before she went to bed she thought about their dinner table conversation and realized there was much she did not know about Roland. She realized too that she had told him a great deal about herself, about feelings and thoughts she had not yet entirely worked through or told to anyone else. And she thought very little about Etienne.

Roland pulled the chair in his room over to the window for a better view of the dark sky, but his mind was entirely on Summer. The sky served merely as a black screen on which he would play back the night's events as if he were a third party observing the two of them at their amber lit table. There was a shyness about her he had never before seen and a modesty he hadn't quite expected. He pictured her looking awkwardly around the dining room searching for a place, a diversion, somewhere else to cast her eyes until finding no such place, she looked right into his. He felt pulled into her and she into him, and he loved the power of it. He was in love for the first time in his life. He thought about her words, all that she had revealed to him. She trusts me, he thought. She never would have said so much if she did not. He swore he would never betray that trust; it was sacred to him. And he felt a kinship with much of what she had said. His life had been much different than hers but in some ways similar. He had earned what he had achieved, and he knew the draw of adventure, more adventure than she could ever imagine. She could be his life partner.

He rose from the chair, turned out the light, crawled under the white-sheeted goose down comforter, his body now entirely relaxed. He knew there would be many obstacles to their relationship, but the one that loomed the greatest was Summer herself. Would she accept him? Would she give up Etienne for him? Tonight he believed that possible.

Stuart and Barry dropped Etienne off at his hotel around midnight. He thought perhaps he should wait until the morning before speaking to Summer about what had happened that day, but he felt wide awake and full of desire, much more so than had been common to him. He went to her room and tapped softly at the door, but there was no answer. He thought she must be asleep. He tapped again, but again there was no answer so he turned away from her door and went alone to his room.

Chapter Thirteen

Light filtered through the edges of the draperies of the otherwise darkened room in the morning when Etienne opened his eyes. His head ached. He rolled over, picked up the receiver, and phoned Summer. There was no answer. The clock read seven-thirty. He fell back to sleep until he awoke again at nine. He phoned her room. There was still no answer. He took aspirin and threw on his pants and shirt from the day before and walked down the flight of steps that separated their rooms. He knocked on her door then pressed his ear against it. Silence. He scrambled to the dining room where his grandmother sat at a table with Hans Bueller.

"Where is Summer?" he asked.

"Is she not with you?" his grandmother said.

"No, I left her here with you."

"Why, we have not seen her since yesterday morning before you left," Madame Conti said looking first at Hans and then her grandson. "We assumed she went with you to Geneva."

Etienne dropped into a chair at their table. "She was to go to the lake with Roland. He was going to take measurements."

"You do not suppose something could have happened to them?" Madame Conti asked.

"Excuse me," he said and rose from the table. "I had better phone Barry."

"I did not mean to upset you!" she said her voice raised as he walked off. She looked at Hans. "I knew there was something wrong. You know that too."

"Zere's nothing wrong with Summer," Bueller said. "She's a very sweet girl."

"I know that she is. But something is wrong nonetheless."

"Summer did not answer the door when I got back last night," Etienne said into the phone. "I assumed she was asleep, but this morning when she still did not answer I got worried. I thought maybe she had already gotten up and was having breakfast with my grandmother, but

118

she was not. Grand-mère said she has not seen her since early yesterday morning before we left."

"Now calm down," Barry said. "I'm sure she's fine."

"Do you suppose something could have gone wrong when she went to the lake with Roland?"

"That's highly unlikely," Barry said, although he really was not sure. "Here, I'm passing the phone over to Stuart."

"Hey Etienne, Stuart here. Look, is your car there?"

"I did not think to check."

"Go check. I'll hold on."

Etienne stepped out into his balcony where he had a partial view of the parking lot. He did not see the car. But to be sure he left his room and went out into the garden to get a full view."

"The car is not here," he said into the phone when he returned.

"She didn't go missing at the lake then," Stuart said. "She returned and took the car somewhere. You say she didn't mention anything to your grandmother?"

"No, nothing."

"Hmm," Stuart said. "The next question I have is whether she left by herself or with Roland."

Etienne grew somber. The desire that had inflamed him when he had returned to the hotel took a sudden turn into something else—anger, verging on a desire for revenge. "How do we find out?"

"Stay in your room. I'll give Luc a call and phone you right back."

Luc met the inquiry with momentary silence, and then said, "I have not seen or heard from Roland since yesterday morning. I thought he was going to hitch a ride with you two out to Etienne's hotel so he could take further measurements out at the lake."

"He rode out with us, but we don't know where he went after that."

"He didn't come back here so I assume he took the train back to CERN. He's probably there now. I could give him a call."

"Do that," Stuart said. "Etienne is worried as hell. When you reach him ask if there's anything Summer said that would hint at where she might have gone."

Luc called Roland at his apartment, but there was no answer. He phoned his lab thinking he may have gone in to do something with the

119

measurements he had taken.

"Halo," a voice said.

"Is Roland in?"

"No, he's not been here for days. I believe he's taken a short leave of absence."

"A leave of absence! When do you expect him back?"

"I don't have that information," the voice said.

"Thank you," Luc said and hung up.

He went into the kitchen and put the kettle on for a cup of tea. The water was partially warm so it boiled in no time. The tea ball steeped for only a few minutes while he thought about what he should say.

Lately he had noticed something different about Roland, something those who did not know him well may not have seen, the evidence being so subtle. Roland had taken a keen interest in Summer. Luc was surprised, having always imagined him to have made some sort of informal pledge of celibacy much like his own more formal vows, only Roland's to science rather than to God. This was an assumption on his part. Roland was not the type of person to discuss personal matters; nonetheless, based on Roland's behavior Luc had thought that was the case, until now.

His suspicions peaked when Roland changed his plans and decided to go back to the lake. That had not been his intention until they met Stuart and Barry for dinner the night before and learned they were to go to Geneva and leave Summer behind. In fact, Roland had already purchased his train ticket and was to leave for CERN the very next morning.

This was not like him, Luc thought. Roland is methodical, a planner who rarely acts on impulse, and now this. No, no, he thought. Summer is very attractive and Roland is after all human, but nothing will come of it. It's a passing infatuation that is all, impulsive and brief. He sipped his tea and wondered if he should tell the others his suspicions. Not just yet, he decided.

"Stuart, this is Luc. Roland did not answer when I phoned. Yes, I think it's quite possible they are together, but I don't know where they would have gone."

"Do you think she may have driven him back to CERN?" Stuart

asked.

"That is possible," Luc said. "But I did phone his lab after getting no response at his apartment, and he isn't there either. I also learned he has taken a leave of absence."

"A leave of absence! For how long?"

"The person I spoke with did not know but suspects it's brief. I assume he didn't want to try to divide himself between his work there and the investigation here once he learned the potential danger Etienne faces."

"I'm surprised he didn't say something about it," Stuart said.

"Roland keeps a lot to himself," Luc said. "Not to change the subject, but how did the conference go? I didn't expect you back so soon."

"Oh, man that conference was a dud. Didn't spend a single night there."

"That probably explains it," Luc said.

"Explains what?"

"Summer. She thought you were going to be gone all weekend. She probably didn't think to leave a note or tell anyone where she went because she thought she would be back before you. When is that conference scheduled to end?"

"There are sessions scheduled all day today and a few morning sessions on Sunday, and then some kind of closing dinner or something."

"She will be back tomorrow, before nightfall."

"You're probably right," Stuart acknowledged. "She probably went off somewhere with Roland. I don't know if that's gonna make Etienne feel too great, but at least we can assume she's safe. That's something."

"Yes, at least we can assume that," Luc said. "You say the conference was a dud?"

"Oh, was it ever. Here, I'll hand you over to Barry."

"Hello Luc. Stuart's assessment is correct with one exception, Dr. Claudio Postremo. I wonder if you know him?"

"I've heard the name, but I'm afraid that's all."

"Well, I wish you had been there. He was quite brilliant. We had dinner with him."

"Why not come over for lunch and tell me all about it," Luc said.

"I'll see. First, I should speak to Etienne."

"Tell him the best thing he can do is calm down and wait until Sunday," Luc reiterated. "Tell him he can come over to my place for lunch if he likes."

"I think you're right," Barry said. "I'll phone you back when I know what we're going to do."

"The good news is that Summer is probably with Roland and quite safe," Barry said to Etienne over the phone. "Luc called his apartment and the lab at CERN, and he wasn't at either place so that's our surmise."

Etienne was quiet at first. "If that is the good news, what is the bad news?" he said sarcastically.

"I wouldn't look at it that way. Summer thought we were going to be gone all weekend and was probably looking for something to do. That's all. The bad news is we don't know where they are, but I bet she'll be back tomorrow. Hey, Luc wants a full report on the conference. He has asked us over to lunch. We could come out there and pick you up."

"Yes, you would have to. She has my car."

"It's no trouble."

"I think not. I will stay where I am just in case," Etienne said. "Anyway, my grandmother phoned just after we hung up and asked me to join her for bridge today since I have nothing else to do. She's got someone who needs a partner. I could not say no."

"I didn't know you play bridge."

"I can assure you, my game is quite rudimentary."

"Well, try to relax and have fun if you can. I'll talk to you tomorrow."

"How did he take it?" Stuart asked when Barry hung up the phone.

"I think pretty bad. He's not coming with us today. He's going to stay back at his hotel and play bridge."

"I see what you mean," Stuart said.

Summer and Roland met up in the hotel dining room for an early breakfast, but after thinking about it for a minute or two, Roland thought it best to skip breakfast so they could beat the thundering herds that were sure to ascend to the mountain top. The first train from Grindelwald to Kleine Scheidegg was nearly empty when they boarded. It meandered up dewy green foothills, dotted with lush evergreen trees, and sprinkled with wildflowers that grew alongside its tracks. Glassy lakes lay in the distance, tidy chalets were scattered here and there, and cables that in winter would transport skiers to the slopes hung unused in the air. The train proceeded to climb higher and higher until trees and flowers and most signs of domesticity gave way to craggy mountains.

Roland opened the window across the aisle from where they sat letting in the chilly morning air. "Listen," he said.

"I'm cold," Summer said shivering in her seat.

"Listen," he repeated.

Summer heard the deep clang of bells that echoed through the high rugged land the train now passed through. "What's that?" she said. She got up and came to the window.

"Look over there," he pointed. "Those are mountain cows."

Summer put her hands in the pockets of her jacket for warmth and studied a herd of white cows standing lopsided on the rugged hill eating the sparse grass. "How can they stand there like that at such a steep vertical angle? They're not mountain goats."

"They are used to it. You would be too if you lived up here."

"It's lonely," she shivered.

"It is quite isolated. No cars even, but they have the train and these mountains."

They stood together taking in the scenery for the rest of the journey to Kleine Scheidegg where the train came to a halt.

"Come on," Roland said and grabbed Summer's hand to help her out of their car. "We have to switch trains now."

They leaped out of the yellow train that had brought them this far and boarded a bright red train destined for Jungfraujoch. It left within minutes as the trains were perfectly timed to each other. Roland did not open the window. Instead they huddled together for warmth while the temperature continued to drop as they climbed higher and higher towards the clouds and mountain peaks. The train halted once again, but they were to remain inside if they were not to get off for hiking. Summer crossed the aisle to the window to get a better view of the mountain peaks. A sign read, Eigergletsch, 2320 meters, 7612 feet.

"7612 feet!" she said to Roland. That's higher than Mount Pilatus!"

"Take it in. We go into the tunnel now."

The train entered a long tunnel excavated late in the nineteenth and early twentieth centuries. It stopped twice before arriving at its destination, allowing passengers to get off for a few minutes and look out at the scenes below and above them through plexiglass windows. Each stop also gave the adventurers a few minutes to acclimate themselves to the thinning air, which seemed to have done Summer no good when her legs gave out from under her only a few steps into the rarified atmosphere of the Top of Europe.

Roland caught her. "It's all right; it's just the altitude.

"I feel so dizzy," she said.

"You need something to eat." He guided her through a concession area inside the train station, past shops that sold postcards, Swiss watches, army knives, and cowbells to an elevator that took them up to the Crystal Dining Room. A waitress seated them next to one of the windows that looked out over the mountain peaks.

"Something light," Etienne said.

The waitress looked at Summer. "You could use something warm. We have a lovely cream of leak soup today."

"That sounds good," Summer said, her head resting against the window glass.

"We just got here," Roland said to the waitress. "She's still dizzy."

"You should drink a cola," the waitress said, "the caffeine and carbonated water will fix you up."

"Okay," Summer said weakly.

"I'll just have coffee," Roland said, "along with the soup."

The waitress brought the cola and coffee right away, along with a basket of pretzel shaped rolls and fresh butter.

Summer took a bite. "Hmm, a soft pretzel," she said. She sipped most of her cola. The waitress refilled her glass and brought out the soup, a creamy pale broth with a dollop of sour cream that spread out over the top as it melted.

"This tastes really good," she said.

"You look better. I was beginning to worry."

"I'm fine now. I just needed food" she said and turned her attention to the outside. "I can see why they named this restaurant the Crystal Dining Room. It's shimmering white out there. How high up are we?"

"11,333 feet."

"I've never been so high except in a plane. Can we go outside?"

"Finish up, and we'll go out onto the glacier."

The morning sun beat down on the glacier making it wet and slippery, which was not a good match for the smooth leather bottoms of Summer's shoes. At first she walked methodically, her eyes looking downward to where her next step would fall while she held on to a rope fence designed to keep visitors upright and prevent any from accidentally sliding off the glacier edge. But as she got further out on the glacier she grew more surefooted and took in the view. Billowing clouds, snow capped mountain peaks, icy glaciers exploded in a winter white brilliance that nearly blinded her vision. She got out her sunglasses and looked down from where she was perched on the glacier ledge. The valley below was obstructed by low clouds that had begun to fill in the windy void between her rock perch and the next peak. She instinctively grabbed the rope but looked more exhilarated than frightened.

"This is fantastic!" she said, all signs of altitude sickness now gone.

"The thin air is good for you," Roland said as he noted the pink roses in her cheeks.

"I feel better out here. Where's the observatory?"

"It's up there," he pointed to a higher peak. "We will have to go back inside to get there."

They reentered the train station and followed the signs leading to the observatory platform.

"I'm glad we got out there before all of these people arrived," Summer said.

"That's the wisdom of taking the first train. By the second train it begins to fill up and stays that way all day unless the weather is bad."

"I'm glad we came when it's clear enough to look out and see the mountains," Summer said.

"On a cloud free day you can see much farther. You could have seen all the way down into the valley."

They wandered past indoor exhibits featuring the history of the construction of the railroad and honoring the memory of those who had built it, most particularly those who had died building it, until they came out onto the platform of the Sphinx Observatory that was much higher

125

up.

Instead of standing on ice and snow with nothing but a rope for a fence, they stood on a metal grated floor walled in by grated fencing. Initially it felt safer until Summer looked down and discovered the grates rested on nothing but thin air. Looking up she saw the observatory's silvery dome still catching sunlight even as more clouds moved in.

"Take a look," Roland said, pointing down.

She could see the glacier they had just stood upon now dotted with throngs of people who had taken the second and third trains to Jungfraujoch. The wind picked up, whipping her hair across her face. She shivered as the dome of the observatory went from silver to gray.

He looked up into the sky. "The weather is changing. We should go inside." He pushed a button to an intercom. "Roland here," he said. The door unlatched.

"Did I tell you this is a meteorological observatory?"

"No," Summer said. "I wonder if they can do something about the weather?"

"Unfortunately, they're not that advanced," he said and broke out into a broad grin. "But maybe they could do something about their predictions. I wasn't expecting this today."

Roland was met by a bright young man, a doctoral student he had originally met at CERN who was now doing research at the observatory.

"Congratulations for getting some time up here," Roland said.

"Not much else was going on right now so they gave me time to work with the Lidar project," Ned said.

Summer looked around the place and was struck by how full of electronics it was. Wires and equipment were everywhere arranged in what looked to her like haphazard order.

"It does look like a mess," Ned said. "But believe me it's not as chaotic as it seems. I know where everything is."

"I believe you must," she said. "Where's the telescope?"

"Yes, Ned. Can you show it to us?" Roland said.

"Do you want me to open the dome?"

"That would be good."

The dome slowly opened and the telescope went into place.

"This looks different from the telescopes I've seen," Summer said.

126

"Of course, the ones I've seen are of the backyard variety."

Ned laughed. "This is a Cassegrain 76 cm telescope, a little more powerful than that. I spend most of my time shooting laser beams up into the atmosphere to measure the vertical distribution of temperature and humidity."

"What? Laser beams?" Summer said, properly impressed.

"Yes, thirty at a time, and then I measure the echo when the light's reflected back."

"What problem are you trying to solve?" Roland asked.

"Why this thing hasn't been working correctly. The whole point is to get more reliable data for weather predictions, and they were getting it until recently. There have been many anomalous events lately, like what's going on out there right now. I'm trying to figure out what's wrong."

"I was planning to ask you about that," Roland said. "This rain coming in was not in the forecast."

"Precisely! And from the looks of it we're in for a big one. We've had a repeated pattern of non-predicted rainstorms, six since I've been up here. All six have been dramatic with plenty of lightening."

"Do you think it could be the effects of climate change?" Summer asked.

"That's possible. But that doesn't explain why we can't predict them."

Roland looked worried. "How long do these storms last?"

"They're short, severe, and frequent."

"Have you noticed any other activity associated with them?"

"Like what?"

"I don't know. I haven't noticed any of this over at CERN."

"Or in Évian," Summer added. "We've had some rain, that's all."

"That's the other oddity," Ned said. "These storms are highly localized. Something must be going on around here that's triggering them."

Roland looked up through the open dome as if he hoped to see the answer in the sky.

"I'll turn on the Doppler radar system and take a look right now," Ned said.

The screen lit up all green, yellow, and orange.

"Look at this!" Ned said. "This is massive and not localized at all, and it's heading this way."

Roland and Summer looked at the screen. "It's moving into CERN and Évian right now," Roland said.

"What's that red?" Summer said.

"That's the worst of it," Ned said. "Same with the orange. The yellow is stormy but not too bad. The green is just rain. We don't usually see red. That's real bad."

"It looks like that red is near Évian," Summer said, "but Geneva looks okay."

"I think we should head back down before the storm comes," Roland said.

"I'm going to shoot off lasers in another twenty minutes if you want to stick around and see it work," Ned said. "We can go have some coffee while we wait."

"I want to see his laser beam," Summer said. She looked around the place again, at the control panels, the lit up Doppler radar screen, the telescope, and all the other unnamed equipment. Her second, better-informed glance was full of approval.

"We might as well stay for a bit," Roland said. "The train's probably jammed full anyway. We will get the next one."

Etienne sat across the table from his bridge partner, a dark haired young woman of about twenty-seven. Madame Conti had never met Juliette, but she knew her as the granddaughter of a very dear friend so she felt obligated to help keep her entertained at her grandmother's request.

The new pair had already lost a number of hands of bridge to Madame Conti and Hans Bueller before late afternoon teatime. Juliette had taken the opportunity of the break for tea to counsel Etienne on the weakness of his game with the goal to improve their chances of winning at least one hand. They were right now very close to that achievement.

She looked at him from across the table, her eyes cautioning him on his next move. He read her perfectly, and the play passed to Hans without any damage to their team. Hans made a minor mistake that

Juliette capitalized on, and she went for the kill. This hand of bridge was done, and Etienne and Juliette had finally won. She got up from the chair, went around the table, reached over Etienne's chair and hugged him, the sweet scent of her perfume informing his senses.

"That was a lucky turn of events for you," Madame Conti said to the couple.

"I think it was skill as much as luck," Juliette said. "We are getting pretty good."

"I'm sorry, I'm distracted," Hans said. "I have been z'inking of Summer. I worry if she is all right. Z'e weaz'er!"

"I'm sure that scientist fellow is taking very good care of her," Madame Conti said.

Etienne's face darkened. "I will check at the front desk to see if she has phoned."

"Who is Summer?" Juliette asked after Etienne had left the table.

"A very dear friend," Hans said.

Juliette rightly suspected that Summer was her competition. She began to see the picture was more complex than what she had been led to believe when her grandmother had phoned her in the morning to ask if she would be available for bridge. Her grandmother had said that Madame Conti's grandson was without a partner. Juliette understood the code to mean without a partner in life as well as bridge; and knowing her own grandmother as well as she did, she suspected that a little matchmaking was going on. She was quite relieved when she was introduced to him and found him quite handsome.

Etienne pushed the door open that led out into the parking lot to see if his car was there, although he knew it highly unlikely that she had returned since she could have easily found him in the dining room. He squinted and lowered his head to protect himself from the swirling pine needles and old brush that blew across the empty space where his car had been parked. He turned back to the hotel just as a violent gust of wind began to tear at the flowery vines that covered it.

Chapter Fourteen

Thunder shook the building. Lights went out, leaving the dining room quite dark. Teacups lay on the table, along with plates, knives, butter, and the empty teacake basket. Bridge was over. Madame Conti called for the waiter to bring them a candle.

Etienne's attention was drawn to the snap of a ripped vine whipping against the window glass, which when mixed with the incessant noise of beating rain, created a cacophony that grated against his nerves. Anger mingled with worry. He hoped she was not out on the road in this weather. He desperately needed another headache pill. He excused himself to go up to his room so that he might look out from his balcony window. Juliette stealthily followed. When he turned the knob to enter, she put her hand on his hand, startling him with her touch and scent. "I do not want be left alone in the dark," she cried. "Please?"

They dared not open the door to the balcony, the force of the rain being great enough to soak the room. They peered instead through the panes of the rain-glazed glass as best they could. It was nearly dark although it was not night, but dark enough nonetheless to shroud the garden from view. They assumed by the condition of the visible vines now hanging limp, stripped of their flowers and most of their leaves, that the garden below was heavily damaged. What they could see with utmost clarity was bolt after bolt of lightening striking down into the meadow and woods beyond the parking lot, the same meadow and woods that Etienne had walked through to the lake.

"Is that smoke out there?" she said after the crack of a massive bolt of lightening.

"I think so, and it is very near."

"Fire!" she said.

"Don't worry. The rain will put it out."

"What if it strikes us?"

"The hotel?"

"Yes!" she said.

"We would have to evacuate."

She drew nearer to him.

"Don't worry. It won't strike here. The center of the storm has moved on."

Within minutes the rain stopped, and the shroud that had enveloped the outdoors began to lift. Etienne and Juliette stepped out onto the balcony to survey the storm's aftermath. Rose bushes lay beaten into muddy puddles, but they looked like they would recover with warmth and sun. The flowering vines took the greatest damage. What remained of them would have to be stripped from the building and new seedlings planted.

"My car!" she said.

"Let us go out and see."

Tree limbs, twigs, and pine needles were strewn about the parking lot. One nearby tree was entirely uprooted while others had lost branches.

"You are lucky," Etienne said at the sight of a heavy limb that lay on the ground just inches from her car.

She opened the door and looked inside to reassure herself. It was dry.

"You go back inside the hotel," he said. "I'm going to take a walk."

"I will go with you. I don't want to be alone."

Etienne took the path from the parking lot up into the meadow towards the lake. Their shoes were wet, but the heavy grasses had been beaten down into a mat that protected their feet from the mud. The pine forest smelled intense, its fragrance amplified by the myriad fresh needles newly shaken down. The trees however were intact, protected by their close proximity to each other. When they got to the lake the situation changed. Charred remains of trees and grasses surrounded its circumference. Smoke still rose from the log Etienne had sat upon.

"Here was the fire," he said.

"It burned quite a lot before the rain dampened it," she observed.

They were silent for a few minutes. Etienne could not hear the frogs. No insects were in the air, and no diving birds were in the vicinity to catch and eat them had they been there.

"At least it didn't spread," she said, breaking the silence.

"Yes. Let us go back to the hotel."

Ned had methodically arranged his instrument before opening the dome.

"This might not work too well with all those clouds up there, but I'll give it a shot since you two have honored me with your presence," he said with a crooked smile.

The three adjusted their goggles to fully protect their eyes and stepped back from the now opened dome. Ned pressed his thumb against a hand held control switch.

"Wow!" Summer squealed in delight after a green laser beam shot up into the sky, exploding the interior of the dome in brilliant white light.

"It is impressive," Roland said.

A second beam shot upwards, and then a third and a fourth.

"Fantastic!" Summer said.

"It is pretty neat," Ned agreed.

A fifth, a sixth, a seventh, eighth, ninth, tenth laser fired upwards, and then something went wrong. The eleventh beam boomeranged down onto the instrument, bursting it into fire. Ned froze for a nanosecond before swatting the flames with his coat. Roland moved closer in and looked through the dome opening. He caught a glimpse of an object in the sky. It flashed silver and moved fast.

"Close the dome!" he shouted.

Ned immediately complied, but even with the instrument dead and the dome closed, laser beams rained down on the observatory. Seconds later the lights went out.

"What's happening?" Summer screamed.

"We've lost power," Ned said. "Those beams I shot up are coming down on us."

"We had better get out of here!" she said.

Roland shepherded Summer towards the door leading out onto the observation platform. Ned followed on their heels. The three of them scrambled towards the door that had brought them out onto the platform from the train station when a laser beam struck the grated metal flooring they were standing on, severing it from its supports. Roland shoved Summer through the exit door leading to the train station platform just before the floor gave way from under him. He grabbed the door threshold and lifted himself to safety. Ned dangled from what was left of the corner support.

"Here," Roland said and stretched out his arm for Ned to grab hold of.

"Thanks, buddy," Ned said after Roland pulled him through the doorway. "You must be lifting weights or something. I thought I was going to die by free fall."

"Adrenaline," Roland said. "Keep moving."

They ran through deserted hallways, past displays commemorating those who had died building this tunnel to the sky until they arrived at the concession area where people milled about shopping for last minute trinkets. Roland led Summer and Ned at a swift pace past the crowd towards the train that stood ready to be boarded. A blast hit the building they had escaped into, as if the beams had some uncanny awareness of where they had gone and were intentionally firing on them. They climbed into their train car seats.

"Can't they make this thing go now?" Summer said.

"Not until everyone has boarded," Roland said, as he watched the now panicked crowd shoving and pushing its way through the open car doors.

Another laser beam hit, rattling both the windows and the passengers who raised their voices to a crescendo.

Roland tried to comfort Summer who sat next to the window weeping. Finally the weighted down train began to chug through the tunnel under the mountain.

"This is the safest place we could be right now," Roland said.

"What the hell is going on?" Ned said. "These aren't the beams I shot up. We're under attack!"

Roland did not reply.

"Why do you say this place is safe?" Summer asked.

"The mountain is thick. Lasers cannot cut through."

"Who's shooting at us?" she asked.

"Yeah," Ned said. "Who's shooting at us and why?"

"I don't know who, but whoever they are, you must have struck them and they're retaliating."

"Who retaliates with laser beams?" Ned said. "The Chinese? The Russians? They don't fly over Swiss airspace."

"I don't know who it is or why they're here, but we hit them and they're hitting us back."

"I was shooting blind with all that cloud cover, but who would have thought someone was up there, equipped to shoot laser weapons no less. And why would they bother to spy on a mountain top in the middle of Switzerland?"

"I can't answer your questions," Roland said. "For now I'm more worried about what will happen when we pull out of this tunnel and head towards the station at Kleine Scheidegg."

"Pray?" Ned said. "There's no other way down the mountain."

The train came out into the open air at Eigergletsch, but instead of stopping as was its custom, it continued on to Kleine Scheidegg at breakneck speed through a driving rain.

"The engineer must have had the same worry as you," Ned said to Roland.

"I wonder if he knows anything? If he's getting any reports?"

"I hope NATO planes are up there chasing them out of here," Ned said.

"Let's get as close to the door as possible."

The three gave up their seats to passengers happy to take them. They pressed through the crowded aisles as best they could, swaying from side to side as the fast moving train raced down the mountain. The train slowed, Kleine Scheidegg, the sign read. Train to Grindelwald, another sign read across the platform.

Roland pointed upwards when they crossed the platform to the Grindelwald train. "Look!" he shouted. Streaks of fire shot through the clouds.

"Green lightening!" Summer said.

"No, an air fight," Ned replied. "When did NATO get laser weapons?"

"I'm glad they're firing them at each other and not at us," Summer said just before a shimmering green beam descended from the sky and struck nearby. "I spoke too soon!"

"We better get out of here," Roland said marching towards the train to Grindelwald.

"There's no tunnel from here on out. We would be sitting ducks on that train," Ned said.

"Is there another way down the mountain?" Roland asked.

"We could hike, but the trail is tricky and it's dark and raining."

"That won't work. They're tracking us somehow. Do you have a cell phone on you?"

"Yeah, here," Ned said and pulled his phone out of his pocket.

"Get rid of it."

"Get rid of it?" Ned said.

"That may be how they're tracking us. If you get rid of it, that could buy us some time."

Ned looked at his phone. "Sayonara good friend," he said and placed it gently inside a trash container.

They boarded along with other passengers whose destination was further down the mountain. The train chugged forward, but before Kleine Scheidegg station was out of earshot, they heard an explosion coming from the platform where they had just been. The train, like the one that had brought them down from Jungfraujoch, rapidly picked up speed, fleeing the mountain.

"I wonder who's winning?" Ned said.

"What'll we do when we get to Grindelwald?" Summer asked.

"Get in your car and go to the safest place I know," Roland said.

"Where's that?" Ned asked.

"Under the Alps, the Gottard Tunnel."

"That's a good hour and half away!" Ned said.

"Good!" Roland replied.

"But even if you can get there, you can't park in there."

"We'll walk," Roland said.

"Walk inside that tunnel! You're crazy! It's 16 kilometers long."

"Exactly, the safest place I know."

A voice over the train intercom advised passengers to listen to a very important announcement first in German, then in French, and finally in English. "Due to circumstances beyond our control," the train conductor said, "Grindelwald will be our final stop tonight."

"But we need to get to Interlaken," a frightened man sitting behind them yelled. The intercom of course did not answer, but his complaint let loose a torrent of others and fearful cries from those too terrified to speak until a woman shouted, "Shut up, will you! We will be lucky to get to Grindelwald alive. Count your blessings if we do."

"It doesn't sound good," Ned said.

"How much farther do we have to go?" Summer asked.

"It's hard to say," he replied. "I've been making this trip a lot lately, and it usually clocks in at about thirty minutes on this leg. But we're traveling much faster than usual."

"We will get there Summer, don't worry," Roland said. "The last blast we heard came from back at the train station. If they took out Ned's cell phone, they may think they took him out. At the very least, they've lost our location."

"Thanks! Maybe you could read my eulogy."

"Don't be so sarcastic," Summer said. "Thanks to Roland's quick thinking you're still here, even if your phone isn't."

"I know. I'm sorry. I'm depressed, that's all. There's something very disturbing about thinking I'm being tracked for extermination because I did a weather test, admittedly in very bad weather, but a weather test just the same. It's weird, very disconcerting."

"Yes, it is," Summer said, and turned to Roland. "You do make it seem like it makes sense when it doesn't. Ned shot off laser beams, hit a plane or something, and they're firing back. Like that's normal!"

"I didn't say it is normal. I just gave the most obvious explanation I could think of."

"But NATO doesn't have planes that fight with laser beams," Ned said, his head having become clearer in the few minutes of relative calm. "Neither do the Chinese or the Russians, at least none that any of us have heard of. And I can't believe we wouldn't have heard something about it if they had those kinds of weapons."

Roland had to relent. "I never said they were NATO planes or Chinese or Russian planes. You did. I saw an object, a silvery object when I looked up through the opened dome."

"A UFO you mean?" Summer said.

"What?" Ned said, "What did you say?"

"She said a UFO," Roland answered, "which is absolutely correct. What I saw was an unidentified flying object. It didn't look like a conventional jet."

"You've got to be crazy! What have I gotten myself into?"

"He's not crazy," Summer said. "A friend of mine was taken on board one, and later I saw it myself."

The train halted at Grindelwald station.

"I'm getting out of here. This is nuts!" Ned got up from his seat and pushed himself through the crowd to the door leaving his traveling partners behind. But before he left the car he turned to them and shouted, "Be careful! Maybe we'll talk about this later."

Sadness swept over Roland's face. Summer wanted to comfort him but restrained herself offering only a remark. "He just can't handle the truth. Don't let it bother you."

For all of her feelings of sympathy, Summer could not know how deeply Ned's reaction distressed Roland. How isolated he felt. He was one of the few scientists to recognize a reality that for most was inconceivable and for others would mean the death of their careers if they should come forward and acknowledge the truth, that we are being visited. These closeted believers were the worst, ready to pounce on others lest anyone suspect their own private thoughts. She could never have fully understood this, she having lived in the world of art where everything is possible and no thought too fantastic or uncertain.

He pulled her near to him, held her close as the last passengers left the train. She knew with that embrace what he felt for her, which up to then he had carefully concealed. He loved her. She knew that. What she did not know was what she felt.

Chapter Fifteen

"I should drive home now before it gets too late" Juliette said when she and Etienne arrived back at the hotel parking lot.

"The roads will be hazardous," he said, pointing to branches, limbs, and evergreen needles scattered about as well as deep puddles of standing water. "Wait until tomorrow."

She easily acquiesced.

"Will they be able to prepare dinner tonight?" he asked his grandmother who was seated in the hotel lobby when they returned from their walk.

"Only a limited menu until the electricity is restored. For tonight they will be using auxiliary power."

"Juliette will be staying on to avoid a hazardous drive home. She will join us for dinner."

"Juliette dear, then you must check into your room and take advantage of what's left of the light to freshen up."

Etienne returned to his own room to rest and to phone Barry and Stuart to see if they had learned more about Roland's whereabouts. Not only was the electricity out but the phone lines were down. He felt like a fool for having suggested that he and Summer leave their cell phones behind in Paris. His motive had been to leave Paris behind, not Summer. How could he have known they would be parted like this? His mood continued to vacillate between worry and anger.

The hotel dining room looked far more beautiful than he had ever seen it when he came down for dinner, lit as it was in soft, white candlelight. Gone was the card playing. Gone were his grandmother's nosey friends. He stood alone at the window looking out on a golden sunset visible on the horizon when Madame Conti and Hans Bueller arrived.

"How lovely the sunset, and after such a terrible storm," Madame Conti said. "Let us take this table right here by the window."

They ordered aperitifs and awaited Juliette who minutes later flooded into the room wearing a white chiffon dinner dress billowing softly with

138

each step, the bodice of the dress revealing tanned shoulders, arms, and chest. Her dark hair was pulled back into a wispy French twist, unmasking a fine bone structure. Etienne was embarrassed by his reaction. He tried to refocus his mind on Summer, but all he could think was how she never dressed like this, Summer never having practiced the art of dressing for dinner, as his grandmother would say.

"My dear, where did you ever get such a dress?" Madame Conti asked. "I did not believe shops would be open after such a dreadful storm."

"I brought a small suitcase with me."

"I thought you were to return home today?"

"That was my plan, but I like to pack just in case I should need something."

"I suppose you are wise in being prepared just in case your plans should change, and as it so happens they did. Who would have ever imagined such an awful storm? I do not believe it was forecast."

"That is what they told me at the desk," Etienne said. "They say it grew even worse when it blew into Switzerland. Emergency radio reports that the observatory at Jungfraujoch has been severely damaged by lightening and fire. Train service has been knocked out so there is no way to fight it. They are calling it a disaster of the first magnitude."

Juliette looked over at Etienne. "Did you tell them what we saw at the lake?"

Madame Conti offered a strained smile and then turned to Etienne. "You walked out to the lake?"

"After the storm ended, we went outside to check on Juliette's car. Then we walked out into the woods to see if we could find where the smoke we saw from my balcony window had come from."

"Ah, you saw it from your room. And what did you find?" she asked.

"The lake was struck by lightening. Or at least the area around the lake if not the lake itself. It looked burnt, but by the time we got out there the rain had doused the fire."

"Burnt to a crisp," Juliette said. "The whole circumference of the lake is simply charred."

"How very unusual," Madame Conti said.

"Yes," Hans agreed. "Very unusual, and given your experience z'ere somewhat suspicious."

"What experience did you have?" Juliette asked.

"Oh, let us wait until after dinner for that," Madame Conti said. "Waiter, could you bring another bottle of champagne?"

"No, I want to know," a curious Juliette demanded.

"My grandson saw an airship or something he could not identify."

"He was taken aboard," Hans added.

"Oh, be silent. We do not know if that really happened or if he simply fell asleep and dreamed it."

Etienne was surprised that his grandmother had so soon become a skeptic.

"What are you saying?" Juliette said and began to laugh. "Are you saying you were taken aboard a UFO?"

"That's what some believe," Etienne said.

"Why, that's absurd!" Juliette spit out before she had a moment to think better about the likely reception of her remarks.

"I would not call it that," Madame Conti said. "The event is under investigation by a scientist from the CERN laboratory."

"Oh, my," Juliette said in a sudden reversal. "I've heard about such things but never believed them, but if a scientist is investigating...well. Does he think you could have dreamed it?"

"That is always a possibility," Etienne said. "But I believe Roland leans toward the abduction theory."

"Why, whatever for?"

Her question was slightly misunderstood by Hans who answered her quite honestly, "Roland researches z'ese z'ings and believes Etienne could be in danger."

"He has just warned me to be cautious," Etienne explained. "He said that others who have claimed to have been abducted have met untimely accidents if their identities became widely known through newspaper articles and such. He has advised me to avoid publicity in this matter. But beyond that, he merely is investigating. He knows no more about such incidents than you or I."

"Then why does he think you were abducted?" she asked.

"I initially had no recollection of being taken. But there were several hours I could not account for, and then I began to remember things."

"Your grandmother must be right. You fell asleep, which would account for the time lapse; and then you dreamed the whole thing, which would account for the experience you believe you had. You will be far better off if your grandmother is right and if you do what the scientist advised. Keep it to yourself. You have a reputation to maintain."

"Yes," he said. "You are right."

The subject was dropped. They dined on roasted lamb cooked on a spit in a gas cooker. They drank several bottles of Bordeaux and ate berries and cheeses for desert. Juliette became animated as the night progressed, teasing Hans Bueller whenever she had a chance and flirting with Etienne at every turn of her pretty head.

"I think we should all retire now," Madame Conti said.

Etienne rose from his seat and kissed his grandmother on the cheek. "I shall come up soon."

"Do not dally," she warned.

Only Juliette and Etienne remained in the dining room. The waiters had extinguished all the candles but the one remaining on their table and stood in the rear waiting.

"I think they want us to leave," Etienne said.

"Oh, so soon?"

"We can go out into the garden if you like."

"That would be lovely," she said.

Heavy rain had beaten down the rose bushes, but it had the effect of unleashing their fragrance as if they were very much in the process of revitalizing themselves under the dim moonlight that peeked out behind a still cloudy sky. In the near dark, the string like vines left dangling from the building took on the aspect of ropes suspended from the gallows. The scene went unnoticed by the couple, so engaged they were with each other. Etienne recognized what he was feeling and vainly attempted to right himself.

"I should go up to my room," he said. "It's very late, I'm very tired, and my head has begun to ache."

"Oh, my poor boy," Juliette said. "Let me rub your back."

She walked around behind the bench where they had been sitting together and began rubbing first his shoulders, then his back, and then his neck. He stiffened under her unfamiliar touch, but the more she massaged his tight muscles, the more he relaxed. She bent over, brushed her cheek past his cheek and kissed him. He impulsively swung her around onto his lap and kissed her hard.

Summer could hardly look at Roland when they got off the train, so embarrassed and puzzled she felt not only by his behavior but her reaction to it. He took off his jacket and covered her head to protect her from the rain.

"Thanks," she said, with a quick glance towards him before looking straight ahead.

"We should hurry to the hotel and get our things and get on the road," he said. "The sooner we get to the tunnel the better."

"It seems quiet now. Can't we stay here for the night? I'm really tired."

"Look up there." He pointed up to the fiery mountain peaks. "We will be better off in a safe place."

Summer collapsed on the bed in her room, spent from excitement and terror. She knew not to shut her eyes because she was sure she would be unable to open them. Instead, she roused herself and attempted to call the hotel in Évian. She thought Madame Conti could forward a message about her situation to Etienne who she imagined was still at the UFO conference in Geneva. She believed he was bound to phone his grandmother when he learned about the terrible storm.

The phone line was dead. She once again flung herself across the bed and weighed her remaining options. She could refuse to leave with Roland and stay in her room until she reached Etienne who would come rescue her, or she could leave with Roland. She got up and went to the window. Fire raged in the mountain peaks. Ribbons of green light shot across the sky. She must leave, she feared. Resigned to her situation, she arrived in the hotel lobby where Roland waited for her.

"We should go," he said. "You were up there quite a long time."

"I nearly fell asleep."

"I will drive. You can rest in the car."

They drove down the mountain to Interlaken where large numbers of emergency vehicles were gathered to take action once they determined what actions could be taken. Roland filled the tank at a gas station.

Summer watched as he talked to the attendant.

"They are reporting that the observatory was struck by multiple bolts of lightening and a fire of gigantic proportions is raging," he said to Summer when he got back into the car.

"They don't know about the attack and the fighting?" she asked.

"They're not reporting it. Let's get out of here."

Roland drove the car along rain drenched country roads following the river Aare. Summer was absolutely quiet. Finally, the rain let up.

"Are you sleeping?" he asked.

"No, I'm awake," she said, turning her face from the window towards him. "As tired as I am I can't seem to sleep. I've never been good at sleeping in cars."

"You're feeling anxious. That's understandable."

"What's going on Roland? You know more than you're saying. How do you know these are spaceships fighting each other?"

"What else could it be?"

"I understand why you think that, but the thought hasn't occurred to anyone else. Ned didn't even believe it when you told him, and he was right there the whole time. So how do you know?"

"I've been studying these things for a good many years, and I've learned something from it. Remember when I suggested that there may be more than one extraterrestrial race visiting and they may not like each other?"

"Yes, I remember you saying that."

"It wasn't just an idle speculation on my part. There is a war going on, and this planet is unwittingly right in the middle of it."

"How can you say that so confidently? I can understand speculating about something like that, but you're not speculating."

"No, I'm afraid I am not."

Roland pulled the car over to an observation point that had it been daylight would have offered a view of the river, meadows, and mountains. "Let's take a break," he said and climbed out of the car. He went over to the passenger side and opened the door for Summer. "This place is very pleasant even at night." He helped her over the road barrier putting her down in the soft green grass that grows along the riverbank. He sat down beside her. "Listen," he said.

143

"I can hear cow bells!"

"Yes, it seems such a wild place until you hear the sound of the bells. I think there are few truly wild places left on this planet."

"The bells are comforting," she said.

"They are. They remind me of the things in life which are the most meaningful." He looked at her closely. Her eyes could not escape his eyes, so deep and blue. "I know because I've made contact with some of these beings," he said. "They've warned me that someday this might happen, that someday we could face invasion. So I watch. That is what my interest in UFOs is all about. I'm watching and trying to piece together whatever activity might be going on. That's why I involved myself in Etienne's sighting. I'm not trying to find out what they are. I know what they are. I keep tabs on what they are doing so I can better predict what they might do in the near future."

Summer turned away from him. This was too much to absorb even for an adventurous, opened-minded girl.

He caught her chin and turned her face back towards his. "You cannot turn away from me now," he said. "I'm telling you this because I trust you, because I think you are capable of both understanding and accepting the truth."

"It sounds crazy, you know."

He smiled. "I know it does. You are good with sayings. What do they say? 'Truth is stranger than fiction.'"

"Yes, or 'you can't make this stuff up!'"

They both laughed. She could not turn away from him any longer so drawn she was to his eyes. They were the most beautiful eyes she had ever seen, such a deep blue. More than their color was what they revealed about this man to a sensitive woman like Summer. His stiff and formal appearance was his shield, she realized. His eyes were warm and full of love and full of mystery, so unusual was their color.

He wanted to kiss her but restrained himself. There was a time when men like him would simply take a woman like Summer, but that time was past. He wanted her to want him as badly as he needed her. He got up and put out his hand to help her up. "We should be leaving now."

Etienne lay in Juliette's bed. He pressed his mouth to hers and stroked her dark, silky hair that had unraveled and now lay loose upon her shoulders. There was no time for conversation, not yet. He pulled away for a moment and looked at her lying on the bed under the dim moonlight.

She was a fine looking woman, tall and perfectly proportioned. But there was something else, something she aroused in him that was almost indefinable. She awoke in him something new and different, something that inflamed a part of him that hitherto had remained unknown. She excited him. He felt on fire, her fire having ignited his own.

Nothing dainty about this passionate woman, he thought. She has no need of my protection or instruction. She was bred to be knowledgeable of the world, quite capable of protecting herself and getting what she wants. And it is me that she wants. He reached down and kissed her again. Worldly yes, but there is nothing hard or crass about her, and she would know full well how to comport herself in lofty circles. She would be an asset, a social equal yet without the silly affectation that had spoiled too many women of my rank. She is a thoroughbred. He kissed her again and again.

After a moment of intense lovemaking Juliette asked, "What about Summer?"

The thought of Summer had escaped him once the lovemaking had begun, and he did not want to be reminded. He turned away.

"You must tell me," she said.

She was quite right, he thought. He must tell her.

"We were—We are engaged," he said. "But we have had some difficulties. It seems I do not understand her."

"And she is with another man," Juliette said.

"How did you know that?"

"Your grandmother told me."

"It is not fair to put it that way," he said. "We suspect she is with Roland, but it is not like that. Summer is not like that."

"What is she like?"

"She is very pretty, independent, industrious. She is an American."

"She's a woman, isn't she? And he's a man. What about me?" she said and kissed him again.

"You are very beautiful, so beautiful."

145

They made love again, this time more intensely as if she feared something would tear them asunder if their bodies did not now fully wed.

"And what about me?" she whispered again, her lips pressed against his ear.

"I cannot give you up," he said.

Tears flowed from her eyes. He touched her face gently, wiping them away, and saw with all of her worldliness she was still quite vulnerable. He saw his own image in her dark eyes. He saw their children. He made his decision.

The perpetual throbbing that had been in his head since he had been abducted finally subsided as these new feelings overpowered even his headaches. He picked her up and joyfully spun the two of them around the room. Now able to put aside obligation and those moral compunctions that once restrained him, he took what he wanted, and what he wanted was her.

Chapter Sixteen

"Wake up!" Roland said.

She yawned. "Where are we?"

"Near the tunnel. They will find us here if we don't get away from this car."

"It's storming outside," she said.

He opened the rain-spattered window so she could see. "Look up there."

The cool rain blew in on her face as she studied discernible objects in the sky. "They look like what I saw out at the lake only they're flatter, not so egg shaped."

An ominous whirring sound buzzed overhead. Beams of white light reflected downward, searching along the road they were just on. That's when she noticed the car was wedged into a thicket of trees and brush.

"I pulled off the road when I spotted them looking for us," he said. "They'll fix on the car in a few minutes."

"How did they find us?"

"Do you have anything electronic on you?"

"No, nothing," she said.

"Neither do I. They probably learned they had not killed me in the explosion at the train station in Kleine Scheidegg and did a search of their photo monitoring records. They discovered what we are driving and are tracking this car."

"Photo monitoring records?" Summer said. "What's that?"

"They could not do an operation like this without first gathering data. They must have recorded us leaving Grindelwald in this car. Quick, let's go."

Her heart racing, she followed Roland through the thick pine trees that provided a partial canopy from the rain while thinking she should have stayed back at the hotel. "Why you?" she asked. "Why do they want to kill you?"

"Because I know a lot. Maybe my learning about the lake was too much for them."

147

"You mean the lake where I..."

"Where you saw them, yes. I'm sure that was also recorded. We are almost there. Keep moving."

"Then I know too much too!" she shuddered to think.

The entrance to the tunnel was well lit. To evade their trackers they waited until the searchlight was far down the other end of the road before they darted out of the trees and into the tunnel where they concealed themselves in shadows inside the tunnel's entrance. A huge explosion came from the direction of the car.

"They think they got us," he said. "We will stay here for the night. They should be gone by daylight."

"They blew up the car!" she sobbed.

"All that will be found tomorrow is a charred hull."

They walked along a narrow walkway towards the middle of the long tunnel, their pace now much slower.

"You mentioned the lake," Summer said.

"They probably recorded me out there taking measurements."

"Of what? Do you know what that ship was doing in the lake?"

"The lake's probably a portal. I could tell when I walked out into the water that the drop-off is steep. Who knows how far down it goes."

"A portal? To where?"

"It had to be important for them to come after me like this. It must be one of their bases."

Summer was beginning to feel some sympathy for Ned when he called the whole thing nuts and rushed off the train, but there was no place for her to rush off to. She wondered if Roland's description of events could be a fantasy. She had read about certain personality types prone to making things up. Maybe it was just a very bad storm, or maybe NATO was fighting off spy planes or drones coming from another country, a terrestrial country, not outer space, she thought. But when Roland opened a door concealed in the stonework of the tunnel, any doubts about the veracity of what he had told her disappeared.

Walls were covered with three-dimensional star maps that appeared self-illuminated. A map of the globe stood out, surrounded by individual maps of the four continents and something that looked to her like transmission equipment.

"Where are we?" she asked.

"A safe room."

She looked about. "These are star maps."

"Yes."

"Who made this place? Not you."

"You're right. Not me. I told you before that I had made contact. They gave me access to this location in case I should need it. Well, we need it tonight."

"Permanent UFO bases beneath lakes. Secret safe rooms hidden inside road tunnels. It sounds like an invasion!" she said.

"It is of sorts; up to now a quiet one. They've been here for thousands of years, at least as long as humanity."

She sat down on the floor and leaned back against the wall of the cave like room. He sat down next to her.

"I know this is a lot to take in, so you shouldn't try all at once. But it's true." He pointed to one of the star maps. "There is life out there, more than you can imagine and older than you can imagine. They have been watching this planet since humankind emerged."

"Why? If they wanted to take us over, they could have done it long ago when humanity was completely defenseless."

"Most do not want to take over, only some. And those who do have been successful on other planets, forcing the natural inhabitants into slavery while they plunder their planet for everything of value. I've seen pictures of it. It's tragic. Whole planets stripped of their beauty, turned into deep mining operations. Intelligent life so subjugated into labor they've become stunted, unable to undergo the natural processes of social and biological evolution, which is the hallmark of universal possibility."

"And they're here now and after us?" she asked.

"After me. But they will go away soon. They won't want to be seen in the daylight." She shuddered in fear, and he continued, "Thousands of years ago friendlier planets formed an Alliance to protect the Earth from such a travesty. You could say that I am a part of that Alliance. I am a watcher."

"Where does this Alliance come from?"

"Over here," he pointed, to one of the star maps. "Near the double star Albireo."

149

"How far away is that?" she asked sleepily.

"Nearly four hundred light years."

"Oh," she said and shut her eyes, afraid to even begin to comprehend that number. She opened them again and looked into the ocean of his eyes and knew instinctively that as fantastic as his claims were, he was telling her the truth. She was tired, too tired to explore his story further. She needed rest and time to absorb all that she had learned. She said nothing more, leaned against the cave wall, and was about to drift off when he spoke her name.

"Summer," he said. She opened her eyes. "Whatever you think of me now or in the future, I implore you not to give me up. I am telling you all of this because, well, soon after I met you I perceived you are, well, I think you are a quite exceptional. My instincts told me I can trust you. I hope I have not deceived myself."

"Whatever happens in the future," she vowed, "you can trust that I would never give you up. Your secret is safe with me."

He knew she meant it. He wanted to kiss her but restrained himself.

"I'm sorry this accommodation isn't exactly comfortable," he said. "Here, put your head on my jacket and go to sleep. I'll wake you when it's light."

He balled up his jacket and placed it on his outstretched legs. She rested her head in his lap and was soon asleep, this time in a deep sleep. He smoothed her damp hair, gazed at her face, and never closed his eyes.

Her beauty reminded him of his mother. She too was golden haired, blue eyed, and slender. That is how she looked when she was seventeen and wandered into a meadow not far from the village where she lived in France's Massif Central. She would go there alone to read, she had told him. When he was very young she would tell him her story but much in the way of a fairytale about an anonymous young girl, a cautionary tale he had thought, meant as a warning to him not to wander off alone. But as her health declined under the stress of abandonment by her family and the struggle to raise him alone, she wanted him to know as much of the truth as she could tell him about his parentage. Eventually, the character of the oft-repeated tale changed from some anonymous girl to herself. And finally the story changed from fairytale to personal history.

She lay in the grasses, she had told him, when she saw a white swan flying high above her. She was not accustom to seeing swans in flight and sat up to look at the bird. He would hover above her; and then to her delight, turn in great circles in the sky, until he swooped down upon her, violently ripping her dress open with his beak. Terrified, she screamed, but there was no one to hear her. He was merciless, his feathered wings holding her tightly to the ground. Finally, he flew off, leaving her limp body still wearing her torn dress smeared with virgin blood. Her parents did not believe her story when four months later she could no longer conceal her pregnancy. She was sent off to the East, near Switzerland, to work for a family who had agreed to hide her family's shame.

His mother never fully recovered from this event of her youth. She was frail and lovely and subject to acute illness. He loved her desperately and would search out teas that should have strengthened her. She died of pneumonia at the age of thirty, leaving him alone when he was only twelve. He was taken in by the family of a boy from his school who he had tutored in the summertime; his continued tutoring would earn him his room and board. Later, his academic record won him scholarships that secured his education and career. But after his mother died, he was quite alone.

He never really believed it was a swan that raped his mother. His reading in psychological literature convinced him that her rape was so traumatic she had constructed a veneer of fantasy that allowed her to cope. He swore he would never grow up into the kind of man that would forcibly take a woman, and yet he felt the strong urges that afflict all young men, urges that he buried in the strict formality that came to characterize his appearance and what little there was of his social life.

Later the story of his mother and the swan would reemerge when he made contact, or more accurately, was contacted by a fellow scholar and scientist who claimed he wanted to discuss some finer points of an article Roland had just published from his dissertation. He was flattered by the offer, never having won many accolades from scientists, his essays appealing more often to philosophical types like Luc.

The two men talked and drank their wine into the wee hours until Roland finally opened up and began telling this man about his background, including the story his mother had told him of his brutal and miraculous parentage, a folk tale, he explained, the sort common among village people in the remote areas of the Massif Central.

The man looked deeply into his eyes as if to secure his trust. "We used to do that sort of thing when we were less civilized than we have become," he said. "Some thought it wise to beat our genes into the human species, to blend, mold, and elevate. That was their rationale, at least. What was really at the bottom of it, I'm afraid, was simple lust. Human women can be very desirable. The practice stopped hundreds of years ago so it surprises me that a man as young as you was conceived in such a way. Your mother must have been very beautiful."

Roland, barely able to speak after this news, answered, "She was. Very young, very lovely, and very unprotected." He looked closer at the man and asked, "Who are you?"

"We have used all methods of concealment," the man announced. "Many are found in folk tales or even in the greatest literature. To conceal, it is believed, is more humane and safer for us."

"But who are you?"

"I think you know already. All it usually takes in interviews such as this is a gentle nudge for self-awareness to crystalize. But you have the trauma of your childhood to overcome. Be proud of your heritage," he said. "Your are the product of the beautiful mother you knew and a highly intelligent father descended from a race that is usually far more compassionate. I thought as much from reading your essay, although I imagined the coupling that produced you had been more conventional as is the practice today."

It was during this interview that had occurred three years earlier that Roland learned who he really was. Meetings such as this one continued for the next year, Roland learning more about the history of the paternal breed that had spawned him without learning much about his actual father. Eventually, he met others and the topic changed from history to present day circumstances. He was recruited and trained to become a watcher.

He looked down at Summer still sleeping. He longed for her. He could even imagine his father's abandonment of restraint the day he saw his lovely mother, still a girl, alone in the meadow away from her village. To pin her down as his father had pinned down his mother with his feathery wings would be the grossest imposition of the will. Yet seeing her laying there, beautiful and tempting, just to touch her, just to reach down and touch her. He pulled his hand back. Years of self-discipline and the tragedy of his mother's short life was a powerful enough antidote to restrain him. Besides, he wanted much more from Summer. He wanted her love.

She opened her eyes as if she sensed him looking at her, pale blue eyes meeting deep blue wells. He bent down and kissed her gently. She put her hands on his shoulders and pulled him nearer and kissed him back, momentarily letting go of her own passion, her judgment temporarily moonstruck. But in what seemed to Roland like a split second, she pulled away and stood up. "I cannot do this," she said. "I've been with Etienne almost a year now. I am engaged!"

Roland sighed, resigned to the difficulty of the situation. "It should be light outside by now. Come, I'll take you back."

Chapter Seventeen

Swiss police phoned the hotel in Évian where records showed the rental car had been delivered only days before to one Etienne de Chevalier.

"I can assure you he was not with the car. He is here and was so yesterday," the hotelier said.

He took the investigating officer's phone number and promised he would have Monsieur de Chevalier call as soon as he awakened. He then attempted to connect to Etienne's room, but there was no answer. On a hunch, he phoned the room of the lovely guest Etienne had asked him to assist the day before. A man's voice answered.

"I'm very sorry to disturb you sir," the hotelier said. "I just received an urgent phone call from the Swiss police concerning your rental car."

"How did you know I was here?"

"You did not answer when I tried to reach you in your room, sir."

Is it that obvious? he thought. "Lucky you caught me. I just dropped by here to invite the lady to breakfast. Well, what about my car? I loaned it to someone, and I'm not sure where she drove it."

"They found it alongside a highway in Switzerland about 300 kilometers from here. I'm afraid it is entirely burnt. They assume it was hit by lightening strike powerful enough to have ignited it."

"And Summer?"

"They said nothing about a person, sir. I have the phone number of the investigative officer at my desk if you would like to call him."

"I will be right down."

"Who was that?" Juliette asked.

"Just the hotel desk with a message for me. I'm going down. You should dress. Grand-mère will be looking for us."

"Alright," she said and turned to him with outstretched arms. He reached down and embraced her. "I will meet you at the desk."

The police offered him little more information than what they had told the hotelier. When pressed on the issue of Summer, they said it did not look like anyone had been in the car, unless of course, they had been entirely incinerated. They assured him they would check all nearby hotels to see if she had checked into a room. As soon as they learned anything new, they would advise him promptly.

Where she went and why she went there was as much a mystery to him now as it had been when he had first returned from Geneva. All that he knew is that she had gone off with Roland. Perhaps the violent storm that had swept over the region had led to tragic consequences for them both, he thought. He immediately phoned Barry.

"The Swiss police just phoned. They found my rental car burnt up on the side of the road somewhere in Switzerland. No, they know nothing about Summer or Roland. They said the car appeared to be empty, unless —and it would have to have been a very bad fire—unless the passengers were incinerated. They doubt that though. They will be looking for her in nearby hotels."

"Oh, Etienne, I'm so sorry. I'm sure she's all right. Tell you what. We'll put on some clothes and come over to your hotel for breakfast if you can wait for us."

"You need not put yourself out."

"It's no trouble at all. Breakfast at your hotel is far more appetizing than what they serve here. This is a health establishment, you know."

"All right. I will look for you in the dining room."

"Stuart, get up! We've got an emergency."

Barry phoned Luc and apprised him of the situation. He arranged to go along in case his ministries were needed although he doubted that would be the case. They arrived at Luc's townhouse in less than twenty minutes, having forgone morning coffee and a shower. Barry combed his hair in the visor mirror while Stuart drove. Luc was waiting outside his front door eager to get on the road.

"How did he sound?" Luc asked when he got inside the van.

"Okay," Barry said. "A little emotionless, if you ask me, flat, sort of matter of fact."

"It's a protective mechanism that comes into play when the mind cannot absorb a situation. A common symptom of shock," Luc said.

"Sort of like numbness," Stuart said. "You can go kind of numb. But if that goes away, you can get kind of crazy too." He pressed his foot hard on the accelerator.

155

They were silent for several minutes. "I'm sure she's okay," Barry said. No one replied.

Forty-five minutes after Barry had hung up the phone with Etienne, they entered the hotel dining room only to find Madame Conti and Hans Bueller. It appeared that neither of them was yet aware of the situation so the talk was casual. They chatted about the storm and compared notes on how their respective hotels had weathered it. Barry remarked that he was happy to observe that the storm had carried off the suffocating flowery vines. When Etienne arrived, surprisingly he was not alone.

"Juliette dear, I thought you were to have returned to your home by now," Madame Conti said, looking suspiciously at her grandson.

"I asked her to stay on for breakfast," Etienne replied before Juliette could speak. She remained quiet while he proceeded to report the phone call he had just had with the Swiss police.

"Have they found Summer?" Madame Conti asked.

"No, Grand-mère."

"Well, then they must look!"

"Calm yourself. They say they will check all nearby hotels."

"Maybe the car was stolen?" she said. "Yes, I am sure that must be what happened. Some hoodlums drove off with it, wrecked it, and left it by the side of the road."

"That very well could have happened," Barry said. "The weather was quite bad and there was that massive fire nearby. Stealing it might have presented an easy opportunity under those conditions."

"Chaos reigned last night," Luc added.

"See, Grand-mère! Summer is all right," Etienne said.

"Or maybe not," Stuart said. "Maybe these thugs took her with them."

"Kidnapped!" Hans said.

"She never should have left here alone with that man. You should have taken her to Geneva!" Madame Conti chided her grandson.

"We are all letting our imaginations get the better of us," Barry said. "I'm sure she wasn't kidnapped, and she will turn up soon. For now we must wait."

The men's attention turned to Juliette. They agreed that she was a good looking woman and charming too although they were perplexed that she should have shown up for breakfast with Etienne.

Madame Conti had become very quiet for a woman who usually takes center stage. She looked on disapprovingly as Juliette worked the table full of men. Wily, she thought, as she observed the granddaughter of one of her old friends make Hans blush, show a keen interest in Barry's work, and maneuver Stuart into giving up classified tales of his undercover operations. Towards Luc she acted the part of a wayward penitent in need of guidance. Her behavior confirmed all of Madame Conti's suspicions about what had gone on between her grandson and this woman. She rightly speculated Juliette had seduced him. And he her? Maybe, she thought.

She had to acknowledge Juliette's beauty. And she noted this young woman was born into the same class and lineage as her grandson, which would ensure the purity of their bloodlines if they should have children. She quieted that thought when once again she envisioned poor Summer in trouble. She nearly wept as she considered what such a betrayal by her grandson would do to such a very sweet American girl whom she had grown to dearly love. Yet she had to admit that Juliette would make a more manageable wife, which might make life for him far easier. She would not demand a wedding in the mountains with goats. She would not prefer backpacks and trains to limousines and jets. Her flirtatious manner could even be an asset when dealing with his business clients; that is if her grandson could keep her excessive sexuality under control. Hmm, she thought. She was not so sure of that given that his temperament and demeanor had always leaned towards the more serious and refined than towards the lascivious. Juliette could prove to be a handful.

She turned her attention to Etienne. His eyes did not look so gentlemanly now as he gazed upon this woman who to his amusement was keeping the whole table of men entertained. Instead, he looked upon her as if he were showing off his conquest. This is not like him, Madame Conti thought. What could have happened to him? Only yesterday he was in love with Summer. How could he have changed his mind so fast?

Her thoughts turned back to Summer. She had begun to suspect that Summer did not desire marriage after she quickly through a wrench in

157

Madame Conti's ideas for a wedding befitting their family name. Should not an inexperienced girl have gladly submitted to her counsel on such an important matter? Summer is to be admired in many ways. She is a lovely, intelligent, independent, and a self-starter. She has raised herself up on the basis of merit not birth. Her grandson had thought her a queen. Maybe she is in her own way. Hmm, she thought. Maybe life has more in store for her than a conventional marriage could offer. Maybe her grandson sensed this after he made the proposal, which might explain how he could be so easily and quickly lured into the arms of a beautiful—she hated to even think the word—sexpot.

Juliette stood up from the table. All four men followed with their eyes and then their feet. She smiled, "I must drive home now. My family will be looking for me."

"Must you leave?" Etienne said.

Madame Conti was incensed by his reaction. Here his rental car was burnt to a crisp and his fiancée lost, and this woman is all he is thinking about. It was not like him, even if Summer has proven a bit difficult. She had not failed to notice Juliette's innate eroticism when she had arrived for dinner in that white chiffon dress she just happened to bring along, just in case, she had said. Just in case she chose to seduce my grandson! Madame Conti thought. It was a plan, and she knew the girl's grandmother had something to do with it. But she had not imagined that her fine, respectable grandson would be so vulnerable to such shenanigans, not such an intelligent, serious man as he is or as he had been.

"You will come back for dinner with us tonight, won't you?" Etienne said.

"Why yes," she said. "Thank you for inviting me."

"I will walk you to your car," he said and excused himself from the table.

Luc, quick on his feet, determined to get to the bottom of this odd circumstance. He peered out of the glass of the hotel door that looked out onto the parking lot to witness Etienne press Juliette against the car and her respond with a passionate kiss. It was a prolonged kiss, long enough that Luc understood this had been no one-night stand. He quickly returned to the table before Etienne came back.

158

The conversation grew awkward as Madame Conti continued to berate her grandson for having left Summer alone with Roland. "This never would have happened had you not done so," she said.

"Grand-mère, this is not the time!" To change the topic Etienne brought up the lake. "Did I tell you it is all burned?"

"No, you didn't mention it when you phoned," a subdued Barry answered.

"Juliette and I walked out there yesterday after the storm subsided. Earlier we had seen smoke coming from the woods. The very log I had sat upon was charred black. The whole circumference of the lake looked like a burnt ruin."

"That's strange after everything else that's happened there," Stuart said. "What did you make of it?"

"I am sure the fire was the result of a lightening strike," he said. "The storm was ferocious."

"But isn't it an odd coincidence that it was that lake," Stuart said. "I wonder if the fire could have had anything to do with the UFO and your abduction?"

Etienne was quiet at first, and then he let loose with a second shocker. "I have been thinking about that. I believe I must have dreamed it all. I believe I went to sleep out there at the lake, and that explains both the experience and the missing time. It was all a dream induced by the letter from Barry's nephew. Juliette thinks that all the other influences, you, Barry, Luc, and most particularly Roland's bias caused me to imagine the details of an abduction that never occurred. It was all a confabulation. That is all that it was."

"But those eyes that you drew, the fish bowl like tube," Barry said.

"The mind can do many things," Madame Conti said. "The imagination is very powerful."

"But I saw the damn thing too!" Stuart said. "And Summer saw it, and you saw it a second time."

"I agree with my grandmother."

"So you are saying I imagined the whole thing too?" Stuart said.

"I would not care to speculate about what you saw. I can only tell you about me. I am done with it. Do you not see, the more we talk like this the greater the chance of confabulating future events. You saw those people at the conference. They were out of their wits."

"I'm sorry you feel that way," Barry said. "I thought Claudio Postremo was quite eloquent."

"He was far better than most, but it was all speculation, idle speculation. Remember that boy I spoke with, the one who believed in an alien war? Well, I went to his group's website as I promised him I would. Madness! Sheer madness! I cannot afford to get caught up in such things. I have important work to do."

"And you do have a reputation to protect," Madame Conti said, thinking back to the mockery from her bridge friends.

"And I will have a wife whose social standing I likewise must protect."

"What's that? I assume you are speaking of Summer?" Barry said, although he had his doubts based on everything else he had seen and heard that morning.

"A lot happened yesterday," Etienne said.

"I guess so," Barry said, already furious at the words he knew were coming.

"Hear me out!" Etienne said. "Summer was not here. She left with Roland. Juliette came last night and consoled me. I fell in love."

"In one night!" Stuart said.

"I would not have imagined it myself, but yes, in one night. I have never known such love. She gave herself over to me entirely. I do not know if you can possibly imagine what I mean, but everything she did, she did for me. And she did everything!" he said with a sly smile.

"How dare you!" Madame Conti said. "I think you have said enough about Juliette with poor Summer lost and alone somewhere."

"Lost yes but not alone! It is inconceivable to me that Summer would give herself over like Juliette," Etienne continued in spite of his grandmother's protestations. "Barry, you know all the trouble I have had with her, her constant complaint that I do not understand her, her constant demands that I must understand her when I cannot. I do not understand her! Yet, I was about to give her my name, my wealth, my family; and that was not enough for her."

"She didn't want your name, your wealth, or your family," Barry said. "Summer wants a relationship on an equal footing, that's all. She wasn't after what you've got."

160

"But that is who I am," Etienne said. "I am my name, and I must protect it. I am my family, which I must preserve. And because my duty is to sustain our family, I am my wealth, and I must protect that too."

"Couldn't Juliette be just another gold digger?" Stuart said. Etienne raised himself from his chair in a huff. "She's a knockout, I have to admit," Stuart said. "Maybe it's just a trade-off. You take complete possession of her, and she takes possession of your money and the family name. It sounds like she'll probably service you pretty well too."

Fists up, Etienne took a several steps towards Stuart.

"Don't be so crass Stuart," Barry said, as he stood between the two men. "He's in love, and Summer is better off without him. Let's get out of here."

"I hate to see a friendship end like that," Luc said once they had retreated from the hotel. "But I saw for myself what's going on between the two of them when I saw them together at her car."

"That old black magic," Stuart said.

"It makes me wonder who took possession of whom," Barry said. "He didn't seem like the same man. Poor Summer."

"I think you were right the first time," Luc said. "Summer is better off without him, but she probably won't feel that way for a time. It's her employment I'm worried about. He pays her salary, doesn't he?"

"Not him personally, the foundation does," Barry said. "It pays my salary too."

"Who controls the foundation?"

"His grandmother, Madame Conti."

"Oh, that's too bad," Luc said. "That could put the two of you in a precarious situation. In the case of Summer, I have my suspicions that a better man might soon step in if he sees an opening."

Barry turned around to look at Luc who was seated in the back of the van. "Are you planning on giving up your priestly order?"

"I wasn't thinking of me. I am thinking of Roland. He's a better man than me."

"Roland!" Stuart said.

"It surprised me too. I never imagined him in love with anything but science until I saw how he looked at Summer."

"I never noticed, and I notice things like that," Barry said.

"You would have to know him as well as I do. And even then I have to admit that I hardly believed my own eyes until you phoned and said they were off together." Luc paused. "He's pretty subtle all right, secretive some would say. But he's a good man. He could make her happy if she accepts him."

By now Stuart's mind had turned to Natalie. Could some undisclosed man, who knows, maybe a surgeon this time, or a politician, a senator, he thought, could some other guy already be trying to step in while I'm not there? That's how I lost her to the attorney with the BMW, he realized. "You run a big risk if you neglect your lady," he said to the others.

"Who's talking? Remember it was your big idea that Etienne go to Geneva without her," Barry said.

"I know," Stuart said feeling contrite and vowing that from this day forward he will stay out of other people's business. Natalie, on the other hand, was his business, and he wasn't going to keep out but jump right in.

Chapter Eighteen

Car horns ricocheted throughout the Gothard Tunnel directed at the couple sidling along the tunnel wall. An irate driver slowed next them. "Wollt ihr euch umbringen?" he shouted. Summer was about to answer when Roland stopped her. "Don't try. It's a waste of breath and could lead to more trouble." They emerged from the side opposite from where they had entered the night before and continued down the road unaware that their burnt out rental car had already been reported and hauled away. "Airlo is only a short walk," he said as they paced the four miles to the train station.

Summer remained silent, partly because of the noise and partly because of the awkward situation she found herself in. She had determined to return to her fiancé unashamed and unsullied, which required a good deal of denial. She dismissed her feelings as temporary, as having arisen out of an extraordinary situation. Yet she could not deny that this man she found herself with was likewise extraordinary, as extraordinary as the story he told and as the adventure they had shared. She would never forget him.

Etienne is extraordinary too, she reminded herself: a humble aristocrat, a chaste lover, a chivalrous knight, a man always there to take charge of every situation, including her. She bristled. She did not like being taken charge of. Had Prince Charming lost all relevance? But if Prince Charming lacked relevancy, what about herself? There had to be a place left in the modern world for virtue, she assured herself, and it was her own virtue she now struggled to maintain. She had pledged her troth when she reluctantly agreed to the marriage and was determined to honor that vow no matter how difficult it became.

Over the course of these last few days, Roland had come to understand her deeply engrained sense of honor along with a naiveté he found surprising. It had never occurred to her how others might have construed her willingness to travel with him alone or how he might have construed it. That became evident the first night they were alone together in the candle lit hotel dining room. He had soon realized that any expectation he might have had for a conventional seduction to follow dinner was very unlikely. And yet that recognition, while not flattering to him, only increased his love for her along with his frustration. Having watched her take in the world, particularly the natural world, was a joy for him. Nature had never been made distant or insignificant by the repetitiveness of her witnessing it. She found a way to see things anew, to make the world fresh. Now that he understood her, how could he ever allow himself to become the instrument of her diminishment? She is the only woman he had ever met who so perfectly pleased him, who he believed could so perfectly adapt to what he acknowledged would be a highly unusual set of circumstances. He saw in her the possibility of a far richer life than he had ever known, which was hard for him to give up once it became tangible

The train trip would take about six hours. He was confident that by his calculation she would arrive in Évian before Barry, Stuart, and Etienne returned from Geneva. First they would go to Lucerne where they would change trains, and from Lucerne they would travel to Lausanne. From Lausanne they would take a ferry directly to Évian.

When they arrived at Lucerne they recollected their first meeting.

"I remember that bird that relieved itself on the table. It just missed you," Summer said. "The look on your face! I thought you were going to flip, but no, instead you calmly ordered us inside the hotel dining room."

"It had happened to me once that I was struck on the head by bird droppings," he admitted. "It felt like the agents of nature were intent on embarrassing me. And I didn't want it to happen again in front of all of you."

"That would be embarrassing," she laughed, "particularly if you're trying to impress someone."

"Which I was." They laughed together. "But what about you? I thought if I did not get you inside you might overreach and fly off the edge of the terrace."

"The view is beautiful from Pilatus, but I'm not that reckless."

"Reckless no, but you've got a little of the dare-devil in you." She smiled at that. "I had just met you and learned that you were assaulted while trying to protect that statue of yours."

164

"Gitane Marie," she said.

"I will have to go to Paris and see her. When I heard that you dodged bullets outside Saint Sulpice and pinned one of those bandits down, well, what was I to think?"

"I think you warned me to be more careful," she said and laughed. "But then look what happened when you took me to Jungfraujoch."

"Pretty dangerous business, I have to admit." He looked at her longingly. "We never would have gone to Jungfraujoch together if it had not been for that first meeting."

"Yes, you showed me its peak when we were up on Mt. Pilatus. You told me its name." She turned and looked into his deep blue eyes. "As dangerous as things got on Jungfraujoch, I wouldn't trade the experience for my life."

He moved towards her. Their lips nearly met, when the train began to move out of the station and jolted him back. As it rolled towards Lausanne, he realized this would be their last train ride together. That thought nearly chilled him to death.

"Is your life always so dangerous?" she asked. "Do they come after you often?"

"No, not most of the time. Most of the time I simply gather information, collate it, and make my reports. Rather dull actually. There are others like me doing the same thing. So my would-be assassins have other fish to fry."

"You're learning new idioms!" she said in delight.

"I'm trying."

"What are they like?"

"Who?"

"The people you work for, and the others too, the people you work against."

"That's an interesting question. How should I explain them, my friends that is? They are a very old race, much older than ours. Very intelligent. They arose on a planet light years away. Very fine people if you ask me. They could have just let the others take this planet. It really would not have affected them much, but instead they expend enormous resources to keep us safe."

"Why?"

"They may feel a certain obligation like parents feel for their children; but more than that, they feel love. They have an enormous capacity for love. That is what so impresses me about them. And not the empty kind, not the self-serving kind. What else can I say; they love humankind."

"Why?" she asked again. "People do so many horrible things. Think about all the wars we have. And there's so much greed and selfishness."

"They don't love us because we are perfect. They love us because they think we can become better. That is why I used the parent child analogy."

"Could that change?" she asked.

"I suppose it's possible they could give up on us, but I think they would rather have to change themselves for that to happen. They would have to adopt another point of view, maybe something similar to those who want to conquer this planet."

"What makes their enemies different?" she asked.

"I'm not altogether sure, but it could be their basic assessment of us. That coupled with their goal to acquire and control as many resources as they can."

"I don't get it," she said. "I don't see how those two points work together."

"Most people do not want to steal from a friend," he explained. "Better yet, most do not want to think of themselves as thieves, whether they are or are not. So I think what happened to them is they rationalized the situation in such a way that they can steal without thinking of themselves as thieves. From their point of view, they are taking what they rightfully deserve from people who do not deserve it. And to make the argument that we don't deserve it, they've concocted the worst possible characterizations of us. They didn't feel bad about trying to kill me last night because in their minds I'm some kind of beast intent on lying, stealing, and murdering for the pleasure of it."

"But you're none of that!" Summer said. "That's entirely false and completely irrational."

"I didn't say it was rational or true. I said they've rationalized in order to justify their own behavior. Maybe this better explains why my people are so committed to protecting us. In us they see hope. In them

166

they see nihilism. What will this universe be, is the question they regularly ask themselves. And here is their answer."

"Hope!" she said, sinking her eyes into his. "The universe is hope," she declared as she saw the two of them afloat together on a raft of deep blue water.

"Full of possibility, unrestrained hope, burgeoning hope, a fountain of hope. Expressions like these are the core of their philosophical position."

"What you are doing is so profound."

He blushed a little. "Would you not do it too if you were called upon?"

She held that question, afraid to respond given all the implications of an answer.

The train arrived at Lausanne. They walked to the ferry and boarded for the short trip across Lake Geneva to Évian.

"What will you do now?" she asked.

"Go back to my work in CERN."

"I mean right now, when we get to Évian?"

"That's as far as I will deliver you. You can call your hotel and arrange transportation before Etienne arrives back. I will spend the night at Luc's. I'm not in the mood to take another train today."

"No, neither would I be," she said imagining herself alone in a passenger car.

When they arrived at the ferry landing in Évian, Roland waited while Summer called the hotel.

"Mademoiselle Summer, is this you?" the hotelier said. "We thought you might be dead. Wait, I get Monsieur de Chevalier"

"He's back already! They thought I was dead!" she whispered to Roland while she waited for Etienne to come to the phone.

"Hello," she said. "I'm here at the ferry landing, and I'm not dead. The car was hit by lightening, but we got out before it exploded. When did you get back? Oh, you came right back. Yes, I've been gone all weekend. I thought you were going for the whole weekend too. I went to Jungfraujoch. Yes, with Roland. What are you saying? No, It wasn't like that! We, I mean the observatory up there came under a lightening attack. Roland was driving the car when it was struck by lightening. He was trying to get us to a safe place. We had to hide in a tunnel. Don't accuse me of such things! Okay, I will look for the hotel car."

She hung up the phone shaken and began to cry. "He's really angry. He accused me of running off with you."

He wanted to put his arms around her to comfort her but restrained himself. "I will explain to him."

"I don't think you should try to explain anything to him right now."

"Let me call Luc."

She walked away from the phone so he could make his call in relative privacy. When he was finished, he came over to where she stood sobbing.

"I'm so sorry Summer," he said and patted her shoulder. "Luc and I don't think you should go back there alone."

"He won't listen to you," she said. "He blames you and me for everything."

"I think you're right about that. Luc is phoning Barry at his hotel right now to ask him to pick you up and take you out there. I'm going to Luc's for the night. You can call me there if you need me."

"When are you going back to CERN?"

"I have to go back very early tomorrow. I took a short leave, and it's over."

Barry pulled up in just a few minutes, surprisingly without Stuart.

"Where's Stuart?" Roland asked.

"He caught a plane back to the States to meet up with an old girlfriend," Barry said. "He thought he would be more useful there than here."

"I'm sorry to see him go," Roland said.

"Oh, he'll be back. He always comes back."

Summer climbed into the front seat of the van. "What about the hotel car?" she said.

"I'll stay here long enough to send it back," Roland said.

She could not bring herself to say goodbye. Instead, she forced a smile and said, "Thank you." Then she crossed her heart. "I will never give you up."

He knew that she would not. He knew he could trust her loyalty, just as Etienne would have if he had really known her. While he waited for the hotel car, his attention turned to what Luc had said to him on the phone. He had indicated sternly and in no uncertain terms that the actions Roland had taken in regard to Summer had had dire consequences. When the car arrived, Roland begged a ride to Luc's house before sending the car on its way.

"Would you like some wine?" Luc asked Roland when he arrived.

"Several bottles if you've got them," Roland answered.

Luc went to the kitchen and brought out two bottles of table wine. He uncorked the first, and poured two glasses.

"You should have known better. You're a grown man!" Luc said when he handed Roland a goblet. He sat down across from him. "What did you think Etienne would think?"

"Well, to tell you the truth, that was not what was on my mind."

"What was then?"'

"Summer, only Summer. I wondered if I had any chance with her, and I took the opportunity of Etienne's absence to try to find out."

"What did you find out?"

"She's a nice girl, too nice perhaps."

"So you didn't get anywhere."

"No, she is loyal to the bone. But I had a wonderful time with her in spite of all the trouble. She's a very brave woman, you know. When the lightening was pounding the observatory, she never panicked, not once. Her conduct was admirable."

"And you wished it had been less so," Luc said.

Roland stared at him for a minute as he considered the implications of Luc's remark.

"I never would have expected this from you," Luc continued.

"I'm not a priest," Roland said. "But I'm not a rogue either."

"You love her then," Luc said.

"Yes."

"That's what I thought. Well, you've made a mess of it for her. I doubt my ability to convince Etienne of what you say."

"How long has he known her?" Roland asked rhetorically. "A year? How after a year could he know her so little? It only took me a weekend. If he knew her at all, he would never question her integrity. Never! Never! Never! Now mine, that's another matter, but not hers."

"I believe you," Luc said. "But much happened while you were gone.

It's irreparable. He will throw her out."

"Of their hotel?"

"Out of everything. He controls her employment. She lives in Paris with his sister."

"Would he go that far on the basis of a mistaken idea? I can explain it all to him. I will take full responsibility. I can with total honesty testify that Summer is the most virtuous woman I've ever known."

"I think it's too late for that," Luc said. "He won't want to hear it."

Roland stared at him unable to grasp what he could possibly mean.

"While you were gone, Etienne, under the impression that Summer ran off with you, involved himself with another woman."

"This is Sunday," Roland said. "We have only been gone since Friday. How far could it have gotten?"

"I know it's hard to comprehend. I wouldn't have believed it if I hadn't seen it for myself. But it looked to me that he has entirely transferred his emotions, all of his desire to this new one. This is why I wanted Barry to take Summer out there. I didn't want her to be entirely alone."

Roland sighed. "That bastard!"

Luc opened the second bottle of wine, and the two men continued to drink well into the night. Finally, Roland told Luc his life story, all of it. And he told Luc what had really happened at Jungfraujoch. Luc listened in rapt attention, never questioning his veracity.

"I always thought there was something different about you, but I never would have expected this," Luc said. "Does Summer know?"

"She knows some of it. She was witness to the attack at Jungfraujoch. And since they kept coming after me well after we left there, I had to tell her about my role as a watcher. But she doesn't know about my parentage."

"I wouldn't tell her that," Luc counseled. He emptied his glass. "That could be too much for her. Let her continue to think you are only a man."

"I am!" Roland said.

"Only?" Luc said. "You are too modest." He refilled his glass.

"I pledged her to secrecy, and I have every reason to believe she will honor it. But I think I was unfair to expect her to hold such secrets with

170

no one to talk to. So if you will, would you be her counselor?"

"You can count on me. There is a certain irony in you telling me all of this right now. Yesterday, Etienne renounced his entire experience: the sighting, the abduction, everything, declaring it all a dream."

"That's not uncommon," Roland said. "And he's probably better off for thinking that."

"And there's another oddity I must report in light of what you've just told me. According to Etienne, the lake area was struck by lightening. He described the whole circumference as burned."

"That's interesting," Roland said and paused to think about it a moment. "It was probably an attack."

"On what? What was going on at that lake?"

"I believe it is a portal. They have many, but I think this one is significant. I think my being there is how I came to be a target."

"Portal, portal to what? The next thing you will be telling me is there really is an underworld."

"There is of sorts. Bases at least. It looks like this one may have been taken out. That would be good for Etienne. No need to come after him if the damage is already done."

Their glasses were empty and there was no more wine left in the bottles. Luc bent over and put his head in his hands. "I'm drunk," he said. "I must be."

Roland could see that he had already told him too much for one sitting. "I should go back now if I want to keep my job. We can talk more later."

The two men shook hands and embraced, and Roland walked to the train station to catch the early morning train back to CERN.

Barry let Summer do most of the talking while he drove her to the hotel. She tried to convey the danger she and Roland had been in without betraying his secret. It was lightening not laser beams that pursued them, she said. Lightening had struck their car and set it on fire forcing them to retreat into a tunnel to get out of the storm. She did not mention the attackers. She did not mention the concealed room. But she did convey other events as fully and accurately as she could without giving Roland away. She described the train trip up to the peak of the

171

Jungfraujoch, how she swooned from lack of oxygen, and later recovered enough to go out on the glacier. She described the weather experiment at the observatory in which Ned had shot laser beams into the atmosphere. She told him how the atmosphere, as if in retaliation, rained fire down on the observatory. She told him she had not meant to cause so much worry. She had assumed she would be back before the three of them returned from Geneva and even tried to call Madame Conti from Grindelwald but was prevented from doing so by downed phone lines.

When they arrived at the hotel the desk clerk greeted her with her luggage. The hotelier, embarrassed, went to fetch Etienne from the dining room where he was playing bridge. Etienne walked into the lobby looking stone-faced. Barry, Summer, and Etienne stood alone together, the hotelier having found some task or another to perform in the kitchen.

"The Swiss police phoned here this morning and reported the condition of the car," Etienne said.

"It was struck by lightening and caught on fire."

"That's what they surmised. They saw no evidence of where you were."

"I was inside the tunnel for protection."

"From the lightening?" he said.

"And the rain."

"With Roland?"

"Yes, with Roland, but as his friend, nothing more."

"You stayed with this man for two nights and you expect me to believe that?"

"Yes, I do."

"You never told me you planned to go off with him."

"I didn't know I was going before you left. I went with him to the lake to take measurements and the subject of Jungfraujoch came up. Remember, I had wanted to go there when we were in Switzerland. In a spur of the moment decision we decided to go. I didn't know how to reach you. You left so quickly I didn't even know what hotel you would be staying at."

"If you had wanted to know where I was, you could have looked up the conference on the internet. The hotel was listed."

"I didn't think of it, and I assumed you would be staying there for the full length of the conference."

"So, what are you saying? You planned not to tell me at all? You planned to sneak off with Roland while I was gone and return before I got back?"

"No, nothing of the kind. I would have told you my plans if I had known how to reach you. What I'm saying is that I didn't mean to cause you worry. I thought I would be back sooner."

"You could have told my grandmother where you were going. Ah, but you knew exactly what she would think. What anyone would think!"

Summer did not know what to say. The truth is that if she had thought about it, she would have guessed that Madame Conti would have objected to her going. But the truth was she had not thought about it. If she had considered how she might react, she never would have tried to call her from the hotel in Grindelwald.

"You have shamed me! You have shamed my family!"

"I never meant to," she said, her voice growing weak.

"Now, Etienne, don't be so hard on her. I believe she is telling you the truth," Barry said.

"Stay out of it!" Etienne shouted.

"I only meant to help."

"You have helped quite enough! Summer, our affair is over."

"Affair? We were engaged!"

Juliette came out of the dining room into lobby. Barry, expecting fireworks, backed away towards the exit to the parking lot.

"It's your turn," Juliette said. "You're holding up the game."

"Who are you?" Summer asked.

Etienne awkwardly answered for her. "This is Juliette."

She looked at Juliette and then at Etienne. "When did this happen?"

"I proposed to her today," he said.

"Before you broke off our engagement?"

"You broke the engagement," he said.

She studied Juliette, the tall, dark haired vessel in which she sensed something new stirring. Her jealousy subsided when she looked closely into Juliette's eyes and saw a woman who was a little lost and a little desperate, who had taken the risk of what could have amounted to no more than a one night affair to secure a place for herself in a society that plays cards in pairs.

She turned to Etienne and imagined his night of gratified lust. She could see it as if she had been there. She could see it in the transformation of his demeanor: so tall, so strong, so virile, and so hard. Prince Charming was gone. There was nothing left here for her now. She would end the standoff. She pulled the diamond engagement stone from her finger and threw it at Etienne's feet.

"I never asked for it back," he said.

"Keep it as a reminder of our affair," she said and walked towards her luggage.

Barry followed and quickly grabbed her bags, and the two of them left the hotel.

She braved the situation until they had driven out onto the road from the parking lot. Then she broke down in deep, heaving sobs. Barry pulled the van over and Summer collapsed on his shoulder in tears.

"That's good; let it out" he said. "It will be all right. Tomorrow we'll figure something out."

After a few minutes she pulled herself together, sat back up in her seat, and stared quietly out the window. Barry drove on.

Chapter Nineteen

Luc woke up with a headache, a result of too much wine and a heavy dose of Roland. His friend's revelations required a stretch of the imagination even for him, but it excited him too. In fact, if it were not for the direction of his own studies, Roland's story would have been impossible for him to believe. But in an odd sort of way it made sense to Luc because it acknowledged an historic legacy that others believed only the product of ancient, untutored imagination. He went to the kitchen to make strong coffee, but before he ground the beans he changed his mind and made herb tea, not wishing just yet to jolt his consciousness into wakefulness with high-powered caffeine.

He carried the teapot into the dining room and went to his bookshelves and pulled out volumes of art history, turning first to nineteenth century painter Gustave Moreau's Leda, a painting he had seen in Paris. There she was in full golden glory, the white swan behind her resting its head upon her head as if to bestow a crown. Off to the side, with their eyes closed as if to grant Leda and her swan some privacy, two winged cherubim fly towards her carrying the golden crown of heaven that she would soon wear. He understood Moreau's painting as an annunciation, marking the moment when Zeus so pleased with Leda's beauty disguised himself as a swan and flew down to mix his blood with her blood and the blood of all of her descendants to come. Leda was not the only beauty to meet such a fate, he thought.

He poured himself a cup of tea, added honey, and sipped as he studied the painting. He noted that Moreau's Leda seems to accept her fate if not welcome it. There is none of the story in her demeanor of Roland's young mother's trauma and her subsequent early death. He looked about his bookshelf and pulled down a volume of ancient art. There was Leda again in a fourth century AD relief. She held the swan by its long neck as if to fight him back. Yet ironically, by their side stood winged cherubim placed there as if to consecrate the rape. More shocking was a first century BC cameo that showed the couple in the act of copulation with the cherubim seeming to urge them on. He closed the

175

book.

He poured another cup of tea and opened a volume of the works of Leonardo. He found the copy of a now lost masterpiece very different from the coarse work he had just seen. Leda stands next to her swan, holding him like a beloved pet. Below are her babies newly hatched from the eggs the coupling begat. While the painting is more tasteful, he thought, it completely misses the point of Roland's story. He went back to the first art book and found a watercolor by Theodore Gericault, painted in 1800. This is closer, he believed. There is no cherubim, no crown of heaven, but there is the image of the menacing swan charging as Leda unsuccessfully tries to hold it back.

Art books open and laid out upon the table, he grabbed a book of poetry and turned to William Butler Yeats' "Leda and the Swan" and read.

> A sudden blow: the great wings beating still
> Above the staggering girl, her thighs caressed
> By the dark webs, her nape caught in his bill,
> He holds her helpless breast upon his breast.
>
> How can those terrified vague fingers push
> The feathered glory from her loosening thighs?
> And how can body, laid in that white rush,
> But feel the strange heart beating where it lies?
>
> A shudder in the loins engenders there
> The broken wall, the burning roof and tower
> And Agamemnon dead.
>
> Being so caught up,
> So mastered by the brute blood of the air,
> Did she put on his knowledge with his power
> Before the indifferent beak could let her drop?

Here is the utter violation of Leda, he thought, the terror and violence of the rape. And yet with all of her suffering, Yeats asks a question in the final stanza that adds dimension to the crown of heaven in Moreau's painting: "Did she put on his knowledge with his power/ Before the indifferent beak could let her drop?" He pondered that line. The experience of Roland's mother answers Yeats' question with a profound no. But Roland, on the other hand….

His meditation was interrupted by a knock at his front door. He put down his tea and found Summer there.

"I hope you don't mind me dropping in like this, but I was out for a walk and, well, this is where I ended up."

"No, no, come in," he said as he looked about outside. "Where's Barry? I thought you were staying at his hotel."

"I am," she said as she entered the parlor. "But he has an appointment with Etienne. I wasn't invited."

"An appointment! What for?"

"Etienne phoned him this morning and asked him to come out and settle the terms of our separation as my representative."

"Like a father?"

"Sort of, I guess."

"But you were not married."

"We were betrothed. At least he gave me that. Yesterday he described our relationship as an affair."

"I'm sorry. This must be very painful for you."

"I don't know what he thinks he could give me. I don't want anything of his."

"Maybe your continued employment at the museum," naming the loss he most worried about.

She bit her lower lip and shook her head in ascent. "That's what Barry said."

"Have you had lunch?"

"No."

"Well, then have lunch with me. I would love your company."

"I'm not such good company now," the usually bright-eyed girl proclaimed.

"Yes you are. I have some things to talk to you about."

She looked at him quizzically. "What?"

"First, let me get lunch."

177

He heated up some fresh vegetable soup he had in the refrigerator, sliced some bread, cheese, and some newly picked apples and brought them out to the dining room.

Summer saw the opened books spread all over the table.

"Here, let me help you," she said and began picking them up. "Leda and the Swan," she said when she moved the book of poetry into the parlor. "I know this poem." When she came back to the table she noted the opened books displayed artwork on the same subject. "You must really like the poem. Is it all right if I close these books?"

"Thanks. I had forgotten the table is covered with them. Yes, I like the poem. I was comparing it to the various visual representations."

She studied the Gustave Moreau before she closed the book. "Interesting. This one is my favorite."

"You should go see it in Paris."

"It's there?"

"That's where he lived. The Gustave Moreau Museum is inside the house where he lived and worked."

"I'll be sure to do that," she said as she and Luc sat down at the table.

He served the soup from a large tureen, and passed her the bread, cheese, and apple slices. "Roland was here most of last night and into the morning."

"He told me he was coming. After all the trains we took he needed a break before he got on another."

"He told me the truth of what happened in Jungfraujoch."

She looked up from the table waiting to learn what truth he was told before she spoke.

"He told me about the attack, about the beings who are visiting here and waging war with each other. He told me he is a watcher and that they pursued the two of you."

"I'm surprised he had not told you before given the closeness of your friendship," she said.

"And he asked me to let you know that he told me these things so you would be free to talk to me about it."

She said nothing more, only looked at him in expectation of what he might say next.

"He said he believed he had put a burden on you by telling you these things and then making you pledge not to tell anyone. That's why he told me."

"He couldn't help but tell me. I was witness to it all."

"He wanted to give you someone besides himself to talk to."

"That was sensitive of him," she said. "He's right. It's hard. I've even had to keep it from Barry."

"Maybe someday he will allow you to tell Barry, or maybe he will tell him himself. But right now you have me."

"And Roland has you. I know you've been good friends for a long time. You must have been shocked." She laughed nervously.

"The odd thing is that I wasn't. I've known Roland for three years now, and I've always found him quite remarkable. I have to admit, I didn't realize how remarkable; but yet he has always been special, above the fray, so to speak."

"Yes, he is. He is, well, extraordinary."

This last remark gave Luc encouragement. He did not know how to broach the subject of Roland's affection for her at a time so close to her breakup, so instead he skirted around the subject.

"I'm sure it means a lot to him that you know the truth and can still accept him."

"Why wouldn't I?"

"Not everyone would. It must have been very lonely for him. It may explain why he has kept himself so isolated."

She thought back to Ned's rebuff when Roland told him the fighter jets were not jets at all but extraterrestrial craft. She remembered the moment Ned got off the train, how Roland had held her close to him. "I guess you're right. Not everyone would accept it. Barry tells me Etienne now believes he dreamed the whole thing."

"Yes, that's true. I heard him say so myself. Roland actually believes it's better for him."

"Well, I guess it is now that he is..."

"With a woman who would never believe it," Luc said.

"Yes, I guess so."

"That's what makes you so remarkable Summer."

"Not remarkable enough for Etienne, evidently. Juliette is very beautiful."

179

"Compared to you she is common. I'm going to take a chance here."

Summer looked up from her now empty plate and bowl wondering, well, worrying about what he might say next.

"Roland loves you Summer."

"Oh! I know," she said and looked down at the table.

"May I ask what you feel about him?"

"Roland asked you to do this?"

"No, I'm on my own now. I wonder what I should say to him. If I should give him hope."

"I care for Roland a lot. But it's too soon to trust what I feel."

"You're worried you are on the rebound."

"Something like that. I misjudged once so I could do it again. I need time on my own."

"That's understandable that you feel this way,"

"But thank you for trying to be my counselor and his." She got up from the table. "I should get back to the hotel now before Barry gets back."

Luc walked her to the door. "Have Barry call me. And Summer, whatever you do, good luck."

"Thank you," she said with tears in her eyes. She kissed him on the cheek and left.

Luc understood why Roland loved her. It is her sweetness, he thought, and she has a freshness about her, and most of all she is utterly honest.

He put on another kettle of water, cleared the table, cleaned up the dishes, and carried the fresh pot of tea back into the dining room where he opened his art book once again to Moreau's Leda. He was not surprised that this was Summer's favorite. It was his too, so beautiful Leda is. He noticed something he had not seen before. Leda's upward arched arm parallels the swan's downward arched wing, joining the two figures into one compositional whole. He took the book over to a shelf and left it there propped open while he removed himself across the room and squinted his eyes. Leda, the swan, and the brilliant sun behind them with shafts pointing upwards and outwards together formed a larger golden shaft of light when looked at this way. A unity! A trinity! he thought. Leda, Zeus, and sun combine to show earth brought to heaven and heaven to earth united by spirit. "Yes!" he shouted although there was no one to hear. Why of course, he thought. The swan itself inhabited by Zeus is the identical representation.

He went back to Yeats's poem reading again the final lines. "Did she put on his knowledge with his power/ Before the indifferent beak could let her drop?" Yes, she did, he thought. The swan may have been indifferent, but the sun, the spirit that animates the earth, is not. How many intercessions have there been? he wondered. How many more to come?

He took his cup of tea into the parlor and sat in his comfortable leather chair where Dante lay on the table next to it. Before he could open the volume there was another knock at the door. He thought maybe Summer had returned, but when he opened it, there stood Barry. He looked about outside. "Where's Summer?" he asked.

"She's back at the hotel. She thought she would take a nap. I don't think she slept well last night. She told me you wanted to speak to me so I thought I would drop by rather than phone if you don't mind."

"No, not at all. I was having tea. Would you like to join me in tea time?"

Teatime was not something Barry indulged in very often, and truth be told, neither did Luc. Rather, Luc drank tea all day, but he thought it would be polite to offer Barry something and Barry thought it would be rude to ask for a beer instead. Luc went to the kitchen and heated up the kettle and searched through his cupboard for something to offer. He had biscuits. That would have to do.

"So, Summer told me you had an appointment with Etienne this morning."

"He only called this morning, and I drove right out there. I'm getting too old for this."

"For what? What did he want with you?"

"It seems I've become everyone's go-between, advisor, and such. I don't feel so good at it either. If I were more talented maybe the breakup would never have happened. But things are as they are, and who would Summer have now if I weren't here to do it."

"I know the burden," Luc said.

"I imagine you do, being a priest and all."

"What did Etienne want to speak with you about?"

"Summer, of course. He said he wanted to end this thing more honorably than he believed he had yesterday. He said he's had time to think about it and believes he was too harsh. To tell you the truth, I think he regrets losing her."

"He should," Luc said. "There aren't too many Summers in the world. But if he really wanted her back, as much as I would not like to see it, I think she has a big enough soul to forgive him."

"I'm curious. Why did you say you wouldn't like to see it?"

"I don't think it's the right situation for her."

"It's these lifestyle questions," Barry said.

"I agree," Luc said. "Two things could happen in such a marriage. Summer could free Etienne from the confines imposed by class expectations; or Etienne, without necessarily realizing what he's doing, could press Summer to conform. I think if she were to conform to those pressures, as she would likely do in time, it could snuff out her spirit. I remember in Lucerne when I asked her sun sign. I knew it before I asked. She is fire, a perfect Sagittarius. Such a situation would drown her spirit. I would hate to see that happen."

"Astrology?" Barry said.

"Sometimes astrology has something to teach. Now, if the other were possible, if she could free him, I would be all for it. I just don't think that is possible."

"Well, I was just asking. I don't think he believes he can reverse anything now. He seems to feel a solid commitment to the other woman. I don't know why her more than Summer."

Luc's expression suggested that he had a good guess, but he didn't offer it. "So what does he wish to do for Summer?"

"Talking to him sometimes is like being in another century," Barry said. "He essentially wants to pay her off. He broke his betrothal, he said, and offered a half a million dollars in restitution. I told him I didn't think she wanted his money and suggested instead that he might let her keep her job at the museum. He upped me. He offered to allow her to keep her position for as long as she would like, the half a million dollars, plus he would give her the apartment in Paris that she now shares with his sister."

182

Luc took a hard bite out of his biscuit. "This changes the picture. It can't only be guilt that motivates him to be so generous."

"Honor, love, and guilt. He believes her now. After he saw her yesterday, he knew his suspicions had been wrong. I believe that whatever happened with this Juliette has put him in such a bind that he can't free himself. That's what I think," Barry said. "He's trapped."

"I saw the bind he had put himself in when I saw them in the parking lot," Luc said.

"But why the one over the other?" Barry asked. "He could have just as well tried to pay off Juliette. He owes her less."

"Others besides her may be involved," Luc said, unwilling to be more specific since his opinion was informed by intuition rather than facts.

"Have you presented Summer with his offer?"

"Yes, yes, I did. She cried, and cried, and cried some more. She will exhaust herself crying. It was painful to watch, and I couldn't do anything to console her."

"It will be okay," Luc said as he tried to console Barry, who he could see was himself in a great deal of emotional pain. "This break was meant to happen and something better lays ahead for her."

"You had mentioned Roland."

"You don't know him as well as I do. He's a truly fine person. The best of the best. He loves her, and in the end I think he could make her far happier."

"Well, I hope you're right. But at present she doesn't seem ready for anything new."

"She will have to find her way," Luc said. "I'm sure she will. So what are the two of you going to do now?"

"She wants her job back. She has put so much into that museum it's like her child. But she says she won't accept the money or the apartment. It would make her feel, well, paid off. So, I've offered her my place for now. I can get a room somewhere else. We're going back to Paris tomorrow."

"Tomorrow! So soon! Évian will be very empty for me when you are gone."

"That's why I came over to tell you. To tell you the truth, Paris feels empty to me now. But I should stay there long enough to see her settled and okay."

"What will you do then?"

"I need to go back to doing what I love. I need to find work out in the field. Maybe when I do you can come visit."

"I would like to very much," Luc said.

"I had better get back before Summer wakes up."

"Take good care of her, and stay in contact. I want to monitor her progress."

"I will."

The two men shook hands, and Barry left on what he imagined to be his last walk from Luc's house to the hotel.

When he arrived back at the hotel it appeared that Summer had not stirred. There were no phone messages waiting for him at the desk, so before returning to his room he stood outside her door for a moment and listened. Silence. He decided not to disturb her.

His room was quiet now that Stuart had gone. He opened his computer and composed a letter to Paul.

Dear N. Paul,

I'm sorry that it has taken so long for me to get back to you, but things have been pretty hectic here since I got your letter. I did talk to the realtor, and she indicated there was at least minor interest in the house. But since she hasn't gotten back to me, I guess it must have faded. I will send a check soon to cover your services for the next month. I hope you don't have any more difficulties with mice, but it sounds from your letter that you and your friends have the situation under control.

It's probably just as well that I didn't write you back immediately because to tell you the truth, I was not certain how to respond. But since then I've learned quite a lot on the subject of UFOs. We've had one here ourselves near Évian where I came for some rest and relaxation, although I've hardly had time for either. I didn't see it myself, but Summer did as well as Stuart. And as you know, Stuart's observations are not to be questioned given he is a government investigator and all. It was described to me as being large and egg shaped. It was seen rising from a lake hereabouts into the sky. No one knows its motive or purpose, but a scientist in the area who works at CERN came out to investigate. He thinks it may have been attracted by all of the science going on in the area, which struck me as interesting because that's exactly what your scientist friend said about what would have drawn a UFO to Central Ohio. I think the conjecture about Big Ear and the WOW signal is fascinating. We did attend a UFO conference near here, but it was disappointing, except for one speaker I thoroughly enjoyed.

Tomorrow I go back to Paris. I may come back to Ohio in a month or so to get some real rest and relaxation before I move on to a new job. UFO aside, the trip to Évian has been emotionally exhausting. I hear that has been the case for your grandmother too. Did your family drive all the way to Washington for Natalie's cancelled wedding? Well, we can talk more when I get back. I just wanted to let you know I will be there soon.

> *Yours Truly,*
> *U. Barry*

Barry hit the send button. He took off his shoes, laid down for a nap, and slept through the night.

After Barry left, Luc went to his refrigerator to root around for something with which he could make a simple dinner. He found a couple of tomatoes and thought they would be nice sliced with a plate of pasta dressed in garlic, olive oil, and parmesan cheese. As he twirled the last bits of pasta on his plate, he became fixated on the rotating motion of the fork set against the dark blue china. A vision of the lake popped into his head, the craft sinking into it and then blasting itself through the water as it ascended into the sky. A portal Roland had called it. For Luc the image was Dantesque: The lake a portal dropping deep into the earth's interior. On the other side stood the mountain of purgatory, which is where he believed he now stood, seeking a path to paradise if only he knew how to find it. Maybe he had, he thought. No Virgil had entered his life to guide him, but Roland had.

He cleaned up the dishes and went back to his leather chair and opened his volume of Purgatorio to the lines he had summoned when he first heard about the craft. "Angel boatman," he said. He thought about what Roland had told him about the endless, unseen conflict that had gone on for millennia to protect the treasured Earth and its inhabitants from those who would despoil and enslave it. He reflected on Roland— intelligent, diligent, modest and brave enough to carry out the work of the watchers. All that he had asked for himself in recompense was a companion.

Luc stepped outside under the eternal sky. Above him, the constellation Cygnus was bright and clear on this autumn equinox. He prayed that the union Roland longed for would come to pass, and he prayed for himself too. Perhaps Roland in some odd way might be his guide. And then he opened his eyes to the stars.

Chapter Twenty

Barry sat in front of Gitane Marie in the rotunda at Le Musée de la Femme de la Mythologie. It was late October. Summer and he had been back in Paris for over a month now, and he found himself even less inspired to be a museum curator than he had in August before he left for Évian. He looked at the woman carved in stone and pondered her origins. She did not speak. As if to provoke her into speech, he recited the poem Hans Bueller had found buried with her in the cellar of the old monastery. Summer looked on unnoticed as he read.

> She looks upon herself who is not there.
> But sees instead before her all the world.
> Whatever was, whatever will be is in her care.
> For she is the maker of the world.
> Within her face all faces, all time,
> The cosmic burst of creation.
> She holds the mirror of world.

He recalled his mystic Egyptian dreams: The half bird, half child that led him into the eye of its beautiful mother; the field of Madonna lilies that lay deep within; the woman floating upon a lake, who beckoned him to her. That lake of his dream was very like the lake in Évian, he thought. But none of it fit together. Not Gitane Marie, not the dreams, not the lake, not the UFO. Summer sat down beside him.

"I don't believe I ever told you about the lecture I heard while at the conference in Geneva," he said. "Most impressive."

"I thought the whole thing was a bust," she said.

"It largely was, but not Dr. Claudio Postremo. He believes we have been visited by extraterrestrials for thousands of years. Of course, this wasn't the first time I've heard that belief expressed. You hear that sort of thing quite a lot in Egypt. I've just never had any reason to take it seriously until I heard him. There was something about him that made me believe he could be right. And that might explain her," he said

187

pointing to the statue. "The intricacy of her carving, her refined style. She is so very out of sync with what we believe we know of the art of that period. Who could have been the carver? What were his tools? Who was his model?"

"Maybe you dated her incorrectly," Summer said.

"No, the stone tells it all. The nanodiamonds are the evidence."

"So, what are you saying? Are you saying she was made somewhere else?"

"No, she was made here, all right. The questions are by whom, under whose influence, and why?"

"What did this Postremo fellow say?"

"He wasn't there to talk about ancient art if that's what you're asking. He spoke to UFO aficionados about a subject near and dear to them: disclosure, the belief that extraterrestrials are about to introduce themselves or something like that. He largely debunked the whole idea. He argued that this visiting civilization would not disclose itself because it dare not. Unlike them, we are neither civilized nor easily teachable. He thinks that humanity has a good deal of growing up to do, and we must do it ourselves with assistance perhaps, but only from a hidden hand."

"I bet the audience didn't much care for that."

"They were defensive, all right. They nearly shouted him down. I thought he was brilliant and followed him out of the lecture room. We ended up having dinner together before we drove back."

"Why is it that this is the first I've heard about him?" she asked.

"Probably because you weren't there when we got back, and we were soon overtaken by other events."

"That terrible storm," she said. She wanted to tell Barry what was going on while the storm raged, what Roland had told her, but she had pledged to remain silent and silent she remained.

"That, yes, and the fact that you were missing."

"The phone lines were out," she said in her defense. "Did you ask him about the UFO we saw?"

"Sure we did. Etienne told him the whole story. Postremo didn't seem the least bit surprised. He never questioned the veracity of the claim once he learned that Stuart and you saw it too. But he agreed that it was better not to go public because few people would believe him anyway."

Her eyes seized upon the statue's delicate feather like locks while sunlight flit around its finely chiseled hair, as if a butterfly or hummingbird were about to perch. "So, what's the connection between Postremo and Gitane Marie? Are you saying she is extraterrestrial in origin?"

"I have no idea. That's what I'm saying. Just a few months ago I would have answered no, absolutely not. Now, I don't know. I know she was made here, but under whose influence and why? Summer, the universe has grown far more mysterious than even I had imagined."

"I know what you mean," she said and bit her tongue. She wished Roland were there to tell him. "But why be so depressed about it? Why not see it as another great mystery to solve?"

"Yes," he acknowledged halfheartedly.

She glanced toward the hallway and saw dark brooding eyes looking at her. He turned away and went back into the museum business area.

"This place is getting very uncomfortable for me," she said.

"I've noticed Etienne's been coming round lately."

"I think he is trying to get out of here without having to speak to me. I will leave for a while if you don't mind."

"Going back to the apartment?"

"No, I've been wanting to visit the Gustave Moreau Museum. This seems like a good opportunity. I'll meet you at the apartment later." She threw her bag over her shoulder and exited the front door.

Etienne entered the rotunda from the hallway and paused before Barry. "Hello! How are you?" he said.

"Quite well," Barry said frostily. "And you?"

"Busy with preparations and such. I should tell you because you will find out soon enough. I'm about to be married."

"So soon?"

"Yes, so soon. We are to be married at Saint Sulpice. The museum is to become a good staging place from which to plan since it is nearby. I thought I should tell you before all the activity begins."

"Well, I wish you happiness," Barry said.

Uncomfortable with Barry's frostiness, Etienne sat down next to him. "You will know soon enough so I should tell you the rest to end any further speculation. Juliette is expecting our child."

"I don't know whether to say congratulations or I'm sorry?"

"I believe it was providence," Etienne said.

Barry thought it was something else altogether, but he had the good manners to keep his opinion to himself. "Do you remember Rosa Palazio at the American University in Rome?"

"I never had the pleasure of meeting her, but I do remember her part in defending your reputation. Did she not help you to discover the nanodiamonds?"

"She found the scientist who identified them, yes. She's trying to set me up to explore a newly excavated Etruscan site with her team." Barry paused to look at Etienne's changed expression. He had grown pale. "Are you all right?" he asked.

All that it had taken was this minor recollection to transport Etienne to a happier time and to what he had felt for Summer. As quickly as the feeling came, it went. "I'm all right," he said as he struggled to hold his consciousness in the present, to dutifully transfer what he had felt for her to where he believed such feelings now rightly belonged.

"I'm only mentioning it now because I would like to go back to the States for a while to get my bearings before I begin," Barry said.

"What will become of Summer? She has grown to depend on you since..."

"I've been worried about that too," Barry interrupted. "And what you've just told me makes it all the worse."

Etienne dropped his is head into his hands. "I don't know how this happened." In a split second he regained his composure, lifted his head and said, "My grandmother is planning the reception to be held here since it is so near the church. That was her idea."

"No doubt," Barry said. Torn between pity and contempt, he got up. "If you don't mind, I will be going to dinner now. Again, I wish you every happiness."

"Thank you," Etienne said. He sat sullen and alone before the magical statue for nearly a half hour as sunlight withdrew itself from the oculus above her. He could not hear her speak, but her darkening looks suggested perhaps she had read his mind.

Summer took the metro to the former home now gallery of Gustave Moreau, a fine three-story townhouse located in Paris' ninth arrondissement. Rooms were packed with stacked rows of paintings depicting all manner of mythological and religious scenes. She could see in the broad representation of his work that for Moreau religion and mythology blended seamlessly, which could explain, she thought, the angelic cherubim being in the same painting as the beautiful Leda and the mythic Zeus she had seen in the facsimile in Luc's art book. For Moreau there was no distinction to be made.

When the curator took her to the painting, she gasped, "Fantastic!" The white swan and the maiden he seduced were situated in the foreground; their forms combined to create a glistening white torch, one great shining vision, as if the sun behind them reached round and lit them. The two cherubim in the shadows served as a backdrop that emphasized the brightness of the maiden and her seducer.

"It's about them!" she said. "The cherubim are only a footnote." The curator acknowledged her comments with a wink.

Leda's hair, the color of the sun, elevated her stature. But it was the swan that captivated Summer. It pressed against the woman, not in the rough, overtly sexual way that Yeats's poem suggests, rather gently, as if it desires her affection, her love. It placed its head upon her head not as a lover would but as a creature that sought something more profound, a oneness of mind, she thought. The cherubim, carrying a single crown, moved towards swan and maiden as if the single crown would eternally unite them. That is the painting's essence, she thought. Swan and maiden, Zeus and Leda joined to create something larger, more profound than either one could have been without the other. She bought a print of the painting and left the museum to walk home and dream. But her dreamy state was broken when she arrived at the apartment.

"Sit down," Barry said, "I have something to tell you. I think it better that you know sooner than later, and I think it best that it come from me."

Her body tensed up as her mind filled with the worst imaginings. "What's wrong?" she said. "Has something happened?"

"No, nothing has happened yet."

She felt some relief.

191

"After you left the museum Etienne came over and spoke to me. He explained why he's been in and out of the museum lately. He's getting married. At Saint Sulpice. Very soon. She's pregnant. There, I've got it all out."

Barry expected a flood of tears, but oddly there were none.

"She's pregnant?" Summer repeated. "I thought she might have been the first time I saw her. Did he seem okay about it?"

"Well, he seemed a bit mixed, but he would never admit it to me."

"Or himself," she said. "It happened that very night. I could tell when I saw them, which seems impossible, I know."

"Only because we deny our own instincts," Barry said. "And our insight."

"I could tell by the way he looked at her. He knew then."

"You know him very well."

"Not as well as I thought I did," she said. "And yet I knew then it was over. Juliette really wasn't all of it. She was only the escape hatch. It wasn't working with us, but neither one of us could face up to it."

"I believe he loved you Summer."

"I believe you are right," she said. Then she wept. "He was my knight in shining armor, my prince that would slay dragons for me."

"Those are fairy tales."

"But there's a certain truth in them. That's what the problem is. I was to stay in the castle fortress hotel with the queen mother while my knight went off to Geneva on his adventure. If I had, it would be our wedding being planned."

"And what, spend the rest of your life playing bridge? Summer, that's not who you are."

"I know. I could never have been happy with such a life. I'm not his passive princess; and if I continued to rebel, I would have only made him unhappy. Juliette almost looks like him. They will have a beautiful child."

"And many of them probably," Barry said. "That seems what she's made for, sex and bridge. She knows how to flirt too, but his grandmother will probably put an end to that. Look, I've known Etienne as long as you have and I like him, but this lifestyle has its limitations. He is a man of duty, which can be a good thing up to a point. But when

192

reality is constrained by duty, it becomes imprisoning."

"What do you mean?"

"The reality is he had a UFO experience that he chooses now to deny for fear it could harm his reputation. The reality is that he's confining himself to a life that won't make him happy. Oh, maybe it will," he reconsidered. "He seems so changed. Have you noticed his new habit of smoking and the weight he's put on?"

"I have noticed that he doesn't look too healthy."

"Maybe it's the stress of the situation he finds himself in," Barry said. "The reality is that with you he had a chance at something better. He could have loosened up a bit, gotten off his damn knightly horse, and joined the modern world."

"He climbed off his knightly horse when he made her pregnant."

"You're right," he groaned. "If he ever had a choice, it is past." Barry stood up. "Well, let's get out of here. Come to the bistro with me and get some supper."

Chapter Twenty-One

After years of research, CERN finally confirmed the existence of the elusive God Particle. Roland however was too distracted to join the celebration. Since his return, he had toiled away in his laboratory but with few results, his mind having been taken up with Summer. He pictured her lovely in the candlelight in the hotel restaurant. He recalled her inquisitive nature at the observatory and her bravery when it came under attack. He remembered what it felt like to hold her for that brief moment on the train. He wanted to fly to her but restrained himself each time he thought to pick up the phone or hop on the train, reminding himself that he had interfered enough, that if there were to be a next time, she would have to signal to him that his presence was desired, that he was desired. His heart ached like that of a great wild bird who has mated for life and grieves with each beat of his wings as he soars above the lover he fears may be lost to him forever.

Luc never would have imagined his friend of three years subject to such psychological torment, so stoic a temperament he had had until he met Summer. While he envied Roland's passion, he pitied him too. He stayed in regular phone contact but believed his ministries were of no help since there was little encouragement he could provide. He had not given up entirely, however, thus had no desire to reconcile Roland to his loss, even if he could have, which he doubted. But once he got the phone call from Barry and learned about Etienne's forthcoming marriage and the pregnancy he had earlier suspected was confirmed, he believed it was time to act. He phoned Roland and told him he would be on the next train to CERN. There was something important he needed to speak to him about.

Roland's apartment was as it ever was, comfortable but taken over with file cabinets and neat piles of articles and other materials in need of filing. Roland looked thinner, his hair longer out of neglect. He brought out a bottle of wine and a cheese board and invited Luc out to a restaurant since he had never taken up Luc's hobby of cooking.

He poured two glasses of wine and sliced some cheese. "Take some," he said. Luc obliged.

"I had a call from Barry this morning," Luc said getting right to the point of his visit. "He had just gotten news from Etienne. He's about to be married. As I suspected, the woman is pregnant so they're in a hurry to legitimize the situation."

"And Summer?" Roland asked.

"I advised Barry to tell her as soon as possible. It would be easier for her to hear it from him rather than Etienne or his grandmother. I presume she knows by now."

Roland quit sipping his wine. Instead he drank it down and poured another glass. "I hope she is okay."

"I think it's time you do more than hope. It's time you act."

"I acted once and look at the mess I made."

"Your timing was off, that's all. Now is the right time. That is if you still want her."

Roland looked up at his friend and counselor amazed that he could think otherwise. "If I still want her!" he shouted.

"Well then act, but do it right this time. Be direct. Ask her."

Roland looked away for a moment then back at Luc. "Do you think she would?"

If he were being fully honest, Luc would have had to admit that he did not know. He thought so, but he could not be sure. That is the risk of a proposal, he would have said. But he was aware that any vacillation on his part would further dampen Roland's confidence. So he trusted in his God and his own instincts and said, "Yes, I think she will."

The two men left for dinner. While at the restaurant Luc explained the customs associated with a proposal, as he understood them from books he had read and plays and films he had watched.

"It's very important to be sincere, romantic but sincere," he explained. "If you think about it, it's a lot to ask of a woman. I don't know that I would want to do it."

"That may be why you became a priest," Roland said and smiled. "But you could be right. Life with me would be dull most of the time, not always, but sometimes."

"I didn't mean you in particular. I meant such a commitment to any one person for the rest of your life is a lot to ask. So, the custom is, as I

195

understand it, to get down on your knees and ask for her hand."

"Like praying?"

"No, like this." Luc slid off his chair and demonstrated the position.

"I see, only one knee. And I ask for her hand."

"In marriage. And you must have a ring for her, an engagement ring. It must be very special."

"Expensive," Roland said.

"Yes, a beautiful ring. And you hold it out to her when you make the proposal."

"Like payment in kind."

"No, the ring is an expression of your love. That's why it must be special."

"I see. But this all seems rather unnatural. Why can't I write to her and ask?"

"It's supposed to be unnatural!" Luc said. "It's supposed to be memorable and romantic not like a dinner invitation. Look, write to her and tell her you are coming to Paris. That will be enough to gauge her attitude if that's what you are worried about. Propose only a meeting, a date, and see how it goes from there. But whatever else, be sincere. Nothing is more important than being sincere."

"All right," Roland said, trying to imagine how he could be both unnatural and sincere at the same time. But the first part of it, writing her to say he was coming seemed simple enough. And finding a ring, well, he thought he would give himself a few extra days in Paris for that.

After dinner the two men walked to the train station. Luc wished him good luck before he departed for Évian.

When Roland returned to his apartment he sat at his computer and realized that writing this letter was a little more difficult than he had thought. He would have to give a reason for his coming to Paris, and he did not want to tell her she was that reason unless he was sure she wanted to be. He could say he had work there, but that would necessitate a whole series of lies. He hit upon an idea.

My dear Summer,

I have been thinking about you lately and hope everything is going well. I have a few extra days off soon, and I thought I would come to Paris. I have wanted to see that statue of yours, Gitane Marie, and I hoped you might have the time to show her to me. Please advise me if that would be possible.

Yours Sincerely,

Roland

In less than two hours he got a reply.

Roland, I'm so glad you wrote. I've been thinking about you too, particularly since Barry has been going on and on about a lecture he heard at that conference he went to in Geneva. He seems so close to knowing what's going on, and it's been hard not to say anything to him. Even if you don't tell him everything, you should tell him something. Maybe we can all have dinner together. Maybe I could cook!

Things are not going that well for me right now. I don't think I can stay at the museum much longer, so it would be good if you come before I leave. I look forward to it. Advise me when you know your dates.

> *Summer*

Two typed sentences wiped out his entire romantic vision of the two of them alone together eating by candlelight at an elegant Parisian restaurant. Her feelings for me aren't entirely clear from what she's written, he thought. Does she want me to come for her or for Barry? He reread the last paragraph and wondered what could be going wrong with her work. He surmised that it had something to do with learning that Etienne will be married. She must be upset, and then he considered his part in undermining their relationship. He felt awful. He wondered if she would ever forgive him. Then he read, "I look forward to it." As tepid as the closing was, it gave him hope. He decided to act on that hope; and as for the rest, he would play it by ear.

Summer tried in vain to stay engaged in her work at the museum. She had abandoned her office, moving a small desk to the museum's interactive area. Madame Conti had become a permanent fixture in the offices, planning menus, interviewing caterers, choosing flowers, and employing the whole office staff, except Summer of course, to handwrite five hundred formal invitations after she had coached them in the art of calligraphy. It already was being whispered around the museum and certain quarters in Paris that Juliette's family was about to lose everything in the financial crisis that had swept across Europe, and it was only the prospect of this fortunate marriage that would save them. Madame Conti ignored the rumors that Juliette was being traded for cash, and she looked on Summer with gazes of pity.

The situation had grown unbearable. Summer's only consolation was knowing that eventually the wedding would be over and perhaps Madame Conti and Etienne would go somewhere else. But she soon realized the museum would never be the same. As if by slight of hand, the ownership had been transferred from everyone who had worked so hard to establish it to the de Chevalier family alone, a family that would evermore see Summer's presence as an awkward intrusion, a story with a sad ending.

If it were not for Gitane Marie she would have had no reason to come to work. Most of her duties had been transferred to the new staff Etienne had hired before they had left for Évian. So when she was not at her tiny desk in the interactive area, she sat in the rotunda looking at the goddess when the sun shown through the oculus and danced upon her mirrored crown. During those meditations, Summer detected a slight impish look on the goddess' carved face that betrayed she held a secret that she was not yet ready to reveal.

When the wedding planning grew particularly intense and spilled over into the rotunda, Summer would steal out of the gallery and take the metro to the Gustave Moreau Museum, ostensibly to study his other works of art, but always finding herself in front of Leda, as if looking for an encoded message in the silky, white nude. In her imagination Gitane Marie and Leda had something to tell her if she could only hear them. Or maybe they did not, she thought in her darker moods. Maybe it was only her desperation and imagination that made her think so. At moments when such negative thoughts entered her mind, she felt lost, adrift, and alone in a foreign land.

She expected Roland the next day and was looking forward to his visit. She had liked him; but lately after reading his note, she was surprised by just how much she wanted to see him. She was not sure where those feelings were coming from that she had so carefully hidden away that night when she traded her heart for her virtue. She wondered if she were on the rebound. She wanted no more big mistakes, no more heartbreak, no more deluding herself. She pledged that she would be careful, not only for her sake but for his.

To that end she arranged dinner for three at the apartment she now shared with Barry. He had been sleeping on the couch since Summer moved in. He had offered to leave, but she could not bring herself to put him out on the street. Besides, she was lonely. So she took over what had been his bedroom, and he moved his personal belongings into the living room, piling them onto chairs, tables, and the floor. He had promised her that while she was out he would stow his stuff and make the apartment presentable for Roland's visit. She would even cook dinner, which was not something she did very often, Barry and she finding the local bistro adequate for most of their culinary needs. She was prepared to make the one meal she knew she excelled at, roasted French chicken. Barry offered to buy several bottles of Bordeaux, and they agreed to let the bakery make dessert.

Roland had written he was coming to Paris to see Gitane Marie. She was delighted to show her off but Friday, the day he had suggested, was not a good day. Madame Conti had said the purveyors of linen and china for the reception would be there that day, and the whole rotunda would be taken up with their wares from which she had to make her selections. Saturday would be better. Summer had written Roland back and asked him to meet her at the Gustave Moreau Museum late on Friday while the chicken was roasting. From there they would go to the apartment for dinner with Barry, and Saturday they could visit Gitane Marie when much of the office staff and Madame Conti would not be there to be intruded upon. That plan was agreeable to him for more reasons than Summer knew.

Unbeknownst to Summer, Roland had arrived in Paris Tuesday evening to allow him a few days to make himself presentable and find the perfect ring. A stylist at a Left Bank men's shop near his hotel had assisted him with the first task when he arrived there Wednesday morning.

"Keep your hair long," the stylist insisted when he asked her to recommend a barber. "She played with it a bit, giving his brown locks that slightly mussed look, which she assured him all women like. "That suit! You need a new one. The color is good, but you have a very nice body. Why not accentuate it?" She measured him and picked out a trim black suit and sent him to the dressing room. He soon reappeared, pant legs in need of hemming. "See how handsome you look." She chalked up the pants before he could say yes or no and handed him a fitted white shirt and a dark gray checkered one. "Try these on," she said. He came back out in the white shirt. "There," she said, "but you must take them both, one for casual, the other for formal." She looked at his shoes. "Sit down." She measured his foot and went into the back of the store and returned with a pair of Bruno Magli's chukka boots in denim blue Italian leather.

"They're blue!" he said.

"It makes a nice contrast," she insisted. "Very nice leather."

She picked out three pairs of blue and black socks, a black belt, and three sets of silk underwear. "It's an engagement," she explained as she encouraged him to touch the silky briefs. Then she began to add up the tab.

"What about a tie?" he said.

"No tie. Keep your collar open, casual like your hair."

He presented his bankcard.

"Come back tomorrow and your suit will be ready for you."

"By the way, have you any suggestions where I might find her a ring, a very special ring?"

"You haven't found a ring yet and you're seeing her on Friday?" She shook her head. "There are many fine jewelers at the Galeries Lafayette on Haussmann. You will find something there," she said and gave him metro directions.

He thanked her profusely for all of her help, but her last remark troubled him. He didn't want to find "something," he wanted the perfect ring, the perfect expression of his love.

He took the metro to Haussmann Boulevard. There was no shortage of fashionable jewelry shops. But as he passed from one to the next he was struck with how alike the rings looked: variously sized and shaped white diamonds set in platinum bands. He thought them impersonal. He returned to each shop a second time, and finally determined he would have to choose from what was available if he could find nothing else. He found a large diamond set in gold, the color of Summer's hair. He would return the next day, he told the jeweler, if he was unable to find what he was looking for. Of course, he did not know what that was, but he knew he would recognize it if such a ring existed.

When he left the Galeries it was already dark and he was exhausted. He took the metro back to his hotel on the Left Bank, had a steak and frites, and retired for the night so that he would be ready to try again in the morning.

The stylist at the men's shop had been so helpful he believed that she might help him again if he explained himself better. She handed him his suit and other packages and listened attentively as he told her what was wrong with the rings he had looked at.

"Engagement rings are diamonds," she said. "Platinum is very popular right now. I would be very pleased if someone were to give me a big diamond set in platinum."

"But her hair is the color of gold."

"I do not know where to send you," she said. "You don't have the time to have a ring made. Why don't you just walk around and see what you can see."

"Can you keep these things here while I do that?"

"Oui" she said and took his packages and put them behind the counter. "Be sure to return before we close." She shook her head as he exited the shop.

Roland walked up and down the small side streets of the Left Bank seeking the perfect ring. He was about to give up and take the metro back to Galeries Lafayette when he dropped into a cafe for a light lunch. After his second glass of wine he told his story to a sympathetic waiter who offered his own suggestion.

"Something unique you are looking for. Go over to Place Saint-Sulpice. They're having their antiques fair today. You might find something if you want the unique, but it will be pricey."

Roland searched through all the antique finery, the statues, the faiencerie, the beautiful leather bound books. Eventually he found a stall with small glass cases filled with vintage costume jewelry. He told the vendor his plight.

"I do have some fine jewelry, but I do not know if any of my rings are what you are looking for," the vendor said. "You seem to have something very particular in mind."

"Not exactly," Roland said. "It must be special and as expressive as she is."

"Well, I do have some unique pieces, one of a kinds, but they are expensive."

"So were the rings I looked at yesterday that all looked alike."

The vendor pulled out a wooden box he had hidden behind the cloth that draped over his stand and opened it. He looked inside and brought out a Victorian era ring, with a cluster of diamonds mounted in 18 karat gold. "You said you want gold."

"That's the color of her hair," Roland said as he studied the ring. "But this is not her. It's way too fussy."

"I have a yellow stone, but it's set in platinum. Maybe the yellow would do in place of the gold." He brought out a ring with a glittering yellow stone mounted side by side next to a sparkling blue one.

"What are these stones?" Roland asked, holding the ring to the light as the sunbeams worked their magic.

"Sapphires, each nearly two and half carats. Perfect stones. And these are diamonds." The vendor pointed to tiny diamonds embedded in the ring's band. "It's an Art Deco design, one of a kind, made here in Paris in 1925."

Roland was transfixed by each brilliant facet. The stones reminded him of the double star Albireo that marks the head of Cygnus the Swan, home to the planet of the people he had come to love. Seen under a powerful telescope, the stars of Albireo appear side-by-side, yellow and blue, much like the ring he now held.

"The carving in the band is magnificent," he said. "And the stones! They remind me of...."

"It's very expensive," the vendor said, sure now he had made the sale.

202

"How much?"

"I cannot sell it for less than 10,000 euros."

Roland pulled out his bankcard.

"I'm afraid I'm not equipped to take that. You will have to take the card to the bank yourself and get cash."

"Will you hold the ring for me?"

"I will lock it up and put it under the stand so no one will see it."

"I will be right back."

Roland nearly emptied his account to get the cash. When he returned, the vendor had already found a white velvet box to put the ring in. He placed the ring box inside another box that he lined with a rose colored piece of velvet.

"Here," the vendor said as he handed the package over, "for a very special woman from a man I know to be very special. I wish you happiness."

Roland rushed back to the mens store to pickup his suit and packages before they closed. He opened the box and showed the stylist what he had found.

"Mon dieu! Magnifique!" She kissed Roland on the cheek, wished him good luck, and as a further sign of her approval said, "Such a ring! She will love you forever," as he walked out the door.

Chapter Twenty-Two

Roland rounded the corner on to Rue de la Rochefoucauld full of trepidation as he approached the museum. "She will love you forever," the stylist had said. Less confident, he wondered if she could love him at all. His rash actions had spoiled her engagement to a man far richer than he. Can she forgive me?

He spotted a smartly dressed young woman standing at the museum door. It was Summer, her hair ablaze under the late day sun. His trepidation mixed with longing.

She quickly moved off of the steps and walked towards him. "You look great!" she said.

He broke into a smile and spontaneously wrapped his arms around her, his longing having gotten the best of him. "It's good to see you," he said. Thinking he was being too forward he was about to step back but stopped himself. She had not seemed to mind, and it was far easier to be sincere than unnatural so they continued to hug, he nearly melting into the fire of their embrace.

She pulled back. "We can't stay too long. The chicken is roasting in the oven, and I don't want it too dry. But I want to show you a painting I first saw in Luc's art book, and well, I think it's pretty fantastic."

Roland observed that the whole gallery was filled with paintings of the fantastic. He had not known Moreau's work, but he most decidedly liked what he saw. When she brought him to the painting she had wanted him to see, he was stunned into silence. Had Luc told her his story, all of it?

"What do you think?" she said in an effort to draw him out.

After a long pause he said, "You say you first saw this at Luc's?"

"The day after we got back to Évian. He had all of these art books spread out on his dining room table turned to various pictures of Leda and the Swan. This was my favorite."

"Did he say why he was looking at them?"

"Oh, you know Luc. He's always studying something. He said he had been reading Yeats's poem and wanted to compare it with various representations of the subject. Do you know Yeats's 'Leda and the

Swan?'"

Eased that Luc apparently had not spilled the beans, Roland honestly replied that he was unacquainted with the poem.

"It's pretty brutal, nothing like this. I find this painting beautiful," she said looking at it admiringly.

"I'm curious. What do you see in it?"

"I see a representation of the purest form of love. I know the swan is supposed to be Zeus, but I also know something about swans. And it seems to me that Moreau has beautifully captured their nature."

"How so?"

"I once saw two swans mate. It was an incredibly graceful dance. They bobbed their long necks and bills in and out of the water nearly in unison, and then they touched each other gently with their heads like this swan is touching Leda. It's like a kiss. Finally, they pressed their chests together as if to link their hearts, raised their long arched necks and pressed their heads together as if to link their minds, and out of this movement created the shape of one heart using their chests, long necks, and bills to do it. They mate for life, you know."

"No, I did not know," he said, impressed with both her knowledge and candor.

She turned back to the painting. "That's what I see here. Moreau shows it differently, but it's the same thing. Leda's arm reaches upward as the swan's wing reaches down in unison, their heads touch, and the cherubim carry one crown for them both, as a representation of one heart."

He smiled and looked on at Summer with great admiration and unadorned love before he drifted off to a more somber thought. If only his mother had known the kind of love Summer sees in this painting. Torn between the emotional extremes of loss and hope, his doubts soon faded into possibility, life's universal nectar.

"Are you all right?" she asked.

"I'm fine," he said, her question having brought him back to the moment. "I'm glad you showed it to me. It's beautiful."

She looked at him smiling as if he had passed a test. "We had better go now. I don't want dinner to burn."

Barry had set the table, basted the chicken, and clipped and washed the green beans so they would be ready to put on the fire. He was hungry. The fragrance of the cooking only made him more so. He uncorked a bottle of wine to let it breathe for a few minutes when they finally arrived.

"I'm so glad to see you," Roland said and shook Barry's hand.

"It's good to see you too. Please sit down. I'll get you a glass of wine."

"You've done enough," Summer said as she turned the fire on under the beans. "Both of you sit down and talk while I get everything ready." She poured three glasses of wine and carried them to the table.

Barry uncorked a second bottle, and then turned back to Roland. "So I hear CERN found the God Particle."

"It's a huge breakthrough. They are rightfully very proud. " Roland paused briefly before asking, "Have you heard from Stuart? He seems to have disappeared."

"Not without a reason. He went home to patch up a relationship with his girlfriend. He sends me email daily, asks for advice, but he seems to be doing quite well on his own."

"He's engaged to my sister Rosalind's sister-in-law" Summer said.

"He finally popped the question. I've been telling him to do it for years," Barry said.

"Why did it take him so long to follow your advice?"

"Oh, I don't know. Afraid of commitment, I guess. Afraid of rejection. That is until he almost lost her."

Roland could not keep his eyes off of Summer as his conversation with Barry continued. "So Barry, what have you been doing these last several months?"

"Oh, I've just been doing this, that, and the other around the museum. Mainly what I've been doing is getting myself out of this job. A curator I am not."

"Any prospects?"

"Maybe. A colleague is trying to get me on a team to do some work in Italy. A real dig this time. Etruscan stuff. I'm looking forward to it too, but I thought I'd go back to the States and attend to some business there first."

206

Summer brought out a platter full of oven browned potatoes, carrots, and parsnips. Then she brought out a large bowl of buttered green beans.

"A feast!" Roland said.

"I've been smelling it for hours," Barry said.

Roland having been distracted by Summer's comings and goings finally answered, "I hope it works out for you."

"I'd like to go back to Italy. I met a most interesting Italian at that conference in Geneva, a Claudio Postremo. I wonder if you know him?"

"I don't know him personally, but I do know one of his books. 'The Archeological and Anthropological Evidence for Extraterrestrial Visitation,' I think it's called. I'm not surprised the two of you might have something in common."

"Yes, and more than that."

"Tell Roland about his presentation," Summer said as she brought the chicken out to the table to be carved.

"Maybe I should carve first," Barry said. "Let's go over to the table. Let's eat."

"So what did this Postremo fellow say that so impressed you?" Roland asked, more engaged now after this turn in the conversation.

"It was the whole situation, really. He was to speak on the idea of disclosure, which apparently is very popular among UFO adherents right now so the lecture room was packed. Instead of telling them what they wanted to hear, he told them a thing or two about themselves, about all of us really, that I just happen to agree with."

"What did he say?"

"That we're not ready for disclosure. That we're still too dangerous a species to be endowed with further knowledge since we'd probably put it to ill use. All you have to do is read the newspapers to know that."

"The news has been just terrible lately. It gets worse and worse," Summer said. "No one seems able to agree on anything. Nothing but murders, wars, and political fights."

"Well, this crowd had a different view. Full of hubris, if you ask me. He knocked them down a peg or two; and I can tell you, they didn't like it a bit."

"They booed him off the stage," Summer said.

"You cannot prevent the acquisition of knowledge," Roland said in defense of science. "Look at what they've just done at CERN!"

"I didn't mean to denigrate your work," Barry said. "My point and I think his point is that we discover things at a pace we are prepared for. At least generally that's the case. They want it all handed to them by what they imagine to be advanced super beings."

"We seem capable enough of endowing ourselves with knowledge without outside help," Roland said.

"Exactly, and at a proper pace. One thing I'm sure of is humanity in its current state is not prepared to handle anything and everything And if these extraterrestrials, whatever they are, if they are as wise as people think, surely they would know this too. Why would they reveal themselves and hand over the secrets of universe? That was his point, which is counter to current UFO buffs' orthodoxy."

"Oh, I see what you're saying," Summer said. "Our discoveries and our social evolution are in tandem."

"Something like that," Barry said. "Of course, I think if these civilized aliens really do exist, they weren't the first to think this way. I've never talked to you much about my work in Egypt, but I learned quite a bit about the ancients, about Imhotep to be precise. That man was brilliant. He designed the first pyramids, you know. But he knew far more than that. Legend has it that he buried his secrets, powerful secrets with him in his tomb because he knew in the hands of ordinary men they would be far too dangerous."

"What secrets were those?" Roland asked.

"We don't know. Some people speculate that they may have something to do with methods to harness immense power, the power the ancients may have used to build giant stone structures before there was modern machinery. People who make this speculation argue that whatever this source of power was, it could have been extremely dangerous if not tightly controlled. It took a wise man to control it, which by all accounts Imhotep was."

"My sister was in Egypt with Barry," Summer said. "She held a statue of the god Thoth in her hands in the temple at Abu Simbel when the sun shown in on it and she fell into a trance. She said she found herself writing in hieroglyphics although she had no idea what they

208

meant."

"Yes, that happened," Barry said. "And it was a pretty significant message she transcribed."

"What did it say?" Roland asked.

"It was quite simple really. It said to embrace charity and let go of pride, but that simple message had a profound effect on Hans Bueller. You met him. Madame Conti's bridge partner."

"The German. Yes, I remember him."

"That man was an old scalawag until he got that message. It transformed him. It turned him into a nearly moral man."

"Scalawag?" Roland said.

"Roland's not acquainted with our more colorful terms," Summer said.

"Oh, scalawag, oh, he was an old rascal," Barry said

"So you think your study of the past reveals something about the present?" Roland said.

"The past illuminates the present. It allows us to see ourselves in context. It helps us to understand the perils that lie ahead."

"Oh, so it helps you to see the future too?" Roland said.

"Yes, in some ways it does. This Postremo fellow I've been telling you about, he wasn't so unlike his audience except that he has a deep knowledge of the past. That's what separated him from the rest of them. He agreed with them on the basics, but it was his studies of the past that informed his opinion well beyond theirs, that the human race just isn't ready for disclosure. We would make a mess of it."

"Intriguing. I see why you were impressed. Tell me, how can he be so sure that these alien beings, whoever they are, are more civilized than we?"

"I can't answer that question," Barry said. "It's a good one though. I suppose the thinking is if they were not more civilized, they would have attacked us already. But you would have to ask him yourself if you ever get a chance to meet him."

"That would be interesting," Roland said. "And what about this Gitane Marie I will see tomorrow. How has she informed you?"

"Stop talking for a moment while I get the dessert," Summer interrupted.

209

"Here, let me help you," Barry said. He gathered up the dinner plates and took them to the kitchen.

Summer brought out a tray with three dessert plates, each with a lovely piece of brioche that had been soaked in rum and topped with whipped crème and berries.

"Baba au rum," she said. "I didn't make these. I got them at the bakery."

"Now this is my kind of desert," Barry said.

"Very tempting," Roland said.

"Back to Gitane Marie. Well, she hasn't informed me enough, I'm afraid. Oh, she has told us plenty, mostly about women. To understand her is to understand the huge role women played in creation, much greater than the biblical creation stories as they are popularly understood."

"You refer here to Eve?" Roland asked.

"Yes, and to the Virgin. Binary opposites. Yet for several thousand years these two archetypes have had a profound effect on how women are seen and how they see themselves. The Virgin is far too pure to be human so women have mostly been stuck with Eve. You see her everywhere. Far too simplistic if you ask me."

"And wrong!" Summer said.

"Yes, sure, there are temptress types," Barry continued. "But men are just as guilty of that kind of behavior. Worst of all, this story has been the rationale behind women's oppression for hundreds of years. Gitane Marie along with the exhibits we've put together paint a much fuller, richer, and more accurate picture of feminine gifts and power. Yet for all that I've learned, I still have far more questions than answers about her origin. I never would have guessed in a thousand years that I would have ever succumbed to an extraterrestrial hypothesis until I heard Postremo; but that could explain it at least, although the hypothesis is a lot to pin my hopes on. But she's just too remarkable for her age. And there's something else about her I can't quite put my finger on. I've been with her nearly every day at the museum, and I feel like she's trying to speak to me. I guess what I'm saying is there's something sentient about her, not in the ordinary sense, but living nonetheless."

"Well, you've increased my expectation. I look forward to seeing her tomorrow," Roland said. "This Postremo fellow made quite an impression on you."

"Yes, he did."

"Roland, what do you think about the extraterrestrial hypothesis?" Summer asked.

"My work investigating stories about extraterrestrial visitation has convinced me of its genuine possibility. How could I not believe Etienne's story when later you and Stuart saw the same thing at the same location and close up. And yet I am not sure of the origins of this phenomenon."

"Doesn't that make it all the more strange that Etienne no longer believes what he saw with his own eyes?" Barry said.

"It does, but that's another matter. He wants not to believe. The power to not believe is as great a force upon the mind as the desire to believe. You got a dose of the latter at the convention."

"You're right about that."

"I tend to agree with you and this Postremo fellow," Roland said. "Something appears to be out there that has chosen not to reveal itself. Random witnesses observe it on occasion, and it knows that. But the majority of people will not take those random witness accounts seriously so it is as good as not having been seen by anyone. Whatever it is, it chooses to remain in the shadows. Probably for good reason. I also agree with Postremo that it has been here for a long time." He paused for a few minutes, and then added, "I'm intrigued by your study of archeology as a way to know not only the past but the future. I've never considered that."

"At least it gives you the knowledge to make informed guesses," Barry said. He looked over at Summer who was beginning to fidget. "I'm sorry, I've been monopolizing you," he said to Roland. "But let me thank you for acting as a sounding board. I've needed to talk about this, and talking to you has given me a little more clarity."

"Maybe we can talk more later," Roland said.

"That would be very good, but right now I'm going to make a visit to the neighborhood cafe. So, if I don't see you before you return to CERN, I hope to see you at a later date."

"Very good," Roland said as Barry left.

"See what I mean!" Summer said. "That's all he can talk about."

"He's got the bug, but that's what happens when you come in contact with startling information. It forces you to think about everything in entirely new ways."

"You were great with him," Summer said.

"I hardly said anything."

"Well, that's true. He did most of the talking. But what you did say helped him."

"I hope so. I wish I could be of more help to you."

"Having you here has helped me a lot. It's given me perspective."

He was unsure of what she meant but said, "It's been several months since I've seen you, and yet it feels like it could have been yesterday."

"Yes," she said softly.

He was aroused. He rightly understood her to mean her feelings were in sympathy with his. What he did not know, as he looked squarely into her eyes, was their depth. He wanted to go to her, to melt into her as he nearly had outside the museum. That would have been the natural thing to do; it certainly was his impulse. And he thought she would reciprocate. But for how long? He held back. What Luc had said about being both sincere and unnatural in his proposal now made sense. Sex is natural, but true marriage is not; and he wanted true marriage.

"It's getting late," he said. "I should go back to my hotel."

She looked bewildered. Just as the moment had become perfect, after a good dinner, good wine, and after Barry had left, why would he want to leave? He could see the confusion in her face, but this moment, full of the intoxication of wine and desire, was not perfect for what he had in mind. He did not want to confuse her too much though so he took her in his arms and put the wine to good use with a long, slow, lingering kiss.

"Tomorrow I will take you out to dinner," he said, and then he abruptly pulled away and left her alone in the apartment.

She appeared minutes later at the cafe Barry frequented searching him out.

"What happened?" he asked when he saw her agitation.

"I don't know. I did everything right, didn't I? The dinner was good, wasn't it?"

"It was delicious. Did he say otherwise?"

212

"No, it wasn't what he said; it's what he did. He left just as things started to get romantic. Do I look all right? I thought these pants and shirt look good on me."

"You're beautiful Summer."

"Then what could it be? I was obvious enough."

"Roland is a different sort of man, and I mean that in a positive way. He's a bit stiff sometimes, but not as much as he once was. I give you the credit for that. He can be a little too reserved, but I detect that's some kind of cover."

"Oh, it is! When you get to really know him he isn't stiff at all; he's kind of passionate."

"Then there must have been a reason for the reserve, the stiffness," Barry said. "Why would a passionate man want to conceal himself like that?"

"Maybe he feels vulnerable," Summer said. "I wouldn't hurt him."

"Well, then. Why would he not take advantage of an advantageous situation?"

"I don't know! That's what I'm asking you! Maybe he doesn't like me in that way. Maybe we're only friends."

"He loves you Summer."

"How do you know that?"

"Luc. He warned me of that fact when you were missing. He said he has never seen Roland in love before and never expected to. Luc thinks you are quite special too."

She smiled. "If that's true, maybe it explains why he feels vulnerable."

"That could be it," Barry said. "Some people feel love or what passes for love often, and there are others who well, only feel it once."

Chapter Twenty-Three

Ayoung couple sat together in the museum rotunda searching Gitane Marie's eyes silently asking for answers to questions about their future together. But it was she and not they who was in charge of both questions and answers and what she would reveal. The goddess sat in full regalia upon her pedestal in Le Musée de la Femme de la Mythologie under a bright sun when Roland began to feel quite uncomfortable, intruded upon, as if the goddess had bored into him. He flinched and looked away only to see another pair of eyes, dark ones, in the hallway watching Summer.

The sight of them together had dissolved any tenderness Etienne had left for Summer, dampened any doubts about her crimes. Minutes past. Rage boiled up from some remote place in his psyche, a place heretofore unknown, catching him in its maelstrom, leaving him unable to recalibrate or right himself. He was now certain she had slept with Roland those two nights they had been alone together. She had abandoned him as surely as his mother had. She had deceived and humiliated him. She had brought shame upon his family name.

"I'm not feeling well," Roland said.

"What's wrong? Are you ill?" Summer asked.

"I do not know. I cannot seem to keep my eyes open." He slumped over and fell into a stupor she could not penetrate.

"Roland! Roland!" she cried.

Her voice grew distant. He wanted to speak but was held silent. Finally, her voice entirely faded when he came under the fullness of the intense gazes of both the goddess, the statue he had come to see, and the dark eyes peering from the hallway. He lost control of the activity in his consciousness, his psyche caught between Etienne's rage and Gitane Marie's prophecies.

The whole dark picture played out before him, his mind becoming the screen the goddess had projected it on. Her eyes cried danger as she revealed a vision too horrific for the more tender girl to bear. Etienne lay naked atop Juliette that fateful night, beating his hips into hers, thrusting himself again and again, filling her with the child of his rage, a rage of which Summer's absence and imagined infidelity was the cause. The newsreel ceased. Released from its power, Roland saw in the full flesh of life, Etienne approaching Summer.

"We must go now," he said.

"Are you all right?" she asked in tearful anxiety. Before he could answer, her attention was drawn to the dark eyes moving towards her. She immediately stood up, anxiety having turned to terror. "He's begun to frighten me," she whispered. "We must leave."

Outside, free of the shadow that had stalked them and the goddess' gaze, Roland's mood brightened.

"You seem okay now," she said. "I was worried about you. You didn't answer me."

"I don't know what came over me. I'm okay now, but we should get out of here."

As they walked along the street, he told her he had joined a committee at CERN to help raise money to rebuild the Sphinx Observatory. He told her that after talking to Barry last night he had become interested in his archeological approach to the future and would like to follow him to Italy. He reported that the Alliance had won the battle so decisively that they did not expect any incursion soon, which freed up his time. Nonetheless, they had asked him to keep a steady watch to help forestall further hostilities. Finally, he asked Summer what she intended to do.

"I don't know. I have to leave here; that's for sure."

"Yes, you must," he said. "And soon!"

Hearing urgency in his voice, she looked at him inquisitively.

He turned to her, took her hands in his hands, held them to his heart and said, "You can come with me. I could use your help."

She looked into his eyes as if expecting more. And when after what seemed to her a very long minute he said nothing, she finally said, "Is this an employment opportunity or a proposal?"

"Come with me," he said and pulled her along with him up the street past the entrance to the Musée de Cluny and around the side of the building into its medieval garden. He sat her on one of the benches, got down on his knee, picked an autumn rose, and handed it to her. "I have loved you from the first," he began.

215

"Roland, you don't need to do this," she said, smiling and a little embarrassed.

"I want it to be perfect!" he said. "I want our bond to hold."

"Then let's make it perfect," she said, dropping down off the bench onto both knees. He followed, shifting to both. The couple looked into each other's eyes, locked hands, and pressed them against their chests as if to link two hearts. He asked, "Will you...?" But before he could finish she answered with a kiss, a long, slow, enduring kiss, a kiss even the most jaded Parisian could not ignore. When it had ended and the couple pulled back to look into each other's eyes, a small gathering of park sitters applauded, and Summer and Roland laughed.

"When?" she said.

"Now!"

"Now? But a wedding must be planned."

"Why? Luc is waiting for us in Évian. We can all go to Switzerland if you like and marry in the mountains."

"With the cow bells as our music?"

"There's nothing more beautiful I can think of," he said.

She felt sure. She kissed him again, then again, and again.

"I almost forgot," he said and reached into his pocket and pulled out the velvet ring box and opened it.

"Oh!" she said as she looked at the ring curiously.

"Don't you like it?"

"I do," she said and held it up to the light. "The stones are gorgeous."

"They are sapphires."

"The detail is beautiful."

"It's Art Deco."

"I've never seen a ring like this."

"It's a one of a kind."

She looked up from the ring. "What inspired you?"

"I wanted something special, something that could express my love. Remember when I told you about Albireo, the double star system the Alliance comes from?"

"Yes, you showed it to me on the star map."

"Albireo is at the head of the swan in the constellation Cygnus."

"The head of the swan, like in Leda?" she said.

"Yes, like in your Leda. When you look through a telescope at Albireo, one of the twin stars appears yellow and the other blue."

"How did you ever find this?"

"It took a bit of doing. Here, let me put it on your finger. It fits perfectly. It is a perfect fit."

A shadow fell over the couple as they looked at Summer's ring wrapped delicately around her finger. "Whore!" a phantom voice shouted. She looked up just as Etienne forced her up by the hair, struck her hard in the face, and flung her to the ground.

Roland rose up. He looked taller, broader through the shoulders than he had before, his face resolute, his voice powerful, and his proportions seeming to have increased with his fury. "You fool!" he shouted at Etienne. "If you ever touch her again your tomorrows will cease. Do you understand?"

The small crowd who had just wished the couple well gathered around Summer lifting her up into their collective arms to comfort her. Looking on from her vantage point, Roland towered over Etienne, who was by now backing away.

"If you were not such a fool, you would still have her!" Roland shouted as he walked towards him. "Let me add truth to your torment. Summer is of the pure heart. She is far too honorable to have been unfaithful to you. It was you who was unfaithful. You thought her to be what you have become! I knew her better after one short weekend than you did over the course of a year. I will treasure her as you could not."

Etienne looked at Summer who still lay in the arms of strangers. His expression changed from rage to despair and back to rage again as the crowd shouted him off.

Roland bent and kissed her bruised cheek.

"Is that man crazy?" a woman asked.

"He must be," another answered.

"Can you walk?" Roland asked Summer.

"Yes," she said, and he helped her up.

"I cannot leave you here alone. You must leave Paris with me at once."

"Barry's here," she said.

"He would be no match. Let's go to your place so you can pack what you need."

Roland put Summer in a cab and directed the driver first to his hotel and asked him to wait with Summer while he checked out. From there they went to the apartment she shared with Barry.

"What happened to you?" Barry said when he saw the bruised girl.

"I got engaged," she said and held out her ring before stumbling onto the couch. She began to cry.

"I have asked her to marry me," Roland concurred. "Etienne saw us together and flew into a rage."

"Etienne did that? I never would have imagined it from him," Barry said.

"He's changed! He's not the same!" Summer said.

"I'm taking her with me," Roland said. "I don't trust what he might do to her if I leave her here. I'll phone Luc. He has room for her, and I'm sure he will let her stay a few days."

"You're getting married?" Barry asked.

"As soon as we can. In Switzerland. In the mountains," Roland said.

"With cow bells," Summer added, half weeping from the pain of the laceration.

"Do you have anything to clean the cut?" Roland asked.

"I've got alcohol in the medicine cabinet. I'll go get it. That must have been one big wallop."

"I think he wanted to kill me!"

Barry brought out the alcohol and a cotton ball. Roland dabbed it on her face, blowing to try to stop the burn.

"I don't think I'll go back to the museum," Barry said. "If I see that man I might want to kill him myself."

"Why don't you follow us down to Évian. We could pack a small bag now, and you could bring the rest of Summer's things down in a few days."

"I'd like to come to the wedding if you don't mind," Barry said.

"You can give me away," Summer said between grimaces as Roland continued to apply alcohol to her swollen, cut cheek.

"Give you away?" Roland said.

"It's a custom," she said.

218

"Usually fathers do it, but I would be happy to oblige," Barry said. He followed Summer and Roland into her room and watched them pack her bag. "So you want me to pack up the rest of this stuff and bring it down. That'll be a job."

"I'll pay you," Summer said. "I can't do it all now."

"That's okay," Barry said. "I'll just round up a few trunks."

"Good, then we'll see you soon," Roland said. "If we leave now we can make the next train from Gare de Lyon."

"You had better get a cab. I'll call one for you. It will be out there before you get down the stairs."

Chapter Twenty-Four

The pieces would not fall into place. Summer surely never would have involved herself with such a man as brutal as Etienne, Roland thought as the train carried them full speed to Bellegarde Station. He had to have undergone a significant change. He stroked her swollen cheek, as her head lay nestled on his shoulder when he was overcome by a dark thought.

He recalled his second private meeting with the scientist who had first introduced him to his paternal identity and subsequently to the Alliance. Without his knowledge, the man had set out to find his father, so intrigued he had become with the story his mother had told him about his conception. It was true that in the distant past his race of men had indulged themselves as Roland's father had, disguising themselves and taking human women by force, impregnating them, and later rationalizing their behavior as having improved the human gene pool. But that was before they had come to understand the concept of rape and recognized its devastating consequences to its victims. The thought that such barbarous acts had continued as recently as Roland's conception inspired a fruitful search.

He told Roland his detective work had uncovered that his father had died in battle. He had been a member of an elite warrior branch of the Alliance made up of the most aggressive of their kind, but he had not always been so. Roland's father had been "mind stripped" by their enemy. Mind stripping, he had explained, is a technique to get inside the mind of a captive and learn enemy secrets. The technique proved so inhumane that the Alliance prohibited its practice, but their enemies had not. In fact, he reported the enemy uses it with great frequency and abandon. Roland's father had been one of its victims, stripped of his capacity to control his impulses, left primitive by his former standards and the standards of his race. He had been reincorporated as other victims of mind stripping had into an elite warrior branch, the Guardians. No one knew that he had produced a child, but it is now recorded, he had assured him; and he had nothing to fear for himself. As destructive as the procedure is to the psyche of the living victim, it cannot penetrate the genes. The genes he would have inherited from his father were those of his more evolved self.

Driven by curiosity to know more, Roland had learned everything he could about the practice and had become quite expert and capable of recognizing its victims among members of the Alliance. But he had never expected to find victims among human abductees.

This cannot be, he reassured himself. It makes no sense at all. Humans have no secrets of value to races of men so advanced as these. Besides, it's not a battle with the men of Earth they are waging, it's a battle with the Alliance. He shuddered. What if he were wrong?

The train pulled to the stop at Bellegarde when he roused Summer so they could change trains. Once they were seated on the local train to Évian, she noticed the pain had subsided. She pulled out her compact and looked at her cheek and could see that the swelling had nearly disappeared.

"What could have happened to him?" she said when she leaned back into her seat. "He wasn't like this before."

"I suspect he was not. You never would have involved yourself with such a brute as he has become." He quietly said, "Maybe the change has something to do with his abduction."

Luc greeted them at his door when they arrived at his home in Évian, hugging, kissing, and congratulating them both. He welcomed them into the dining room and offered them his grandmother's famous soup, a rich chicken broth full of spinach, eggs, and parmesan cheese.

"Wonderful!" Summer said. "Just what I need after what I've been through."

"Let me see your face?" Luc said, and closely inspected the bruised cut. "Etienne did that to you?"

"How did you know?"

"Barry phoned me soon after the two of you left his apartment."

"It's a lot better now."

"The swelling has gone down," Roland said.

"My soup will fix you up. Let's sit down."

Luc had fresh baguettes that he had just picked up at the bakery that evening, a huge tray of assorted cheeses, his best wine, and a fruit tart.

"I hear that I'm to officiate," he said. "And in Switzerland."

"In the mountains with cow bells," Summer said.

"I hope I wasn't being too presumptuous in announcing your services," Roland said.

"Of course you were not. If you had even considered anyone else, I would have been offended. Where are you going on your honeymoon?"

The couple looked at each other.

"You are going on a honeymoon, aren't you?" Luc said.

"Where would you like to go Summer?" Roland asked.

"Well, we're going to Switzerland for the wedding. I'd kind of like to stay there longer. If you really want to know what I'd like to do, I would love to go paragliding."

Both Roland and Luc burst into laughter. "A true Sagittarian," Luc said.

"All right. I will teach you to paraglide. We will do it together. I know what we can do. We can go back to Mount Pilatus and stay up there at the hotel."

"I would love that!"

They finished eating, cleared the table, and Luc showed Summer to the room he had made up for her.

"I wish I had another room to offer you," he said to Roland when he came back downstairs. "You can have the couch if you would like. I've got extra pillows and blankets."

"I must go back to CERN for at least the next several days. If you can keep Summer here, I truly would appreciate it. I should leave now to catch the last train." He shook Luc's hand. "I can't thank you enough for the advice you gave me. You have deep insight into the human heart. It must be a tremendous asset to your occupation, wise counselor."

Luc blushed. "I'm pleased my advice worked out this time. Unfortunately, that's not always the case. But in regard to you and Summer, my instincts spoke with a resounding voice. He walked Roland to the door. "It will be my delight to keep Summer here. Tell me before you go, what happened? Why did he strike her?"

"Because she is happy, I suppose. Because she is happy and with me. He took us by surprise. We were looking at the ring I had just given her, and before we even knew he was there, he yanked her up by the hair and struck her."

"That violent! I wouldn't have expected it from him."

"Neither did she. I fear he may get worse. That's why I had to get her away from the museum or anywhere else he might see her. I cannot predict what he might do."

"It's hard to believe from such a man."

"Hmm, yes, that is what Barry said. She will be safe here for a few days. After our wedding, we will stay far away from Paris."

Roland grew increasingly uneasy while on the train returning to CERN. He remembered the picture Etienne had drawn of his abduction when his mind was still lucid. He was in some kind of protective pod with a stack of faceless eyes starring at him. He said it felt as if they were looking into his soul. Roland feared it was not his soul they were looking at but deep into his mind. Feeling a growing sense of urgency, he determined he must make contact with the Alliance. To that end, he began his meditation.

Chapter Twenty-Five

"**M**onstrous!" Luc cried out, awaking from a fitful night's sleep. How could a man like Etienne so viciously strike a girl like Summer, particularly when he himself...?

He tried to block the thought but could not block the image of Etienne pressing himself against Juliette in a passionate embrace while Summer was still missing and presumably could have been in mortal danger. The phone rang, shaking him entirely out of sleep.

"Sorry to disturb you so early, but I couldn't sleep a wink. Are Summer and Roland with you?" Barry asked.

"She's here. Roland went back to CERN last night."

"Etienne showed up at my apartment late in the evening looking for her. He knows she has left Paris. I thought I had better warn them."

"Does he know where she is?"

"I told him I didn't know where she'd gone. I told him she had left with Roland, which he already suspected since he had seen them together earlier."

Luc sighed. "How did he seem?"

"Disconsolate, enraged. He vacillated between the two."

"Did you try to speak to him?"

"It wasn't easy. He said he came to apologize for striking her. Said he never meant to do it. I felt bad for him and thought maybe he had returned to his old self. The Etienne I thought I knew was quite a gentleman, you know. But before I could count to ten, he talked himself back into a rage. I swear he would have struck her again had she been here."

Luc was silent for a moment and then he said, "You probably handled it as well as anyone could."

"I tried to talk him down. I really tried. I wanted to give them a heads up. He's acting crazy."

Luc immediately phoned Roland and delivered Barry's message.

"He would have certainly surmised that she had left with me whether Barry had told him or not," Roland said at the news. "He may suspect that I brought her to my apartment in CERN."

"Or brought her here!" Luc said. "If he leaves Paris looking for her, he's likely to come here since he knows we are friends and he's been here before."

"I will come right away," Roland said.

"No, it's best if the two of you are not together if he should come looking at either place. That would only increase his rage."

"He's fading faster than I had thought he would."

"Fading? What do you mean by that? Could his changed behavior be a result of the abduction?" Luc asked.

"Ah, you suspect it too. By all the accounts, he is acting completely out of character and seems to have begun so only after the abduction. And it seems to be getting worse. So yes, I think there must be a connection. The trauma of the abduction might even explain what happened that night with Juliette. But my first concern is Summer. All I knew to do was get her out of Paris. We can only hope that he will not venture beyond the city."

"I will keep a watchful eye on her in case he should come here," Luc said. "And I would ask that you be very careful yourself."

"Thank you friend. I will come and fetch her soon. But before I let you go, I have something to ask you. Summer took me to a gallery to see a painting, Gustave Moreau's Leda. She mentioned that you had shown her a picture of the painting in one of your art books."

"I did. She arrived unexpectedly while I had my art books spread out on the dining room table."

"For a moment I thought you might have told her my secret until she described what she saw in the painting."

"I never would have done that Roland. You know that."

"It was only a brief thought, but you would have to admit that it was quite a coincidence given I had only just told you the news of my parentage. You must have been doing a little research into the mythology behind my tale."

"That I was. I have to admit."

"I'm only telling you this because you might want to ask Summer what she sees in the painting. I'm not sure if it is what Moreau had intended, but it gives me more insight into her. I am the luckiest man in the world."

"She is the luckiest woman," Luc said.

"You will take care of her for me?"

"Of course I will."

Luc put out a plate of croissants on a sunny spot on the dining room table. He ground fresh coffee beans and set up the brewer. He did not want to unnecessarily worry Summer, but he had little choice than to pass along Barry's report. He roused her and asked her to come down to breakfast.

"We may have a problem," he said as he filled their coffee cups. "Barry phoned me very early this morning to warn me that Etienne went looking for you at the apartment yesterday evening and knows that you left Paris with Roland. Apparently, he was highly agitated. Barry fears he could be dangerous."

Her eyes widened, and her skin grew ashen.

"I fear he might come here looking for you. If there's a knock at the door or any other indication of his arrival, you are to go straight upstairs to your room. Do you hear me?" He went into the kitchen and searched around in drawer and pulled out a skeleton key. "Take this key with you and lock yourself in. Don't come out under any circumstance until I come up to get you."

"What will you tell him?"

"I will tell him you are not here, you went to Italy or something like that. But I might try to help him, and that could take time."

"It could be dangerous if he's anything like he was yesterday."

"He has no reason to harm me. Later we can go out to lunch and go shopping for a special dress."

He cleared plates from the table and the two of them carried them into the kitchen. She brought out more coffee and he followed with a couple of oranges. Before they could peel and eat them, they heard footsteps at the door."

"Go hide!" he whispered.

In the doorway stood Etienne, a lessor image of the man he had been only months earlier as if this once dignified man had been replaced with a being far more common. He must have put on weight, Luc thought. His face and posture were quite changed. He had been up all night, Luc realized, as he looked on swollen eyes and a slightly bent frame.

"I thought you might know where Summer is," Etienne said when Luc opened the door.

"She was here only yesterday evening with Roland. They just dropped in to say goodbye before they left again by train."

"Can you tell me where she was going?"

"Italy, I believe."

Luc's heart ached as he looked at the sad figure of a man who stood before him. He invited him in, but as soon as he did he remembered there were two coffee cups on the table so he quickly seated him in the parlor and cleared the dining room.

"You don't look well," he said when he came back into the parlor.

"Is it obvious?"

"I got a call from Barry. He said you came over to his place yesterday evening and were quite upset."

"I struck her yesterday," Etienne sobbed. "I saw her with Roland and struck her hard. I must apologize. She must forgive me."

Luc moved his chair closer to comfort him. "I'm sure she will."

Etienne rose up abruptly his posture now changed. He stood straight and tall. "How could she have done this to me?" he shouted as he raised his fist as if to strike. "I've done everything for her, and look what she did to me!"

"We can talk about that," Luc said. "But let me make us some tea. It's chilly. You must be cold."

Etienne sat back down while Luc put on the teakettle and filled a strainer with his finest herbs: sweet, fragrant, and guaranteed to calm. He brought the honey pot to the table and peeled the oranges he and Summer were about to eat. Out came cups and saucers and a large pot of tea. He went back into the parlor where Etienne sat brooding.

"Come join me at the table. Now, where were we," Luc said as he filled their cups. "Barry said you are to be married."

"In a few weeks to Juliette. You met her."

"I did," Luc said. "A very beautiful woman. Congratulations."

"I suppose you are wondering why I'm looking for Summer when I'm engaged to marry Juliette."

"I was wondering, yes."

"If she had not run off with Roland, it would have been our wedding."

"You saw it otherwise than she did. You must remember she is an American. They think differently. She thought of him then only as a friend."

"She's a woman, and he's a man," Etienne said, echoing the words Juliette had whispered to him.

"And eventually that did come into play, but not that weekend, at least not for her," Luc said.

"He intended to take her away from me. Is that what you are saying?"

"What I am saying is he did not succeed."

Etienne again began to weep. "She abandoned me. She went off with him and died."

"Summer is not dead!"

"Grand-mère told her to stay with her children," Etienne sobbed. "But Mère said she had to be with him, and she died. She never came back. Grand-mère told us she would not. I did not believe her, but she never came back."

Summer, ear to the door, began to weep.

"Are you talking about your mother?" Luc gently asked. By now he realized that Etienne was not just a jealous suitor but a delusional man. He wondered what had happened to him during the abduction.

Etienne pounded his fist on the table. "Yes!" he shouted, and rose up, pacing back and forth until he sat back down in the chair in the parlor.

Luc followed him. He had begun to discern the complexity of the situation, and did not like it. Two lost loves that he accuses of abandonment. One died for her crime and the other? He knew now why Roland and Barry were so concerned for Summer's safety. He would have to calm him. Etienne had committed no mortal sin yet, but if he could not turn him around, redirect his obsession, it was only a matter of time. He must try to reconfigure his troubled logic.

"And Juliette, do you love her?" he asked.

"She is not like the American," Etienne said full of pique.

"Do you love her?"

"I want her," he said, and turned his face away from Luc. Yet in

228

what seemed like defiance of Luc's priestly order, he continued, "I took her again and again. I could not stop myself. I did not want to stop myself. I still do not." Turning back to him he said, "She gives me enormous pleasure."

Luc's eyebrow arched. It was an honest answer, he thought, but not the sort he was accustomed to hearing. With all the priestly authority he could muster he said, "Then it's good that you should marry."

Yes it is, Summer thought. Her ear to the door and her eyes now dry.

"I imagine you have heard that she's pregnant with my child."

"Barry told me."

"It was no accident. I intended it. That night was my nuptials."

"You want children," Luc said. "Do you want them to have a father?"

"Of course!"

"Then you must commit no crime that would deny them their father."

Luc had meant the statement as a warning that Etienne's violent impulses could lead him to prison for a very long time, particularly if he continued to pursue Summer. But Etienne heard him differently, and what he heard seemed a revelation to him.

"It was him! It was him and not my mother!" he said in astonishment and stood up. "He was the criminal! He sinned against me twice. No thrice! He stole my mother and abandoned me, leaving me to the mercies of that tyrant headmaster who had no mercy when he beat me."

He sat back down and grabbed Luc's hands and wrung them tight and grimaced when the hateful face of the tyrant headmaster flashed before him. Then he wept, and with each salty tear his anger towards his mother dissipated until tears done, pain gone, he had reframed the past and invented a future. Juliette's belly flashed before him, the image he had stored in his memory since he had learned she was pregnant. "I will never betray my child as my father betrayed me," the outraged son declared.

Luc realized that while the wound had not healed, it had subsided with its cause. A new cause was substituted, but one that Etienne felt empowered to affect and one that might leave Summer free of threat.

"You must devote yourself to this child you have made," Luc urged.

229

"You must let go of Summer and give yourself to this child you created, as you admit, with intention. Tonight you must pray to the Virgin to give you strength."

"Yes, yes, thank you father!" Etienne gratefully replied. "I will do as you ask."

This penance was a liberation from his torment. The past, no longer a dead, fixed thing that gripped him could be remade; and he could remake it with each new child. And he would make many, he vowed. Already a rich man, he imagined himself a very rich man, his beautiful, dark haired wife's womb filled with possibilities through which he would redeem himself.

He left Luc's home more at peace than he had been since his abduction. He thanked him profusely for his guidance and prayers and asked him if he might officiate at his wedding and baptize his children. Luc declined, leaving it to the priests of Paris. They shook hands and Luc told him his door was always open should he need help or someone to talk to.

Summer ran downstairs. "You were wonderful!" she said full of admiration. "I could hear everything."

"Thank you. It was a challenge."

"Are there any awards that priests get, a Nobel prize of some sort? Because if there are, I'll nominate you."

He blushed. "In my faith they call it sainthood, but this would hardly qualify. I will make you some tea."

He busied himself in the kitchen while Summer continued to talk. "I knew losing his parents upset him. Anybody would be upset. But I never knew he blamed his mother."

"I don't think he consciously knew it either. And he's not himself. He seems somewhat delusional," Luc said when he brought the teapot out to the table. "I would offer you your orange, but I'm afraid Etienne ate it."

"He seems nothing like the person I knew. He seems almost entirely like someone else."

"Here, it's my bedtime tea so it should relax you. Sometimes memories are better left buried, pushed under so they do not drown us, particularly memories that were framed by an immature mind. I believe he was about to drown in them, and perhaps take you with him."

"Why me?"

"Because he had identified you with his mother. When he thought you had betrayed him, it called forth old feelings that he had never resolved, only buried. You have to understand that ending his own pain was what he was really trying to do when he hit you. But striking you only made it worse. His mixed up mind could not comprehend that. The impulse was still there, and you were the only target since his mother is already dead."

"Are you saying he might have killed me?"

"Struck you again, surely. Apologize and then strike you. The worry was he might strike too hard."

Her cheek began to ache as she imagined an even harder blow. "Did I cause all of this? Did I make him so jealous that he totally flipped?"

"I don't believe you are entirely the cause. I'm not sure of the trigger, but Roland thinks it must have had something to do with his abduction."

"That's what he said to me too, and it makes some sense since Etienne never acted like this before."

"All that I seemed to accomplish here was to shift the blame from his mother to his father, but that has changed the whole dynamic of his mental obsession. I believe you are far safer now, but I would warn you not to tempt fate. Keep away from him."

"You don't need to worry about that. The only thing that concerns me is getting into the museum to see Gitane Marie once in awhile."

"That could be difficult. Maybe after this baby comes he will be too preoccupied to spend much time there any longer."

"I heard him talking about it. There he was, still engaged to me and trying to make her pregnant."

"It did sound like a desperate attempt to dislodge himself," Luc admitted. "Something else must have been going wrong in your relationship."

"He wanted me full time, no career. Before we came down here from Paris he had hired a whole new staff to replace me without even consulting me. He just did it. He thought it would make me happy."

"And it did not?"

"Of course not! Who would be happy to have their job taken away without being asked?"

"So, that is all it was. He did not ask."

"No, that's not all of it. I wouldn't have agreed had he asked. I wanted partnership, and he never understood that. That's what I thought we had in the operation of the museum. But he wanted my full time attention. That's the change he thought would come with the marriage. He would never admit it, but he wanted me to become like his grandmother who had been entirely devoted to his grandfather. Well, that's just not me."

"You feel he wanted to circumscribe you."

"Yes! Make me a social hostess, a bridge partner, and apparently available for nonstop sex from what I heard him say about Juliette. I had no idea his appetite was so, well, vast. Maybe I'm just not as sexy."

"It's not as simple as that Summer. Different women excite different aspects of a man. I am sure you were and still are quite attractive to Etienne, but there is a lot to you. You are a personality to be reckoned with."

"Well, I am a person if that's what you mean. I'm not a sex machine. He made her sound like—I stand corrected—he made them sound like that's all that goes on between them."

"It did sound excessive," Luc admitted. "So you might look at Juliette as a kind of blessing."

"I don't know how you can say that."

"He would have expected the same from you as he does from her, and you might have found yourself confined not only to the house but to the bed."

She cringed. "How will Juliette put up with it?"

"I suspect they are much alike in their carnal appetites."

"So he wanted to make her pregnant to get rid of me. He never even tried to understand me, but in one short weekend he understood all he needed to know about her."

"Because they are alike in their expectations, and she is simpler to understand. You must reconcile yourself to this. He did make a choice, and it is better for you that he made it. Consider yourself free, and be glad of it."

"Really I am. I just don't understand. He wasn't like that before, at least not with me. I had thought he loved me, but I guess he didn't, not really."

"He did and still does, but people change. He does not love you in the way you need." Even so, Luc had to admit to himself that the changes in Etienne seemed too sudden and profound to entirely make sense of.

He pulled one of his art books off the bookshelf and turned it to the picture of Gustave Moreau's Leda. "Roland told me you took him to see the original."

"I've been to see it many times. I thought he might like to see it too."

"Tell me, what do you see when you look at it?"

"A lot of things. I studied art while in college. I even painted a little myself. So at first I looked at it from an aesthetic point of view, analyzing its background, foreground, that sort of thing. Then when I visited it again I thought more about the subject matter: Leda, the cherubim, the swan, and their relationship with each other on the canvas. Later, I realized Moreau must have known a lot about the nature of swans, the Mute Swan in particular, because it is the swan's nature he portrays in its relationship to Leda."

"That's interesting. I would never have thought to consider that. What is the swan's nature?"

"Pure love," she answered. "The painting is its very essence."

"I sometimes wonder what would have become of Roland had you married Etienne? He probably would have ended up like me. That's the kind of man I thought he was, that is until he met you. I believe you are the only woman he has ever loved or will ever love."

She smiled. "I wish I could say he was my first love, but I cannot. I can say that my heart tells me he will be my last." She looked up at Luc and made her own confession. "I fell in love with him the weekend we spent together. I didn't act on those feelings, of course. And I never would have if circumstances had been different. I felt honor bound to Etienne, and I had feelings for him too, but not like what I had begun to feel for Roland. I was embarrassed. I didn't want to admit it to myself. But there is something about him I can't quite put my finger on. If I had been free, I would have flown away with him that very night we hid together in the safe room. I feel so natural around him, so fully accepted. It's like we fit together, separate but whole, as if we were two puzzle pieces that somehow got separated by great distance and were miraculously brought together. It was hard when we got back to Évian and I had to say goodbye. I can't imagine life without him now. He's perfect, and I don't mean that in a frivolous way."

The morning ended on that happy note. Summer left to go shopping for her dress. She did not believe she would need a priest's assistance in that pursuit. Luc stayed home so that he might give Roland a call in the privacy he needed to be quite candid.

"Etienne was here this morning and is reconciled to his new life. I don't believe he will trouble the two of you again, but I warn you to be careful. He could revert."

"Are you a magician? What did you do?" Roland asked.

"I appealed to his reason! That's all. That is what's left of it. He seems quite unstable."

"I fear it's worse than that," Roland said. "Remember the picture he drew: himself in a protective pod of some sort, a stacked row of eyes looking into him? Remember he described feeling like they were looking into his soul?"

"Yes, I remember. His descriptions were quite vivid."

"My friends in the Alliance believe they were not looking into his soul. They were looking into his mind. If they are correct, Etienne was mind stripped."

"Mind stripped?"

"It's a technique used to bore into the mind, extracting every thought, every experience. The procedure pretty much destroys the superego, not all at once but gradually."

"But why?"

"Their enemy uses it on captives they have taken, mostly from the Alliance. When there is a prisoner swap the Alliance gets many of them back. They are permanently damaged."

"Damaged how?"

"They remove all the blocks and impediments that are in their way so they could learn everything about their victims, all of their experience no matter how deeply buried. The effect is to strip them of the coping mechanisms that had been built up, probably over many years. Once they are gone, once these blocks and impediments are removed, they cannot be mended. It is as if they ripped the scab off of an old wound that once removed can never again heal."

"This cannot be. There must be a way to restore him."

"In some instances they have been able to halt the regression but only after severe damage has already been done. The victims are left with a personality that is nearly pure id: regressive, primitive, acting on every impulse. They can be dangerously aggressive."

"This sounds Hellish!"

"Even worse, if such a thing was done to Etienne, how many other abduction victims like him are there out there? There is no defense against it, no warning we can give. We would be dismissed as madmen if we tried to sound the alarm. And we are left with no explanation for this atrocity at all. Etienne had no military secrets that might give the Alliance's enemy an advantage. No, this appears to be a direct assault on humanity. But why?"

"Well, this exploration will have to wait. I think we should not mention these details to Summer right now. She's been through so much already. I think she has a right to a joyful wedding."

"Where was she when he came?" Roland asked.

"I hid her upstairs. He never knew she was here. She overheard the whole thing, which was a bit trying for her. She's fine now, out shopping for a dress and waiting for you to come for her."

"I wish I could come right now," he groaned. "I want to go straight to Switzerland and get this thing done."

"You sound impatient," Luc said.

"I'm beside myself," Roland admitted. "I feel like I have been waiting for an eternity."

"Be patient young man," Luc said as if to mock him. "Yours has been a short engagement. Does Barry know when to come down here?"

"Could you phone him?"

"What exactly should I say?"

"Tell him I have the whole thing planned. We will go back to Grindelwald for the wedding. Summer likes it there, and we should have no trouble finding a nice meadow below the mountains. I will only have to make sure we are near enough to a herd of wandering cows to hear their bells."

"I will be sure to wear my boots," Luc said. "I've done outdoor weddings before but never in a cow pasture."

"From there we can go on to Mt. Pilatus. But I thought it right to spend the first night of our honeymoon where it all began."

"I see the justice in that," Luc said, remembering Roland's description of his failed attempt at seduction. He laughed so hard that tears came into his eyes as he listened to his once stoic friend.

"And I thought we would paraglide together from Mt Pilatus where we first met. You remember? You were there."

"I remember," Luc said. "She so wanted to fly. I worried she would dive off the mountain. Make sure you hold her good and tight."

"I will always."

Luc sighed. So much hope, so much love, how can they be sustained? "Roland," he said, "you and Summer have the possibility of something most special if you will always honor each other as you do now."

"This bond will hold," Roland said.

Chapter Twenty-Six

The grassy meadows surrounding Grindelwald were myriad shades of green when Barry and Summer drove past still verdant fields on the way to her wedding. Roland and Luc were at the chosen site, having just paid a curious farmer a few Swiss francs for the use of his land, a rolling pasture near a glassy lake, surrounded by the dark, lofty peaks of the Bernese Alps. Cowbells rang their bucolic chorus in the distance when Summer stepped out of the car in ivory organza, carrying a bouquet of white roses mixed with blue delphiniums tied with a yellow ribbon. Her hair hung loose under a braided pearl tiara and a veil that sparkled with glittering Swiss polka dots.

"I was asked by Summer's family to extend their heartfelt congratulations and invite you to visit them in America," Barry said when he delivered Summer to her groom. "Oh, and Stuart and Natalie send their congratulations."

"Thank you," Roland said and took Summer's hand. "You look beautiful," he whispered.

The couple stood before Luc who smiled broadly, took a serious turn, and began to speak:

I am honored on this day to join you Summer and you Roland in marriage. But as I am bound to speak the truth, I perceive the bond between you is already made by a presence far greater than me. I am merely the humble officiate of this union. Treasure what you have for rare is the union so heavenly blessed and rare is the couple so blessed as you, my dear friends and fellow travelers. May your life together be long and your love endure. May you always be for the other. And may the love that binds you guide you in your worldly endeavors.

Summer has told me she sees in the swan the expression of perfect love. And Roland sees that expression in Summer. The woman and the swan in their perfection, united in love by the holy crown of heaven is the image the artist made for it speaks to us all if we can but open our eyes. Love is the perfection of all that is holy. It is the ether of the universe, which links the stars with our planet, each one of us to the other, the divine with what we call the mundane. All is linked as one: man and woman; the fields, lakes and mountains where we stand; our planet with other planets and all the suns in the universe. All reach their perfection in that ether of perfect love. And so shall you Roland and Summer, from this day forward.

"Roland, do you take Summer to be your wife from this day forward?"

"Yes I do."

"Summer, do you take Roland to be your husband from this day forward?"

"Yes I do."

"You are now husband and wife. You may kiss the bride."

Cowbells rang loudly nearby as if the animals had sauntered over for the express purpose to rejoice in their union or interrupt the nuptials kiss.

"Look, over there!" she pointed to the herd of wandering cattle.

He kissed her outstretched hand and looked at her in smiling amusement, so pleased he was that he had made Summer's wedding just as she had wanted. Barry, not to be outdone by a herd of cows, applauded loudly as he walked over and kissed them both. Luc stood aside, his eyes tearing while he watched the happy couple.

"Don't weep for me. This is the happiest day of my life," Roland said.

"I know it is. I'm not accustomed to seeing you so happy, that's all," he said and wiped his tears.

The wedding party climbed into Barry's rented station wagon and drove back to the hotel for a celebratory feast in the very restaurant where Luc had taken Summer the first night of their weekend away. A photographer was waiting when they arrived. He snapped photos first of the bride and groom together, the bride alone, and finally the four of them united with Jungfraujoch behind them. The party dined on cake and quite a lot of very good wine until night settled in. Summer and Roland looked at each other and then at their guests who seemed reluctant to end the party. Finally Barry rose from his chair and said it was his bedtime. He looked pointedly at Luc who caught his meaning, turned to Summer and Roland, and bid them goodnight. At last they were alone. Candles were lighted in the dimly lit dining room now that sunset was well past. Roland reached across the table and kissed Summer softly and helped her up.

Their first night together was a private affair until Summer was awakened by distant thunder. She lay in bed a few minutes, reluctant to move, so comfortably entwined she was in Roland's arms. But when the thunder grew nearer, she gently lifted the arm that draped over her and went to the large panoramic window that looked out towards Jungfraujoch. It had begun to rain. Thick, black clouds were visible under the glare of lightening.

Roland awoke when the thunder shook the window glass. He reached for Summer; and when she was not there, he searched about the dark room when a flash of lightening made visible her silhouette in front of the window. He leaped out of bed and held her near as if he feared the thunder gods would steal her from him.

"Are they back?" she asked.

"Who?"

"The enemies of the Alliance."

"I don't think so. It's just a late night storm." Silently, he was not so sure. Could they know what she means to me? he thought. Would they calculate what ransom I would pay?

The couple stood frozen in the moment, locked in an embrace before the window in the darkened room as the fearsome storm raged on. He kissed her again and again, face, neck, shoulders, as if each kiss offered her protection. A bolt of lightening struck so near that under its awesome torchlight their bodies shimmered smooth and white. Embarrassed, as if their lovemaking had become a show, they returned to their bed and slipped beneath the sheet, wrapped into each other and drifted off into sleep.

In the morning when Summer awoke she spied a package at the foot of their bed, all shining in silver metallic wrap.

"What's this?" She climbed out of the bed and picked it up.

"I don't know," Roland said as he looked around the room. "Bring it to me."

She carried it around the bed to where Roland lay and sat down next to him. He unwrapped the strange package and inside found a note on top of a metal box. It was addressed to Summer, but she could not decipher its markings.

"It's from the Alliance," he said. "They must have been hidden inside the clouds last night."

"And they came into our room?"

"Apparently they sent a messenger."

She leaped up and went to the door. "No one broke in. It's still locked and bolted."

"Doors and walls are no impediment."

"You mean they can come through them?"

"Like ghosts, but they employ another mechanism."

She reached for the long, satin robe she had bought for her wedding night and covered herself. "And they saw us together in bed?"

"You look beautiful in that," he said. "Come here. I will read you the note.

Dearest Summer. We welcome you and think you be a prize for any man. We know Roland to be such a man who is truly worthy of you. Please accept our little gift, which might relieve the growing doubts of the fine boy we have lately learned to be your sister's nephew. It will bond him to you and you to us. May the joys of life be yours.

"It's a mouse!" Summer said when she opened the box. "It's just like what Paul described in his letter." She studied the creature from every angle. "It's a robotic mouse like the ones he said invaded Barry's house. You know what his means, don't you? It means we're going to have to travel to America soon so I can show it to Paul, and what did they write, 'relieve his doubts.'"

"We should go while Barry's there," he said.

"That would be fun," she said, while turning the mouse round and round in her hand. "You must have told the Alliance about Paul's letter?"

"No, I filed the copy Barry made for me after I read it. I thought I would save it for another day when I wasn't so busy."

"Then how did they know?"

"It was one of theirs. It must have been," Roland said. "Paul saw an Alliance ship."

"How did they know he's a relation?"

"I'm not the only watcher. We are everywhere. They must have become interested in learning about you when they saw us together, and

240

found out your connection to Paul."

"So he's in their files, and I'm in their files." She sat back down on the bed feeling totally exposed. "Will I meet them?"

"I think you will. They have welcomed you already."

"Will I see their ship?" she said as she began to play with the locks of his hair.

"Someday, but you are here with me now." He pulled her down next to him. "First you must learn to paraglide"

She laughed and snuggled close.

Summer and Roland bid farewell to Barry and Luc after a last lunch together. The couple traveled on to Lake Lucerne where they boarded a cogwheel train that carried them upward past a farmhouse that sat diagonal upon the land, past forests heavy with evergreens, until at last they crossed the tree line and arrived at the craggy heights of Mt. Pilatus. Summer ran to the edge of the terrace, reaching over as far as she could stretch to look down on mountains and the land below.

"Wait until tomorrow when we fly," Roland said and pulled her back.

They checked into the hotel, had a light meal, and spent the rest of the evening entwined, not having slept much the night before.

Morning crept through the edges of the window blinds that Summer had pulled shut. They lay together in the dim light like pieces of a puzzle tightly fit. He stroked her as she slept. He stroked every part of her, putting to memory the rise and dip and flow of each curve and the sensations of her silky skin against his hand so if by accident he should become blind, he would know her by his touch. Eventually she was awakened and drew nearer to him, if nearer was possible.

He had once asked a question of one of his Alliance teachers, as he grew in the way of the watchers, as to why humans, unlike the other animals they share the Earth with, were always in heat. Why were they not designed to have the more efficient estrous cycle like the others? His teacher explained that human mating was far more complex than that of their animal counterparts because humans themselves were far more complex and potentially higher in their leaning.

"They don't mate solely for offspring," his teacher had explained. "Nor do they mate only for pleasure. At least not all of them have reduced sex to only this. Mating in humans has a greater goal if ever that greater goal is achieved. It bonds a couple to each other in the highest spirit of love and thus to us."

"You make it sound as if it is part of their evolution," Roland had said.

"Your evolution," the teacher replied. "Remember who you are. And yes, you are quite right about that. Human sex when properly practiced evolves the spirit and thus can be practiced often and always. Thus, there are none of the constraints of a nature imposed cycle."

Intrigued by his teacher's comments, Roland read all that he could on the subject in the library of the Alliance. What he learned only complicated what his teacher had said. For all of the books stated that if this higher spirit of love is to be achieved, more important than the proper application of sex, is choosing the right partner. For without the right partner compatibility at these levels is not possible. He would have to find a woman he was attuned to who was likewise attuned to him.

As he matured and looked about among the women he would meet, he began to think that an impossibility and grew increasingly dispirited. Seeing no use in settling as he had seen others do, he had resigned himself to a life of loneliness and celibacy until he met Summer. In spite of the impediment of her engagement, her image grew in his imagination. He would hear her voice when she was not there. Actions he had seen her take would play and replay in his mind as if they were permanently recorded. He knew she was the woman for him, and the books had stated there might be only one, so finely attuned two people must be. He determined that even if his efforts ended in failure, he must fight for her. And now that she lay beside him, he resolved to forge a bond that would never fail for he could not bear to be without her.

If he should be blind and lose his sense of touch, he would know her by her smell because her smell and his were now the same. There was no flower whose odor was sweeter than this, he thought, as he drew her into his nostrils to be recorded forever in his mind.

And if he should be blind and lose both his sense of touch and smell, he would know her by her thoughts, which she has made a practice of laying open. He was attentive to them, appreciating the quality of her mind, even learning the nuances of her speech, which he soon adopted.

And he had begun to tell her the secrets of the Alliance one by one so as not to startle her too much with their revelation. In time there would be no secrets they did not share. And when the day comes that she meets the Alliance, as he knew that it would, she will not be frightened or surprised for she will have already become part of their family as she has become a part of him and he of her.

And if he should be blind and lose both his sense of touch and smell along with his power of intellect, he would know her by her heart, for his heart and hers were one.

He kissed her again, knowing the full promise of the love they were fashioning. They will always hunger for each other, the wise people had written, as they hunger for life and air, as long as they mate thusly in the spirit of pure love. He had become its devotee, as he was devoted to her, his Summer. There was nothing greater the spirit had to offer.

"Do you want to go fly now?" he said to her as she lay in his arms.

"I feel I already am," she said as she reached up and kissed him.

She lay back down feeling lightness in her being, her emotions elevated to a place they had never been. She touched his chest and then her own, feeling the rhythms of their hearts in sync. She felt a rush of thoughts transport from each to the other minimizing the need for speech. Her body was all sensation as if with each kiss, with each tender touch he had brought her to life.

Summer recognized she had never known love before, only a shadow that calls itself thus. And without Roland she never would have. She reached up and kissed him again and then lay back down in his arms, looking into the deep well of his eyes, eyes a color she had never before seen either in life or art. She wished to dive into them, to swim in them, to be reflected in them. With no necessity for words, she committed herself to him in a way she had thought impossible. She would stand with him and by him, not apart, as before she had thought a necessity in a world that subordinates women. It was no necessity with him. She was free now.

And thus, on the second morning of their marriage, their vows to each other fully made, Summer and Roland entered into the sacred marriage the wise people of the Alliance had written of.

Chapter Twenty-Seven

Roland carefully unpacked the paragliding gear from a rucksack while explaining its various parts as the pair spread the bright blue and yellow wing out on the lawn near the edge of a tall, steep cliff.

"We must make sure these suspension lines do not tangle. These fabric cells will fill with air, slightly inflating the wing that will lift us."

He strapped Summer into a tandem harness so they could fly together; then strapped himself in, attaching the harness to the risers that hung from the suspension lines on both sides of their wing. "Just right," he said, holding his finger to the wind before he studied the rock face to his left and the vast open space in front of him.

"When I say go, run until the wind picks us up. Are you ready?"

"Yes!" she cried.

"Let's go!" he shouted.

The couple ran together down the hill until a gust of wind filled their wing lifting them high and away from the threatening cliff wall. Roland used the brakes to steer them straight off from Mt. Pilatus as they lifted higher and higher. They soared above snowy peaks; green valleys spread below them like glistening jewels in the sun. All was serene for three hours as the couple flew over the alpine highlands until unexpected gray clouds moved in.

"Is it going to rain?" Summer shouted over the roar of the wind.

"It was not supposed to," Roland shouted back.

The weather report had indicated the weather would remain clear and mild, so mild that he had ventured to take them a good distance from where he had planned to put them down thinking they had all the day to fly. He tried to turn them back toward Pilatus, but the wind picked up making it hard to steer the sail. As he struggled with the brakes, out of the corner of his eye he saw something pop out from behind a fast moving cloud before disappearing behind another.

"Did you see that?" he shouted.

"See what?"

"It was probably nothing," he said, although he was sure he had seen a ship.

Gray clouds thickened with blackening skies rushing behind.

"I'm going to have to take us down fast," he shouted. "Grab hold of this brake," he handed off one of the two controls to Summer. "When you hear me shout 'brake,' use both hands and squeeze it with all of your might. I will do the same with the other."

"Where are we?" she shouted.

"I do not know for sure, but the wind is not cooperating. I've got to get us down now before it rips our sail or we are struck by lightening. Hold on tight with both hands as long as you can until you hear me shout. We are going into a spiral dive. Are you ready?"

"Yes!"

"Here we go."

Down, down they dropped, fast spinning and spinning. Their bodies stretched out horizontal as the wind whipped them into a rapidly spinning corkscrew dive. The noise was deafening. The pressure of their speed contorted their faces as they spun mercilessly through the air. The blackened clouds split open as they continued to plummet in a wet free fall.

As they fell in a downward spiral, Etienne's hostile face took shape in Roland's mind. He recalled reports of other abductees having perished in accidents. It could have been murder disguised as accidents, he thought, as he felt the force of their downward plunge. He could not be sure what had happened to those abductees, but he was confident as to what was supposed to happen to Summer and him.

She saw the ground approaching, a small patch of green with a larger deep forested woods on one side and a rushing river on the other. She recognized the Aare by its color. Summer grimaced, imagining herself ripped apart by tree limbs or cut to pieces by river rocks. "Brake! Brake!" Roland's voice sounded like a whisper in the wake of the roaring wind. She let go of her harness and clinched the brake with both hands as hard as she could. The wing gradually slowed their spin and the harnesses righted them into a vertical position. They hit hard in the narrow patch of soaking wet grass.

His hands unloosened her harness and then his own. He spun her

245

around and kissed her hard, she both laughing and crying when he released her, unable to speak so exhilarated and frightened she had been.

"Let's get this gear under the trees," he said. They gathered the wing and lines and harnesses and took shelter under the bows of great evergreens. "We can leave the gear here," he said. "But let us go further in."

They wandered deeper into the forest until they reached a small opening to the sky. "We can stay here until the rain stops." He looked into her face realizing she had not spoken a word since they landed. "Are you all right?" She wrapped her arms around his neck and pressed her head against his shoulder trembling. He made a cocoon for her with his arms, rubbing her back to warm and calm her. "That was a rough landing," he said.

Her trembling nearly ceased. She broke into a smile and said, "We flew like birds!"

"Yes, we did," he said laughing. "Sometimes they have to come in for a hard landing."

"I thought we would crash into the trees or be dragged across the river rocks. You brought us in perfectly." She began to shiver again.

He pressed himself to her to keep her warm and said, "I couldn't have done it without you."

She looked about where they stood. "Do we know where we are?"

"I'm not sure, but we cannot be far from a road with the river so near. When it stops raining we can hitchhike back."

The two sat down together on a pile of soft pine needles waiting and waiting, but the rain never stopped as darkness descended on the pinewood.

"We are going to have to stay here tonight," he said. "It's too dark and cold to try to find the road. Let us gather up some fallen pine boughs."

The violent wind had loosened many, so they gathered up the fullest of them and dragged them back to their campsite below the small opening to the sky. Roland freshened the pine needles they had been sitting on. "We can sleep here," he said.

He pulled the pine boughs over them, and they nestled underneath, atop the soft bed of pine needles. The sky cleared and stars appeared.

"I saw them today, darting behind the clouds," he said.

"Who? The Alliance?"

"No, the others. I think we are being stalked."

"What should we do?"

"Stay vigilant. Stay hidden so they will think we perished in the trees or were swallowed up by the river."

She felt a teardrop fall from his face onto hers and rose up to see tears in his eyes. "Why are you crying?"

"Because I have put you in great danger."

She kissed his tears away. "You've saved me from a greater one," she whispered.

They lay silent asleep while the night lingered on. Cygnus rose high above the opening in the trees, unfolding its wings with a promise of protection. The swan, though gentle and steadfast in love, is fierce in defense of its own.

Epilogue

A nearly imperceptible sky door opened making visible for only a few seconds a silvery ship. Hidden in darkness, the ship dropped down slowly until it threw a wide beam of light onto the tops of a grove of pine trees in the center of the small woodland. Rising up through the beam just above the tree line, two lovers appeared sleeping, entwined with each other. Branches from their pine bough blanket fell away into the chill night. Undisturbed by either light or coolness, caught as they were in the protection of their dreams, they rose gently and disappeared into the ship that vanished through the sky door from whence it came.

Fini

Author Biography

Cygnus is the third in a series of adventure novels by Linda Oxley Milligan. Earlier works are *The Blue Nile Adventure, Gitane Marie: Through the Eyes of the Black Madonna,* and a soon to be published novelette for young readers, *The Shadows that Haunt the Walls.* Milligan's novels draw on her love of travel as well as her background in folklore and literature. She seeks to take the reader to many of the places she has traveled but with a distinct insight that is the product of both a folklorist's eye as well as a vivid imagination that draws from the history and mythos of ancient places.

Cygnus is her second foray into science fiction writing following her completion of *Shadows that Haunt the Walls.* Like her other works, it draws upon knowledge derived from her research. In the case of *Cygnus,* that research was her fieldwork gathering legends about and perspectives into UFOs that resulted in a dissertation, oral papers, and published articles. In *Cygnus* she makes real what is speculated and provides an understanding of how such phenomena might occur under our very noses.

Also By Linda Oxley Milligan

The Blue Nile Adventure
Gitane Marie: Through the Eyes of the Black Madonna
The Shadows that Haunt the Walls: Paul's Story